ELIJAH'S CHARIOT

The Forgotten Children
Book One

ANDREW GRIFFARD

ISBN: 978-0-692-35825-2

PROLOGUE

Red Square lay before him, its far edges seeping into the gray and winding streets of Moscow. His feet shuffled slowly along the gutter as his eyes remained riveted on the plumes of smoke still rising from St. Basil's Cathedral. The smoke and strong odor of burned rubber and spilled gasoline filled his nose and throat, and from deep within tears welled up, filling his eyes. The only sound was the wind.

The cars lining the bridge that led to the square had been smashed aside by some great force. The cleared path continued up to the walls of the Kremlin which were blackened and pockmarked, possibly by some of the twisted pieces of metal and debris that lay at the front gates. Most of the detritus was unidentifiable, but some twisted shapes were all too familiar.

His feet carried him along the path of destruction as if by their own volition, drawing him closer to some inescapable and terrible truth, begging him to draw back the curtain and stare it full in the face. But he feared that if he did it would swallow him whole.

Through the smoke and tears, movement fluttered in the corner of his eye. It looked like a bird, its white wings flapping as it raced along the ground. Wiping his eyes, he took a few steps toward the strange object as it drew closer.

It wasn't a bird, but rather a white jacket or sweatshirt, its owner's arms pumping wildly as he ran. The first figure was followed closely by another and then an additional two, no – three, others further behind. Suddenly the still quiet of Red Square was split by the distinct report of gunfire and the two lead figures instinctively flinched – then kept running.

As the group continued getting closer, he clenched his fists

1

and fear knotted in his stomach as his earlier dread was replaced by a much more immediate concern. He turned his back on the smoking buildings and failures of a now silent people and started running.

CHAPTER ONE

The meteorite descended through the sky, a thin trail of otherworldly white smoke billowing behind, pointing the way from heaven to earth like the finger of God. The kilometer-wide rock struck the ground with supersonic force, throwing up a mountain's worth of dirt and rock in an ellipsoid wave that quickly rained down across the desert plain. A split second later, a wave of heat and light exploded, mushrooming in every direction, incinerating plant life and turning sand to glass. Overpowering gusts of air several times stronger than hurricane winds strafed the landscape, scattering soil and rocks for miles. Moments later, when the sulfurous smoke cleared, the only thing that remained was an immense, charred crater several miles in diameter, surrounded by millions of shattered chunks of blackened rock.

The imagery replayed itself for probably the hundredth time that day in Sean Prochazek's thirteen-year-old mind as he bounded up the path to his front door. Mr. Alvarez had shown the video earlier that week in his eighth grade science class as an example of the type of impact a larger sized meteorite would have. But, Sean knew that Earth's imminent rendezvous with Jerry, a much smaller rock estimated at 100 to 200 meters in diameter, wouldn't be quite that spectacular. It had only been a few weeks since the Near Earth Orbit Program, the group that his father managed at NASA's Jet Propulsion Laboratory site in Pasadena, California, had discovered Jerry's intercept course with Earth. The rock from outer space was calculated to touch down in three days somewhere in Russia's expansive wilderness several hundred miles east of Moscow. And Sean and his father were going to be there to witness the whole amazing event firsthand.

Well, not exactly, Sean thought to himself as he stopped on his doorstep to retrieve his key. They would be in Moscow probably in some dull Embassy conference room watching scratchy satellite photos with all the other scientists until Jerry landed. Then they would fly out to the crash site and get to work with the first response research team to find out all about Jerry – what it was made of, how old it was, where it came from. Although somewhat less interesting, the conference room scenario was probably a lot better since his mom would totally freak out if she thought they were going to be anywhere near the actual landing site.

Sean turned as he heard his sister, Elizabeth, running up behind him. He laid a gentle but firm hand on her shoulder to block her way to the door.

"Not a word to Mom about the fight – okay?" he said quietly.

"But they started it and there were two of them – it wasn't your fault! Kyle Moffett is a stupid bully and everyone ..."

Sean cut her off. "You can't say anything – promise!"

Elizabeth's ten-year old eyes stared up at him for a moment, then she nodded silently.

Sean opened the door and started making a quick dash for the stairs.

"Hey mister, no hello? How was school?" called their mother from the kitchen.

Pausing on the first step, out of his mother's line of sight, he turned slowly and stared at Elizabeth as she set her backpack down by the coat closet.

"Fine – same boring stuff," he said.

Cindy Prochazek stepped out of the kitchen into the entryway holding a plate of celery sticks with peanut butter. "Boring? Wasn't there a math test? I still don't think you studied enough."

Sean left the stairs quickly and grabbed a celery stick from the plate and popped it into his mouth.

"Smoked it – even easier than I thought it would be. Oh yeah," he paused again on the first stair before heading up, still chewing. "Terrorists attacked during second period and tried to take over the school. I had to grab one of their guns and take them all out. Everyone was scared out of their minds but, you know, somebody had to do something."

Cindy stared for a moment at her son. "Sean, that's not even funny."

"What?" he said. "You asked."

"Sean was a real hero, Mom. He even saved the girls first – Jenny Hilton went hysterical over him," Elizabeth said.

Cindy looked back and forth at the faces of her two children. "You guys are terrible. Your dad's upstairs packing – have you finished your suitcase yet? You'll have to before dinner because you need to be in bed early tonight for your flight tomorrow morning."

"I'm almost done," Sean said as his mother turned back into the kitchen. He smiled conspiratorially at his sister. She smiled back.

Sean dropped his backpack onto his bed and pulled out an internet article he'd printed out for the current events portion of his history class. Folding it in half, he pinned it to the corkboard above his bed, covering up the lower half of a diagram of the Mars Reconnaissance Orbiter, the satellite that had made the Jerry discovery. The boy looked slowly over the rest of his collection of articles and solar system posters, making sure that everything was in place and wasn't going to come crashing down on him in the middle of the night. Grabbing a magazine from his backpack he jogged to his parents' bedroom.

"Hey Dad," Sean said as he jogged through the doorway and jumped on the bed. Kevin turned to him and smiled. He was standing near the dresser with a handful of socks, staring at the rows of framed pictures that were hanging on the wall and spilling down onto the polished wood of the dresser itself.

"You've really grown a lot in just two years," Kevin said as he picked up a picture frame from the dresser. The photo had been taken during their trip to Tahoe two summers ago. They'd stopped at a campground outside the resort town for a couple of nights. In the picture, all four of them were sitting on logs around the campfire, with Sean holding a skillet of grease-soaked pancakes. Kevin's hair was standing up in back and Elizabeth still had a big, red crease on her cheek from the pillow.

"Pretty soon, you'll be as tall as me."

"Taller," Sean said, smiling as he kicked the box springs with his heels.

Kevin turned and set the picture frame back in place on the dresser.

"Have you finished packing? You'll need some coats and sweaters? It could be cold in Moscow. They have pretty long winters."

"Yep, got all that. And my hiking boots for the snow."

"Your Swiss Army Knife?"

"Yep."

"The neck cushions for the plane?"

"You said we'd get those at the airport."

"That's right, I did. We can pick some up tomorrow morning. What time do you want me to wake you up?"

"If we're leaving at 6 a.m., then probably at 5:30."

Sean placed the magazine on the edge of the bed. "May issue of *Science* is out – I wanted to bring it on the plane to read."

Kevin glanced at the cover. A round, middle-aged man in a rumpled suit posed in front of a large, blurry photograph of an asteroid.

"John on the cover again – probably all Jerry articles."

"Yeah, I read the one in the *L.A. Times* that they wrote about you and the team from the... what do they call it, Russia's NASA?"

"The RKA, Russian space agency or something like that. It wasn't all about me though, I read it this morning. Most of the interview questions were with John. They just mentioned me toward the end."

"Yeah, Dad, but they know who the most important guy is. You're the Program Director. John just discovered it. And it wasn't just him anyway, the mission guys were all there, too. Besides," Sean said, holding up the magazine, "you don't wear a yellow flower tie and a green suit when you're going to be on the cover of *Science*."

Kevin chuckled and sat down on the bed. "How do you know about suits and ties?"

He shrugged. "Mom told me."

"I'll have to remember that. In case *I'm* ever on the cover of *Science*!"

"You will be, Dad. You're going to make some great discoveries about Jerry," Sean said confidently.

"We'll see," Kevin said as he looked out the window above the bed.

Sean stood up and walked toward the door, holding the magazine. He stopped and turned back, pausing for a moment before he spoke.

"Do you hate John?"

Kevin's eyes rose slowly until he was peering at his son over his wire-framed glasses. He stared at Sean for a second in confusion, not saying anything.

"I mean, because he discovered Jerry and you didn't," Sean explained quietly.

Kevin swallowed and continued to look at his son. "No, I don't hate him."

Sean, seeming satisfied, nodded and turned into the hall.

"Sean," Kevin called after him.

The boy turned and looked back at his dad.

"Do you... never mind," Kevin said as he waved his hand. "I'm almost done packing – I'll be downstairs soon."

Sean smiled at his father.

"Hey, Dad," he said excitedly, "tomorrow we'll be in Russia!"

CHAPTER TWO

Sean watched the tiny, white jet inch slowly across the screen, its nose just reaching the Atlantic Ocean. He'd never been on an international flight before, nor on any plane that had maps showing their progress as they flew. They were definitely a nice feature, he decided.

Sean's father sat to his left, the overhead light shining brightly on the chart in front of him. He yawned and set the stapled sheets down on the tray table, took off his glasses and rubbed his eyes. They'd watched the sun set an hour or so ago and many people had started to pull the window shades down and search for the small pillows and thin blankets.

Sean was about to turn back to the article from *Science* that he'd been puzzling over for the past hour when a round man, with dark wavy hair gathered in a fuzzy ball around his head, stepped into the row of seats in front of them and reached out to shake Kevin's hand.

"Hello, Bob. Whose conspiracy theory are you chasing this time – Drudge Report's, *UFO Magazine's*?" Kevin chuckled.

"Ha, ha. Tim Bailey over at *Astronomy* has me on this one – wants me to do more of a science angle, compared to most of my regular stuff, of course. Most of the other rags already had their own guys headed out this way – people are practically coming out of retirement for this one. Kind of hard to get an assignment, believe it or not."

Bob slowly rotated his head as he spoke, surveying his surroundings, only occasionally focusing on Kevin and Sean. His words came out in brief sprints, then would slow way down about mid-sentence, making him almost sound like a drawling southern gentleman. His choice of which words to rush and which ones to let drag seemed completely random.

"Even after your piece in the *L.A. Times*? I saw it – it was good. Glad you didn't misquote me this time."

A weak smile crept onto Bob's face and he held his hands up in mock helplessness. "Come on! You're still the only one that's called me on that one, by the way. Very few people are as intimately acquainted with the supporting mathematics of string theory as you, *Doctor* Prochazek. I mean, it *was* the *L.A. Times*, after all."

Kevin laughed again and shook his head. Gesturing to Sean, he said, "This is my son Sean. Sean, this is Bob Quidley – part-time world adventurer, part-time wine connoisseur and all-the-time freelance reporter: breaking down science into digestible chunks for the masses."

"Digestible chunks – I like that. I'll have to put it on my business card." He smiled broadly and leaned forward, shaking hands with Sean. "Glad to meet you, Sean. So, you're tagging along to Mother Russia to see the end of the world up close, huh?"

Sean smiled and glanced at his dad, unsure of how to answer. He didn't completely buy Bob's act. His speed-up-slow-down words were telling one story, but his languidly shifting eyes another. He'd pitched the question to Sean casually enough, but his eyes had stopped suddenly on his face at the end of the sentence, narrowing as if he was carefully scrutinizing his reaction, gauging the emotions that were playing across his face. Sean wondered if Bob was using a trick that his dad had taught him about asking questions that you already knew the answers to, just to see how much the other person knew or to find out their opinion of the facts. His dad had also said that it was a great way to throw a person off guard, forcing them to underestimate your understanding of the subject so that they wouldn't notice in time to change their story as your questions became more focused.

"Don't tell me you've fallen for all that alarmist talk, have you Bob?" Kevin said quietly.

Bob spread his hands again, eyes back on the rove. "I don't know, a lot of people are saying a lot of different things. It's sometimes kind of hard for us 'masses' to know what's happening in this big, scary world."

A flight attendant glided by taking drink orders and passing out packets of peanuts. She looked overly eager to serve the few passengers on board, her voice surprisingly energetic for the late hour.

"No, seriously, what's your take on this? I mean, I've read all the reports and NASA's official assessment of impact hazards and some of the speculative literature, but what's it look like from the inside?"

"You want me to tell you that it's all a government cover-up and that Jerry's really going to knock us into some kind of ice age?"

"That would be nice – if it's true," Bob said, a mischievous grin pulling at the corner of his mouth.

"Sorry. Everything's out there, there's no time bomb. We're all still going to be able to grow our grapes and summer squash after it's all through. But, this is still one of the greatest events of modern science – it's the biggest thing since man walked on the moon. We missed our chance at Tunguska, but now – we've got another shot," Kevin waved his hands emphatically as his voice grew louder.

Bob held up his index finger to pause Kevin, nodded, then swung out into the aisle and shuffled toward the back of the plane.

"Tunguska's where that meteorite exploded about a hundred years ago, right?" Sean asked.

"Yes. Well, a meteorite or a comet or something. They never found any sizable fragments, so it's tough to say."

"But, it still blasted everything for miles around, didn't it?"

"Luckily, it was in a sparsely populated area. If the thing had exploded near a city it could have killed tens of thousands of people."

"Wouldn't they have evacuated the city?"

"They didn't know it was coming – it just happened. This time we can be there and study it up close. Plus, technology's gotten a little better since 1908."

"Why do meteorites always crash in Russia?" Sean asked curiously.

Kevin paused. "Large land mass, it's kind of hard to miss with twelve time zones. But, they don't always land there –

there've been lots of others in South America and elsewhere. Plus, with about seventy percent of the planet covered in water, most of them have probably hit somewhere in the ocean. Since it's often very hard to find any fragments or craters, we don't have a very good idea of actually how many have collided with the planet over its life."

Bob hurried back up the aisle with a notepad and pen in hand. Along the way, he stopped the flight attendant, who had just taken drink orders from Kevin and Sean, and placed one of his own. He resumed his kneeling position in the seat in front of Kevin and quickly scribbled on the page, prepping the ink. Kevin sat back calmly, lips pressed together, head resting against the seat and hands languidly curled around the armrests.

"Okay," Bob said, jotting something down. "The Mars Reconnaissance Orbiter picks up an abnormal magnetic field, way out there, on March twelfth." He paused, most of the words dripping out like sweet honey on a summer's day. Then, he quickly shot out, "How'd you know it wasn't something else, maybe from the planet itself, maybe some star exploding way out there."

"We didn't. Dr. Rohrstadt's team noticed an abnormal fluctuation and decided to check it out. He could have just as easily attributed it to any one of those things, or a temporary equipment glitch. But, he decided to find out what, if anything, was going on and called the guys down on Palomar Mountain in San Diego and asked them what they could see."

"And... they saw it out there?"

"They thought they saw something, they weren't sure. It's tough with such a small asteroid. So, they had to check it out with other observatories, get approvals, check, double-check, triple-check. That's why the announcement didn't come out for a couple of days. We had to verify it."

"Why hadn't you seen it sooner?"

Kevin paused. His hands hadn't left the armrests. He inhaled and looked back up at Bob.

"Like I said, it's extremely difficult to see such small asteroids. The Near Earth Object Program is really only equipped to find near-earth-asteroids larger than a kilometer in size, since those pose the greatest threat to life on the planet. Even once we knew something was there, we had to contact observatories all over the world to measure its parallax to see if it was moving at all."

"Parallax?" Bob asked.

Sean, leaning on the edge of his seat, watching his father intently, said, "It's how an object looks like it's changing positions, or moving, when comparing other objects in its distant background from different locations around the world."

Bob nodded and quickly scribbled on the page.

Kevin glanced at Sean and continued his explanation.

"Since it's easiest to detect sideways motion from a stationary object, assuming for the sake of illustration that Earth is stationary... the fact that the planet is actually moving relatively slowly both complicates and eases the calculation..." his voice stopped suddenly, his eyes focusing on some faraway point.

As suddenly as he'd stopped, he began again. "So, it's a great deal more difficult to catch objects that are coming straight at you, making these little guys even easier to miss. There have been several near impacts that we only found out about *after* they passed by us."

"Like 1989 FC? What was it – missed us by only six hours? About as far away as the moon, wasn't it?" Bob threw the words out quickly as he studied the overhead storage bins.

Kevin nodded. "It was about 300 meters across, a bit bigger than Jerry should be. It could have been bad, depending on where it hit."

The flight attendant pushed a thin, gray cart to a stop next to Bob and handed him a Bloody Mary. She passed ginger ales over to Kevin and Sean and continued toward the rear of the plane.

"Alrighty," Bob said after taking a careful sip from his glass and placing it on a tray table beside him. "Jerry's supposed to be coming down around 6 a.m. local time, Sunday, April sixth, at like thirty thousand miles an hour, slamming into the middle of Russia..."

"That's assuming that it doesn't break up in the atmosphere or somewhere on its path down to the surface. Even though it's largely composed of iron – you just never can tell. The Tunguska object exploded about a mile *before* it hit the ground."

"Okay, okay, but assuming it does make it relatively intact – what's going to happen?"

Kevin leaned forward a little, licking his lips. "As it streaks through the atmosphere, its surface is going to begin to melt and the air around it will become electrically charged, turning it into a giant fireball. This is going to be very bright. When it hits, it'll be traveling at about forty times the speed of sound and will therefore explode, sending fragments everywhere, and creating a blast of roughly one hundred megatons, about one hundred million tons of TNT."

"How big was Hiroshima?" Bob interjected.

"About twenty thousand tons of TNT."

Bob whistled and quickly jotted the figures down on his notepad.

Sean leaned forward in his seat. This was usually the most exciting part for everyone and he'd heard the scenario enough times to know his father enjoyed telling it. Sean never grew tired of hearing it again and again.

Kevin cleared his throat and continued, making a bowl shape with his hands above the tray table in front of him. "The impact will create an enormous crater, over a mile wide and hundreds of yards deep. Everything for miles around will be vaporized. This all, of course, depends on Jerry's impact angle, its density, its mass, how much iron really is in the thing. The more heavy iron and less porous rock material, the bigger the blast."

"So, if Jerry's supposed to touch down somewhere in the middle of Siberia, who's in danger? Maybe a couple small villages?" Bob asked.

"Right, as long as it lands in a relatively unpopulated area, most everyone's fine. People for miles around are going to hear the impact, it'll blow out windows, leave some fires, but not much besides that. There'll be a slight tremor in most of the region. And it'll light up the sky for thousands of miles. Most of that stuff you hear about tidal waves and craters dozens of miles across are based on impact scenarios of much larger objects – at least a kilometer in size. Jerry just won't cause that kind of damage."

Kevin took a sip from his glass. "It would be much worse if it hit a more densely populated area. In Moscow, for example, the entire city would be destroyed, plus most of the suburbs around it."

"How sure are you of the impact site?"

"Pretty sure. As long as it continues on its course and at a steadily increasing speed from gravitational force, it should strike within a few hundred miles of where we're predicting."

Kevin unbuckled his seat belt and stood up, stretching out his legs. Bob's pen scratched furiously at the pad of paper. Looking up at the tiny, white airplane on the trip monitor, Sean noted that they were out over the Atlantic. An image of the dark, rolling sea thousands of feet below the plane flashed through his mind. He shivered slightly and reached for the dark blue blanket in the seat next to him.

"Is that why you didn't try to divert the thing, because you knew it wouldn't hit any populated areas?" Bob asked, pen poised on the pad.

Kevin shook his head and continued to stretch out his arms and back. "With barely three weeks' notice, we didn't have enough time or resources. A year or more ago we could have done something, fired off some nuclear missiles to try to turn it off course, but not this late in the game."

"Sounds like it's going to be quite a show," Bob mumbled quickly. Then, more slowly, "Let's just hope that Jerry delivers."

Both men fell silent. Suddenly, the previously unnoticed hum of the plane's engines became noticeably loud in the absence of conversation. Sean shifted in his seat, maneuvering his pillow into a more comfortable position and pulling the blanket up more tightly around his chest.

Bob drew in a deep breath, stretched his arms out, then folded his notepad over and dropped the pen into his shirt pocket.

"Great chatting with you guys, makes the flight go by faster. Sean, you keep an eye on your dad, he knows what he's doing. Say, Kevin, once this bad, old alien rock touches down, let's go have a drink at the Hilton or someplace, okay?"

Kevin gave him a brief nod. As Bob walked by, he slapped a hand on Kevin's shoulder. He continued to stand in the aisle after Bob had passed, his hands in his pockets as he stared at the floor. Sean pulled his earphones out of the armrest jack and dropped them on the seat next to him. He adjusted a pillow behind his head and leaned back already halfway asleep.

CHAPTER THREE

Arriving in Moscow, getting through customs and driving from the airport to the Kosmos Hotel were all a blur of exhaustion for Sean. Despite the daylight that was trying to poke through the oppressive clouds overhead, his body felt like it was the middle of the night. He was too tired to even notice that he'd landed in a foreign country and had just lain down on the hotel room bed when the realization struck him. But, by that point the pillow was already too inviting and he quickly succumbed to the jet lag.

A few short hours later, Sean's father helped him stumble his way down to a taxi and through an official dinner at the U.S. Embassy. The first bite into some kind of chicken dish sent a flavorful jolt through his brain and he was suddenly completely awake and alert. He finished his dinner quickly and tried to sit still for the few remaining minutes of the meal as scientists, administrators and military men all chattered excitedly around him. Soon, Sean and his father set off with a small group for the Russian space agency.

RKA headquarters was a large, gray box of a building buried somewhere deep in Moscow's warren of carbon copy streets and structures. Front-gate security seemed minimal compared to the embassy, but the uniformed guards were equally as somber-faced as the marines had been. The city streets had been completely deserted during the trip from the Embassy.

After waiting in the lobby for what felt like an eternity, they were greeted by a tall, friendly man with a bushy goatee who gave his name as Kondratyev, Agency Director. With him, the group stepped into an elevator and descended for what felt like several minutes.

The elevator doors opened into a large, auditorium-style room, the exact dimensions of which were indeterminable because the furthest corners faded into darkness. Rows and rows of terminals stretched all the way down to a giant screen that appeared to be a satellite-linked map of central Russia. Dozens of men and women were stationed at the terminals, monitoring the gigabytes of data streaming in. The large room was relatively quiet, except for a distinct hum coming from the ceiling and the occasional beeps and blips from the terminals.

Sean had only taken the public tour of the facilities at NASA headquarters in D.C., which didn't include any of the actual communications control rooms that were used to pilot missions, so he was somewhat unsure of how the RKA compared with its U.S. counterpart. From the looks on the faces of his father and the other men, it compared quite well.

Kondratyev led the group down the steps to the front of the huge room. As they neared the giant screen, they estimated that it easily spanned forty feet across. He ushered them over to a display of data on the far, left-hand side.

"Relative velocity, rotation, distance from the moon, distance from Earth, ETA," he said in a heavy accent, gesturing at several numbers and the Cyrillic letters above them.

Kondratyev beckoned the small group over to an adjacent computer screen a few meters away. The screen was large and split into four different views, each showing live video from various locations. Two of the views showed pilots in some type of aircraft. The other two views were dark.

"Live video feed from our Air Force stationed near expected crash location," said the Russian Director.

He gestured to the image in the upper right-hand quadrant of the screen. A middle-aged, uniformed officer was visible in the foreground, with a younger pilot to his right. Both were busy monitoring the complex instrument panel in front of them. "This Colonel Tomak in Airborne Command Center. This one," he continued, gesturing at the other view of the pilot, "of fighter pilot in vicinity. And these others are of night sky from helicopters a little closer to expected crash site. Hopefully we will be able to see light from explosion, signs of meteorite's descent."

"How close are those helicopters to the crash site?" asked

17

one of the NASA officials. "Depending on the size of the blast when Jerry touches down, they..."

Kondratyev waved his hands in reassurance. "They are in no danger at all. Their positions are many kilometers away – completely out of harm's way."

The Russian Director leaned his tall frame forward and pressed a button on the panel, then blurted something in Russian. Colonel Tomak responded quickly in a gruff voice that seemed remarkably clear for coming from an airborne plane nearly a thousand miles away.

"Everything proceeding normally, gentlemen," translated Kondratyev with a smile. "Now it is just question of waiting for meteorite to strike. Please, make yourselves comfortable. There is tea and coffee – couches at rear of room," he said, gesturing.

Each of the Americans glanced around, all obviously unwilling to sit back and relax while the giant asteroid neared Earth. One of Kevin's colleagues stepped forward and whispered something to Kondratyev. He nodded and gestured toward a bay of terminals a few rows down, then turned to walk in that direction. All the others began to follow him.

"Sean, why don't you try to get some sleep on the couch – it's going to be a long night. We're just going to go take a look at some of the read-outs," Kevin said.

"But, I can't see anything from back there! What if something changes – I want to see it!" Sean protested, glancing at the dark, empty area around the couch.

"I'll let you know what's going on. Everything's going to be pretty standard until Jerry gets into the atmosphere and I'll wake you up way before that."

"I slept the whole day! I'm not even tired..."

He stopped short after seeing his father's glance. This was one of those no argument times. Sean hated those. He sat down on the couch, resigned to his fate.

Kevin walked down to investigate the monitors where the other men were now gathered, talking excitedly with one of the Russian technicians. Sean watched him go. They're right there, he thought, only a few feet away. I'll hear if anything starts happening.

He leaned back into the soft cushions of the couch and

listened to the whir of the computers and their series of beeps and pulses as they relayed information from the multiple satellites trained on the approaching asteroid. His watch said it was almost midnight – only six hours away.

Sean's mind began to fasten on that point in time and he wondered what it would be like. He'd been imagining the moment and the entire week that lay ahead of him, for the past month. The fantasy that he'd invented changed slightly each time he returned to it, but a few things remained the same. Sean was completely convinced that this would be the single most important moment of his existence up to that point, possibly of his entire life.

As he stared at the large screen at the other side of the room with its constantly changing sets of data, the image of the meteorite streaking through the sky as a ball of flame leapt into his mind and he imagined the deafening sound of it smashing into the ground, splintering trees and obliterating small hills for miles around.

He tried to imprint the image in his memory, as well as his mood and feelings about the approaching events. Then, he told himself to remember this exact moment in one week's time, to recall everything in perfect clarity – this huge room, the Russians sitting quietly at their monitors, the feeling of excitement in the air. This was a technique that he'd used a few times before so that he could compare his conceptions of something before it happened with the reality of the event as it later unfolded. He hoped that the magic he felt right now would be preserved, that this level of excitement would carry through the next few days as they finally arrived at the site and began studying the fragments scattered all over the Russian steppe. But, somehow he knew that the actual event would never completely live up to his imagination of it. That's how things usually turned out – he could always dream them to be better than they really were. Although the real thing was wonderful and exciting, it never quite carried the same electrifying feeling that the anticipation of it had…

Sean struggled to open his eyes, the last vestiges of the dream slowly receding as he became aware of his body, lying crumpled on the couch. He blinked around as he pushed himself up onto his elbows and looked around at the large room, teeming with activity. How long had he been asleep? He glanced at his watch – 5:45! Jerry was going to be here in fifteen minutes!

He jumped off the couch and staggered as his feet tried to get their strength back. There were many more people in the room than there had been when they'd arrived. They were all milling about the terminals, talking excitedly and pointing to the giant screen at the front of the room.

Sean walked gingerly down the steps, searching the groups for his dad. Few of the Russians noticed him – their attention was riveted to the screen.

He found his father toward the front of the room, leaning back against the terminal bay behind him, his tired eyes fastened on the large, constantly changing map. Kevin looked down at him as he walked up and seemed not to recognize him at first. Then, he made a small attempt at a half-smile and put his hand lightly on Sean's shoulder.

"I think I fell asleep," Sean mumbled, rubbing his eyes. He had no idea what time his body thought it was and, although he still felt rather tired, he could feel his heart beating in his chest with excitement.

"Jerry's going at just over… 10K per second? Is that what those letters right there mean – velocity?" Sean asked, pointing at the left-hand side of the digital map.

"Yep – speed's constant, rotation's minimal, trajectory is right on."

"Won't he speed up by the time he actually enters the atmosphere, in…" Sean glanced up at the screen again, "thirteen minutes, forty-nine seconds?"

Kevin nodded, eyeing the steadily decreasing seconds carefully. "Earth's gravitational force should bring it up to at least 11K. Then, the flash, a quick streak and – touchdown."

Sean smiled and looked up at his dad, all memory of sleep or weariness completely erased from his mind.

A technician seated on Kevin's right toggled a few keys and the split-screen view from the Russian Air Force appeared on the monitor in front of them. Sean saw the same image on many of the monitors around the room. Everyone was tuning in to the action as the meteorite approached.

The two views of the pilots looked the same, as did the

images of the dark Russian sky. Sean thought the sky was just a shade brighter than when he'd seen it a few hours earlier. Dawn wasn't for another half hour or so. If they were able to catch it, the view of Jerry coming down would be spectacular.

The clock now read thirty-five seconds. Sean looked from his dad to the screen and back again. "When is it going to start speeding up?"

"Should be any second now," Kevin said slowly, not taking his eyes off the steadily decreasing numbers that were marking the time until Jerry entered Earth's atmosphere. Beside those figures was another set of seconds, also steadily decreasing, but a little greater than the first – the countdown to ground impact.

Suddenly, the numbers measuring the asteroid's velocity began to change. They went slowly at first, just adjusting by tenths of a kilometer per second, but then started moving faster. There was an audible gasp as the numbers to the right of the decimal point began to pick up speed and the whole numbers started to drop.

Kevin stared incredulously at the screen, glancing around quickly to make sure he was looking at the right figures. They were dropping faster and faster now. Instead of speeding up, Jerry was slowing down.

The asteroid was ten seconds away from entering the atmosphere. A low, rhythmic whisper started mounting from the Russian scientists as they counted down, "Desyat' devyat' vosyem …"

Sean chanced a hurried glance at his father and saw confusion and worry in his face. How could Jerry's speed be decreasing? Didn't he just say that the gravitational force was going to make it speed up?

The last second ticked off and the clock reached zero. Sean noted that right at that moment, Jerry's velocity had dropped to a little over seven kilometers per second.

The entire room was silent as the last few seconds of the atmosphere entry countdown reading slowly ebbed away. The velocity reading continued to drop. Jerry was now speeding along at over six kilometers per second inside Earth's atmosphere.

Sean felt his heart pounding in his chest, almost two beats for every second that ticked away. He thought for a moment that by willing his heart to slow down, he could also slow down the clock, freezing time, bringing the sliding seconds to a trickle, so as to preserve the moment.

With only a couple seconds remaining, there was a brief streak of light, almost a flash, on one of the two dark screens showing the view of the early morning sky over central Russia. Then, the final countdown clock hit zero.

No one breathed. A few of the Russians held their hands out slightly to their sides as if trying to brace for the impact and keep themselves from falling over. But – there was nothing. Deep in the ground below the quiet, deserted streets of Moscow, not a tremor or any kind of disturbance in the Earth was felt. All the numbers that had been racing and changing so rapidly on the screen before were now a long string of goose eggs. It was as if the meteorite had completely disappeared.

As Sean continued staring at the digital readouts, he gradually became aware of a slight pressure that seemed to be building at the back of his skull. At first, he thought it was just the hum of all the electrical equipment surrounding him, but slowly it built until it felt like his head was caught in a powerful vice. The pain of the headache continued to grow, forcing Sean's hands to his temples as if to try to keep the sensation from expanding. A wave of nausea assaulted him and he sagged against the panel, squeezing his eyes shut to try to block out the pain. The sounds of the world around him receded and all he could hear was an overwhelming rushing, like a powerful river was pouring through his ears, carrying his pain-wracked brain along with it.

Suddenly, a host of new smells hit him like a wave: dank earth, vegetation and rotting wood. The pain lessened and he started to straighten up, opening his eyes. Sean stared in confusion at the sight before him. He saw the control room of the Russian Space Agency around him – everything was in commotion. People were running around, shouting commands into telephones. But, overlaid on top of this view was one of a dark, green forest, full of tall trees and dense undergrowth. It was like a double-exposed photograph – both scenes lying right on top of each other. Sean was completely disoriented as it appeared that trees and grass were growing out of computer monitors and

Russian technicians paced quickly through leafy fern beds. None of them seemed to notice what was happening. As Sean continued standing very still in the control room, the image of the forest seemed to be speeding by as if he were running.

The room or the forest or both, Sean couldn't tell, it began to brighten as if a faint light was moving toward him. Gradually his entire view began to be suffused by light, until it seemed that the entire world around him, both the control room and the forest, would explode in a dazzling flash. Just as it started to become so bright that Sean had to turn away, the light winked out, like it had just been switched off. The green forest, the smells, the rushing sensation in his head – everything was gone and Sean once again stood in the control room, everything around him erupting in noise and chaos.

The Russian technician nearest Sean and Kevin was shouting at the split screen in front of him as sweat ran down his face. Each time a phrase exploded from his mouth, new beads of sweat formed on his forehead and his pudgy face shook with the effort. Sean and Kevin stared on in confusion, watching Colonel Tomak and the other pilots on the screen swiveling in their seats to scream orders to their subordinates. The screen views from the two helicopters near the crash site that had previously shown the dark, early morning sky now showed nothing – only gray static.

"Garrett, what's going on? What happened?" Kevin yelled as his boss from NASA headquarters hurried over, heavy strain evident on his face.

The short, round man was nearly out of breath from his short run across the RKA command room. He paused briefly to glance at the screen in front of the still yelling technician before turning to Kevin.

"We've lost the video feed from both of the helicopters – just a few seconds ago. Colonel Tomak says that they lost radio contact right about when Jerry hit and the video cut out just a little after that. They're trying to confirm what…"

"Two radio-men down!" yelled one of the American scientists from a couple rows down. He waved his arms at Kevin and Garrett to get their attention before taking the short steps up to join them.

"Boris down there speaks English and says that two of Tomak's men, inside the Airborne Command Center, collapsed just a few seconds after Jerry hit. They haven't been able to revive them – they're saying that they're dead."

"What? How? What killed them?" Garrett shouted. The commotion in the room was so loud that they had difficulty hearing even though they stood right next to each other.

The American scientist shook his head. "No idea. They just dropped dead. No one else on the plane is injured and the aircraft itself hasn't been damaged at all."

"What about radiation levels?" asked Kevin. "Have they been able to detect anything?"

Right at that moment, a deep Russian voice boomed across the P.A. system causing everyone to briefly stop what they were doing and look toward the front of the room.

The RKA Director stood at a cheap-looking wooden podium, a microphone pointing stiffly toward his bearded face. He spoke rapidly, taking only half a minute to deliver his message, then paused and began in English.

"Airborne Command Center has confirmed at least one of helicopters has crashed. No communication received after meteorite hit. They still try to make contact with second helicopter, but nothing heard yet. Also, Meteorological Observation Center forty-six reports no seismic activity. None whatsoever around impact site or vicinity. There was no explosion from meteorite."

There was a brief moment of near silence after Director Kondratyev finished speaking. The only voices heard were those from the airplane pilots, their tinny chatter echoing off the still, blank faces of everyone in the room. Then, suddenly, the commotion resumed almost as quickly as it had stopped, voices and activity picking up like birds awakening at first light. Soon, the room was filled with a dull roar as technicians and scientists scrambled around trying to discover what had happened.

Kevin, Sean and the rest of their small group of Americans stood motionless, still staring down at the grave face of the RKA director. Seemingly heedless of the activity going on around them, they turned slowly to face each other, each expression a mixture of shock and confusion.

Sean remained immobile, quietly watching his father's face for hints or clues – anything. "Dad – what happened?"

Kevin glanced slowly at the large electronic map display running along the front wall of the cavernous room, then down at his son. "I don't know, son. I don't think anyone has any idea."

CHAPTER FOUR

The corner of the wall bit sharply into his shoulder as his entire body slammed into it. He had been using his left arm for support as he slowly inched down the dark hallway, but it had slipped and his withered left leg was no help. When it wasn't cramped with tension, as was the case now, it usually hung limp, a thin sack of bones and useless muscles dragging behind him, flopping around, wherever he went. His left arm was stronger, but with the tightly clenched muscles so difficult to control, especially with the occasional spasms, it often failed him. The right arm wasn't much help either as it was usually locked in a grisly, exaggerated bodybuilder's curl. His only saving grace, as Viktor thought of it, was his right leg – strong, well-developed and expert at hopping at a steady clip and negotiating turns. The doctors couldn't explain it – why this one limb turned out relatively normal when all the others were wracked by cramping, spasms and poor muscle tone. Of course, they were also unable to completely pinpoint the exact cause of his general condition.

Cerebral palsy had no cure. It was not a disease or an infection, but rather a result of brain damage that usually occurred during pregnancy or soon after birth. The brain injury impeded muscle development and control; symptoms varied from child to child, but most were grouped into various categories depending on the severity and type. Viktor's was a fairly typical case, but, luckily, with the use of his right leg, he wasn't completely confined to his bed. As many victims, he'd learned to use his body as it was given to him, neither waiting around for life to improve nor blaming anyone for his misfortune.

His mother, Irina Timofeyevna, on the other hand, blamed

everyone – the doctors, Viktor's father and, especially, Viktor himself. The small woman's reproach, however, never found its way to her own actions. Her refusal to abstain from alcohol and her beloved cigarettes during her pregnancy was never perceived by her as being remotely responsible for his condition. Nor were the resulting late night stumbles and falls as she returned home from yet another festive gathering of over-consumption. In her eyes, she was blameless. And in the small, dark apartment, her viewpoint was the only one that mattered.

Viktor steadied himself on his right leg and pushed away from the wall, swinging his right arm slightly for balance. He began hopping slowly again, his left leg tucked underneath as it bobbed and bounced with the motion. More saliva dripped from his mouth as his face contorted with the effort, his thick tongue thrust against the inside of his left cheek. He stared resolutely ahead, focusing on the doorway to the kitchen at the end of the hall.

The low muttering of the tiny, kitchen television set reached Viktor's ears as he neared the light-rimmed doorway at the end of the hall. None of his senses were impaired in anyway, something for which he was exceedingly grateful. Although speech was difficult and his words often unintelligible because of his inability to control his tongue and mouth, his eyes and ears functioned perfectly allowing him to fully observe and study the world, if not actually to participate in it.

He pushed open the door. Irina Timofeyevna stood in the corner, staring at the television, a greasy, yellow cigarette poking out of her curved lips as she casually sliced up a carrot. She was a solidly built, squat woman dressed in a dull, flowered smock, her graying hair hanging in strands down the sides of her face. Her lower lip slightly overlapped the upper, hiding a row of dark, yellowed teeth set in a severe under-bite. Her compact, round head and dark, little eyes completed the image of an angry bulldog about to pounce. The beaded eyes flicked over to Viktor briefly, then back to the television.

Dull morning light filtered through the dirty window, driving back some of the shadows that clung tenaciously to the dusty nooks and corners of the kitchen. Viktor's grandmother was sitting on the opposite side of the small room, a thick shawl hung over her stooped shoulders as she stared absently into space.

Two quick hops brought him to a stool beside the table. He looked at the half-loaf of bread sitting on an old, stained wooden cutting board and the dish of thick, yellow butter beside it. He glanced at the television then to his mother and back down at the bread.

Without taking her eyes from the little, black box, Irina Timofeyevna sawed off a slice of the bread and slathered some butter on it with the serrated blade. She stretched her arm across the table and shoved the bread into Viktor's open mouth, cramming in the edges as he tried to chew it up at the same time. She leaned back against the counter, wiped her hand on the filthy apron tied around her waist and resumed slicing the carrot, dropping the pieces into a pot on the stove. Not once did her small eyes leave the television set.

"Your aunt stopped by a few nights ago – I told her you were asleep," she said, the crimped cigarette bobbing up and down as she spoke. "She dropped off some more of those dumb children's picture books, but I'm probably going to have to go sell them to pay for all the food you eat. I'm not running a charity house here, you know."

As Viktor slowly chewed the somewhat stale slice of bread, using his left hand to move it out of the way of his constantly rolling tongue, he heard the door behind him creak open. A figure walked past the table, opened the cupboard and pulled out a cracked, white mug.

Viktor watched his older sister ladle some hot water into the mug from a pot on the stove. She dropped in a tea packet and a couple spoonfuls of sugar, stirring around the mixture as she leaned against the counter, a few feet away from her mother.

"Home late?" muttered Irina over her cigarette, her dull eyes still focused on the news program.

"Not much later than you – your light was still on," answered Tatyana as she sipped the tea.

Viktor pointed to the television. "Uht ahpenned – mete… mete…"

"Meteorite," Tatyana said. "Looks like it came down – somewhere near the Urals."

Viktor glanced up at his mother. She was staring at him, her cigarette burned to a tiny, glowing stub poking upward behind her pronounced lower lip. Her eyes flicked down to the table in front of Viktor. There was a glob of half-chewed bread sitting there, stuck to the tablecloth.

He heard a quick scrape of slipper across the floor and then felt a hand slap him on the back of his head. "Don't spit when you talk – I don't have all day to be cleaning up after you."

Viktor stared down at the small hunk of bread. He lifted his left hand, trying to maneuver it so that he could wipe up the tablecloth. Tatyana grabbed a rag from the sink and picked up the piece of bread.

She took another sip of tea from the mug and looked at Viktor. "Aunt Lydia called yesterday. She said she's going to come by at four o'clock to take you to the museum. She said there won't be as many people there in the afternoon."

"When you see her, tell her to stop buying all those books – we don't have that kind of money around here," snapped Irina.

"She pays for the books, Mama, she never asks us for money," replied Tatyana quietly.

"Well, we don't need her charity either. This is our family, we can take care of ourselves. Just because we didn't go to university and don't have artsy friends, doesn't mean we don't know how to provide."

Viktor glanced over at his grandmother. She hadn't moved. She never moved – at least, not for the last five years. One day they had found her, just sitting in the bedroom, staring off into space. She didn't respond to them at all, no matter how hard they shouted or pushed her. They never knew when she was hungry or when she needed to use the restroom. She had to be spoon-fed and constantly cleaned up after. Even worse than him, Irina Timofeyevna had said.

He looked back to his mother. His mind began to drift again, wondering why she had never allowed Aunt Lydia to take her own mother in, or him, for that matter. Irina had absolutely refused and continued to do so, becoming even more irritable and offended each time Lydia brought it up. She could certainly afford to – her late husband had left her quite comfortable financially and her schedule at the theater allowed for a great deal of flexibility. But, Irina would never give up her invalids, despite her constant complaining about their needs and the time and energy they took from her. Viktor suspected she did occasionally take the money that Lydia offered her, although she would never admit to it. He wondered where her pride stemmed from – her humble upbringing, her misfortune with various men while her sister had won a kind, gentle, wealthy man whose only fault had been dying too young. Viktor suspected it was the pride of the lowly, that he'd read about in some of Tolstoy's writings. That and her complete and thorough, stubborn meanness.

Irina cackled, the mirthless laugh sputtering out of her enormous under-bite in a series of quick, bullfrog croaks. She gestured at the television with the knife in her hand. "They say there wasn't any explosion – they promised an explosion. I bet they don't have any idea where the damn thing is." She laughed again.

Viktor stopped straining to try to see the screen and settled back onto his stool. He eyed the loaf of bread as his stomach grumbled and slowly raised his eyes to try to catch Tatyana's glance. But, she was staring at the television too, still sipping her tea. He didn't dare say anything – he'd already had one slap this morning, and when she started early, even the smallest thing could set her off for the rest of the day. Maybe Tatyana or his mother would bring a newspaper home in the next few days and he could catch up on all the meteorite news. Or, if not, he would just have to imagine how it had all happened, as he did with so many events in life that others simply took for granted.

Besides the occasional trip to the park across the street or an outing with his Aunt Lydia, which his mother rarely allowed, all of Viktor's life happened in the cramped apartment – and inside his head. Because in his imagination, he could go anywhere, do anything, be anyone he wanted. He could be normal, go to school with other kids, ride the Metro alone and see all the world around him however he liked. He knew the imagining of something could never take the place of the real thing, but that was all he had. It had been that way his entire life. And he expected that it always would be.

CHAPTER FIVE

Svyeta walked slowly with the throng of people pouring out of Red Square, her shoulder-length blonde hair swaying gently in the spring wind. The parade on the grounds in front of the Kremlin and St. Basil's Cathedral had just ended. It had been part memorial of some military victory Svyeta couldn't remember and part celebration of the coming of the meteorite, or 'Ilya' as the news reporters had been calling it.

It was a beautiful Sunday – a day off from school for twelve-year-old Svyeta and getting out in the rare sunshine to see the parade had sounded like fun. Plus it was close by her family's apartment so it had been relatively easy to get her six-year-old sister, Zhenya, to go. Their mother was away putting in overtime again at the hospital and their father was out drinking who-knows-where.

Svyeta tugged on her sister's hand as she slipped forward past a clump of slower moving people. The crowd was starting to thin out as everyone made their way home, catching buses or descending into the metro stations. There were a lot of school kids at the parade. They were probably just as anxious to get out and enjoy the nice weather, one of the first sunny days of the season.

She glanced back at her sister to make sure that she was doing okay. She didn't mind having to take care of Zhenya – in fact, she kind of liked it. Zhenya could be impetuous at times, but she always listened to her older sister. And being responsible for her gave Svyeta a sense of purpose – something to be in charge of that helped to keep the loneliness of their small apartment at bay.

Up ahead at the last corner before their street Svyeta saw a few older boys playfully shoving some of the younger boys as they passed, laughing loudly at each other. She recognized some of these older boys – they were a street gang who were always causing some kind of trouble when they hung out together. They were from this neighborhood, although she didn't know exactly where they lived. One of her friends had told her that they called themselves the Black Scorpions. Some of them wore pants and coats that looked like they hadn't been washed in, well, forever. Svyeta wondered if some of them might even be homeless – it seemed like more and more kids were living on the streets nowadays.

One of the boys she knew, Ivan, who was just a year or so older and had spiked white hair, turned and glanced in her direction. She knew him from school where he sometimes showed up for classes. He recognized her and turned to say something to a taller and older teenager behind him. Ivan jerked his head toward Svyeta, let out a short laugh, then turned to stare at her as she approached, a thin smile on his face.

"Hey Svyeta," Ivan said casually as she and Zhenya made their way by the boys. The older teen he'd just spoken to, a gaunt-faced boy with short cropped dark hair, let go of one of the younger kids they'd stopped and pushed him on his way. He stepped toward the girls, smiling broadly.

"I want to introduce you to someone," Ivan continued, gesturing at the older boy. The three other gang members snickered and hung back watching.

"This is Pyotr," Ivan said. "He's the leader of the Black Scorpions."

"Well hello beautiful," Pyotr said as he leered down at Svyeta, ignoring her younger sister entirely. "Ivan says you go to the same school – you live nearby, right? Why haven't I seen you around before? I think I would have remembered..."

"I really doubt that," Svyeta blurted. She'd said it without even thinking, her nervousness making the words sound accusatory, much harsher than she'd meant to. "I mean," she said quickly, "I'm sure there are so many girls your own age."

Pyotr laughed darkly. "There certainly are. But, I can still understand what *some*," he tilted his head toward Ivan, "see in you. Makes me think getting back to school to get some more...

learning opportunities might be a good idea."

"Pyotr's really smart – he doesn't need school. He always knows just what to do," Ivan said.

"Exactly, Ivan my friend, well said. In fact, I've got an idea."

Pyotr stepped after Svyeta as she started to edge away, holding Zhenya's hand tightly by her side.

"Some of us are getting together at Ivan's place right now, for a little party. You know, to celebrate that meteorite Ilya or whatever they're calling it. You should come over. And you can bring her too," Pyotr added as he gestured at Zhenya.

"We can't – my mom's waiting for us," Svyeta lied. "We have to be home now."

"Come on, you'll like it – Ivan's a ton of fun. You just need to get a drink in his hand. Plus," he leaned in, whispering conspiratorially, "I think he likes you."

Ivan either didn't hear or pretended not to as his expression didn't change at all – he just continued staring, his lips forming a tight line.

"I'm sorry," Svyeta said walking past the gang leader. "We have to get home."

"Svyeta!"

Both the girls and the group of gang members turned at the shout that had come from just a few paces away. An unshaven man in his late thirties with shaggy hair hanging over his eyebrows and ears and wearing mismatched clothes staggered toward them, swaying a bit after each step.

"Come here, what are you doing out so late?" His words were thick and garbled as he continued to lurch toward the girls.

Svyeta's heart hung in her throat. She wasn't sure if she was more relieved or terrified to see her father. On one hand she was grateful he was there to help rescue her from this situation and on the other she was scared he was just going to make it worse.

"Papa!" Pyotr yelled, holding his arms out wide before bursting into hysterical laughter and slapping the shoulders of his fellow gang members.

Zhenya ran to her father as he stopped and swayed dangerously, appearing to be on the verge of tipping over as he shifted his confused gaze to the teenage boys. She wrapped her arms around his legs trying to hold him steady.

Svyeta took her father's hand. "Let's go Papa, let's get home."

"Yes, Papa, you really should get home since it's so *late*. It's almost, oh my, it's almost noon! Looks like you've already started your celebration early, old man."

Svyeta's father's face turned red with anger and he began advancing toward Pyotr. Svyeta and Zhenya stepped in front of him, leaning their bodies into his to stop him like they had a hundred times before over the years. It was always better for him and everyone else if he just stayed away when he was like this.

"Papa, Mama wants us home. She's waiting with dinner," Svyeta said urgently to her father.

The man blinked and stopped in place, seemingly heedless of his two daughters still pushing their entire body weight into him. Finally, with Svyeta tugging on his hand, he turned away from the Black Scorpions and started shuffling toward their apartment building.

"Next time then, Svyeta. Don't worry though, we're always throwing great parties. Right Ivan?" Pyotr asked as he smiled after the two girls pulling their father home.

Ivan didn't say anything, just nodded as he stared at Svyeta. His eyes, which hadn't left Svyeta's face during the entire conversation, were wide and emotionless. Svyeta had no idea what thoughts were going on behind them. She found that she was a little afraid to know.

CHAPTER SIX

"We've got six Russian Air Force men dead – with no readily identifiable cause of death. And two reports within the last hour that say there may be similar mysterious deaths within the vicinity of Yekaterinburg," said a strong, slightly east-coast-accented voice. Administrator Leonard Hoffman paused in his loud tirade of the past few minutes to wipe his glasses with a monogrammed handkerchief, a dramatic effect at which the head of NASA was obviously well practiced.

Placing the glasses back on his pink face, he continued, "Now, I don't have to tell any of you here how ugly the blame game is going to get if we don't start coming up with some definite answers to explain these phenomena fairly soon."

Sean, Kevin, all Kevin's NASA colleagues and several U.S. government officials were crammed into a large conference room back at the Embassy. They'd stayed at the Russian Space Agency for a couple of hours after Jerry had landed, trying to find out more about what exactly had happened. After no additional information had seemed forthcoming, they'd all returned to the Embassy for an emergency meeting. Disorder and chaos was so widespread across the usually quiet compound that Sean had been able to walk right into the conference room behind his father and quickly found a seat against the wall at the back of the room. Everyone was too agitated and exhausted to notice the boy.

Jabbing his finger into the open dossier on the table, Administrator Hoffman addressed the large group of Embassy officials and the few representatives from NASA who were gathered in the now too-small and stuffy conference room.

"I need a status report that I can deliver to Washington on

what the hell went wrong and what we're doing to manage this situation. Garrett – what've you got for me?"

The boyish deputy director, his innocent-looking face and nervously darting eyes belying his fifty-three years, stood up from his seat at the table and addressed Hoffman in a somewhat timid voice.

"Well, we have about the same information as we did two hours ago. Asteroid JR0406 underwent a velocity reduction as it entered Earth's atmosphere. The slower speed was apparently not enough to cause the degree of impact and ensuing blast that our team had predicted. Because of this, we believe that there may be a chance that the meteorite is still largely intact. We haven't yet determined why it slowed down, but we do know that it is in the vicinity of the original impact site that we had previously estimated – a few hundred kilometers north-east of Yekaterinburg, most likely very close to the city of Serov."

Taking a deep breath, Garrett Larson continued, "As for the six soldiers, earliest reports indicate that they died of heart attacks. This could have been caused by some type of electrical surge that was generated when Jerry passed by or… it could be something else entirely. The Russians haven't exactly been willing to share much more at this point."

He looked questioningly around the room, possibly hoping that someone else had something to add. When no one volunteered any additional information or theories, he turned back to Hoffman who had been staring at him sternly during his entire report. "Administrator, we are unlikely to find out anything more until the Russian team that has already been deployed is able to find the exact site. Once they do, our people are on standby to fly out there and get to the bottom of this – with your permission."

Sean managed to steal a glance at his father over the shoulders of all the suited men sitting in front of him. He was standing at a table, near the front of the room, his eyes half closed as he listened to information that all of them already knew. Kevin had been complaining about a headache shortly after all the commotion started at the Russian Space Agency. Sean knew his father needed rest – he could see it the way that he was leaning against the table with his shoulders stooped. Sean's nap on the couch the night before was the only thing that was keeping him from falling asleep in his chair. He wondered if the news about Jerry not exploding had reached the television networks yet. Sean could just imagine his mother's fears once she saw that something unexpected had occurred. He hoped she wouldn't worry too much. They hadn't had a chance to call her yet – all communications outside the Embassy were forbidden. It was some kind of security lockdown.

Despite his concern for his parents and his own weariness, Sean was still very excited about Jerry. If large portions of the meteorite were still intact and they were able to get out to the crash site in time, they might even be able to identify some of the various types of gases that were still being emitted from the astral rock and get a better idea of composition and temperature before everything was tainted too much by Earth's elements. Sean hoped he would still be allowed to participate in the initial field research. He just couldn't imagine coming all this way and not being able to learn firsthand about the otherworldly visitor.

Suddenly, Sean was aware of eyes on him. He glanced around quickly and noticed the marine guard at the door, a very young man with blonde hair, was watching him from the corner of his eye. Sean's eyebrows came together questioningly and the marine nodded his head and glanced down at Sean's feet. The boy looked down and noticed that the half-full cup of juice that he'd placed there had tipped over and spilled on the carpet. He quickly grabbed a handful of napkins from a nearby table and began trying to mop up the mess. As he did so, he glanced back in embarrassment at the marine who was now staring straight ahead trying to restrain a smile that was tugging at the corners of his mouth. Sean smiled too and finished cleaning up the juice as best he could. He sat down and glanced over at the marine and mouthed "thank you." The marine smiled and nodded. Sean noticed the name on his uniform – "McCaney," then quickly turned his attention back to the debate going on at the front of the room. Administrator Hoffman was talking again.

"Look, I'm as anxious as anyone else to get out there and see what makes this thing tick, but we are trying to determine how to handle the situation with the international press and everyone back in D.C. They are looking at us as the representatives of the

U.S. in Moscow to explain what is happening here – what are we going to tell them?"

"Tell them nothing," said a loud voice from the other end of the table. Alan Connors, Director of NASA Public Relations, lounged sedately in his chair, hands resting comfortably on his chest as he leaned back. The PR man's eyes were closed and he looked like he was wincing slightly. "Tell them nothing at all happened."

"You can't be serious – we've got to tell them something," protested Hoffman.

"We will – we'll tell them the truth. That the meteorite came down and nothing happened – no explosions, no destruction, no nothing. Oh, and by the way, a few Russian airmen were killed in an accident and no, there's not any substantiated correlation between the two events. Probably just outdated Russian equipment. Then, we remind them that because Jerry didn't explode, there's a good chance that a 150 meter long meteorite is sitting out in the middle of some Russian forest waiting for us to come out and discover the secrets of the universe. And that they'll be the first ones to hear about it when we do."

Connors looked like he was entirely past the point of caring when the last time he'd slept was. His immaculate dinner suit from the night before was wrinkled, his hair mussed and his dry, cynical voice was laden with a strong under-current of apathy.

"Besides," Connors continued, "they don't have to wait to hear the news from us – the world's reporters have been broadcasting everything since early this morning. Sure, they don't know about the deaths yet, but when they do, they'll think for less than five seconds about those poor Russkiy soldiers before they start eating up the next juicy tidbits of Jerry updates."

He had their attention now. Sean thought it was strange that a room full of scientists and other experts were listening to the guy in charge of talking to the media when they were deciding what should be done about Jerry. Especially a guy who seemed like he'd almost given up entirely on the whole thing.

Connors stood up slowly, his eyes sweeping the expectant faces around the room. He walked over to stand beside Garrett Larson, the scientist's boyish face remaining blank.

"That's our position – an air traffic accident, no big

explosion and we're looking into it."

There were a few nods of ascent, mostly on the part of the embassy officials. Hoffman studied Connors' and Larson's faces for several seconds, then glanced in Kevin's direction briefly before speaking. "Alright, I think we can go with that – for now. The best idea is going to be to get Dr. Prochazek and the rest of the team out by tomorrow morning – we've got to get some real answers as soon as possible. We can't float this forever."

The room broke into scattered conversations as the breach-birthed plan began to be put into action. Connors' shoulders slumped and he stared dully ahead, seemingly unaffected by his small victory. He just looks tired and bored, Sean thought. He's not a scientist – he doesn't really care what happened to Jerry. He doesn't have the irresistible pull of scientific discovery to keep him going. Sean looked over at his father again. He couldn't put his finger on it exactly, but his father looked older somehow, like he'd aged a little just during the night. Sean knew he'd be okay once he had some sleep and was able to get rid of his headache. And once they were able to finally start going out to find Jerry. That's all he needed and he would be just as excited and strong as ever.

CHAPTER SEVEN

A blaring siren cut through Sean's dream and echoed loudly inside his head, making his ears ring as he sat straight up in bed. It sounded like it was right outside the room, about to come bursting through the door. But, as the sound faded, he realized it had to be an ambulance or police car outside, flying down the busy street with its lights flashing. He fell back down on his pillow and looked over at the clock – just after six. He still had some time, they didn't have to be at the airport until eleven and the car wasn't coming until a little after nine. A few more minutes of sleep...

Within a couple of minutes, Sean rolled over and sat up. He couldn't go back to sleep. His father lay peacefully in the other bed, not making a sound. Sean stepped out of bed and onto the carpet, making his way quietly over to the window and parted the drape. His fingers touched the glass as he stared out at the deserted, gray street below. There was still frost on the grass in the field a ways down from the metro station. The usual blare of music and din of kiosk owners hawking their wares were absent – the only sound was a dull hum, probably from some appliance or nearby factory. He unlatched the lock on the sliding glass door and stepped out onto the balcony.

It was cold – and starkly refreshing. He quickly walked over to the railing and grasped it. The light, gray metal almost burned his hands it was so cold – he gasped and could see his breath float away in a little cloud. He tightened his grip, whitening his tense knuckles and held on until the pain subsided.

Sean was alone. He couldn't see another living person anywhere around him, not on any of the other balconies or out on the street or even driving in cars. A sharp sense of loneliness struck him, but it was quickly washed away by his excitement for the day that was approaching. Just as he could imagine the slow arrival of pedestrians on the street below and cars heading in every direction and the noise of the metro station pouring across the city, he could see himself and his father boarding the plane, flying over a thousand miles to the middle of mostly uncharted territory, then arriving at the site of a completely new and foreign object, something completely different and undiscovered. This would be a day that he would remember forever.

Another siren started somewhere down the street, beyond his vision. Sean listened to it get louder as a police car raced down the middle of the empty road, its lights flashing. The car sped past the hotel, continuing for some unknown destination. As the blare of the siren was fading, Sean realized that he was still tightly holding onto the railing and was starting to lose feeling in his fingers and toes. He let go and stepped back into the room, walking quickly over to the large bed, just to warm up for a couple minutes. He wrapped the blankets around his white feet and burrowed his head into the large, square pillow, falling quickly asleep.

- -

Sean switched off the stream of hot, steaming water and began toweling off. He quickly got dressed and stepped out into the room where his father was busily packing a few last minute items. Sean switched on the T.V., turning the channel to some kind of Russian news program and started gathering up his things.

"Did you put some of your stuff in my suitcase? It's like it got smaller or something since we left Pasadena," Kevin said as he zipped up his luggage. After getting no response from his son, he quickly glanced over his shoulder and saw him sitting at the edge of the bed watching the Russian news.

"You catching all that?" he joked. Sean didn't respond. Kevin walked over to the end of the bed and sat down beside his son.

A somber looking newscaster in a dark suit was leaning forward on his desk, papers in hand, speaking rapidly at the camera as images flashed on a video screen behind him. Russian paramedics were carrying people out of an apartment building on stretchers and loading them into the backs of ambulances. Other men in various uniforms holding guns and police batons were gathered nearby, chatting with some people in a small crowd lined up outside the building. No one on the stretchers was moving.

"What happened? Was there a fire?" Kevin asked.

Sean just shook his head.

"Don't we get CNN or something? Maybe they've got the BBC?" Kevin said.

Sean switched the station, running through several Russian channels – most had some news report with similar images of people being pulled out of apartment buildings. Several had what appeared to be family members surrounding them, crying and screaming hysterically. They stared at the images, searching for some clue in the faces of the distraught onlookers as to what was going on.

Finally, Sean found the BBC World station. He turned up the volume again, just as a voice spoke over the image of some helicopters flying over a large forest, "…expected to begin securing the site today and starting a preliminary investigation."

The picture switched to a smartly dressed, pale man sitting at a desk in front of a busy newsroom.

"And now, back to our earlier report on the unexplained deaths. For those of you just tuning in, reports began flooding in just a few hours ago of strange deaths all over the Russian Federation, Eastern Europe and in many parts of China."

More images of people being dragged out of apartment buildings and houses on stretchers flashed across the screen. Sean and Kevin watched even more bereaved families attempting to hold on to loved ones as a few paramedics attempted resuscitation before finally giving up.

The newscaster's voice continued as the picture switched from location to location – Prague, Bucharest, Tbilisi, Beijing, Shanghai, Kiev, Moscow. "Officials are saying that it's almost impossible to estimate the number of deaths at this point, but some are speculating that they could total in the tens of thousands, possibly up to one million."

The newscaster was back on the screen again, dark circles under his eyes evidencing the early hour in London. Someone handed him another sheet of paper and he glanced down at it quickly before looking back at the camera.

"We've just received confirmation of similar deaths occurring in Tokyo. Police and ambulance dispatchers everywhere have been assaulted with a barrage of calls and many are already overwhelmed with the task load. All emergency personnel have been called in to help attend to the victims and their families. As of yet, no symptoms or other cause of death have been discovered. All reports indicate that victims died in their sleep. We will continue with updates throughout the hour."

The screen switched to an energy drink commercial and Kevin sunk down to the bed beside Sean. The boy turned to look at his father. Kevin sat staring at the television screen, his mouth open in shock. "What's going on, Dad?"

From out on the street, they heard another siren sound as a couple of ambulances raced by.

CHAPTER EIGHT

Morning rays from the window shone through the glass lamp sending geometric wisps of green light onto the bedroom walls. The sun always rose through her window in the mornings, but Elizabeth had become used to it very quickly and she rarely woke up before her mother came in to tell her to get ready for school. Except for today. She didn't remember when she had started staring at the slender-necked green lamp, but she thought that it must have been quite a while ago. The white walls were definitely lighter than they had been the last time she'd looked. The shapes of green light occasionally danced as the wind blew her white curtains.

Her mother had bought her the old-fashioned oil lamp the day before at an antiques shop near the ice cream parlor. The lamp's neck was narrow at the bottom and the top, but swelled out in the middle. A wick rose up from a round base made of the same glass where the oil was held. There had been many prettier things in the shop, but this one had caught Elizabeth's eye right away – she liked how the light split after passing through the lamp. Its dark green color and gentle curves, for some reason, made Elizabeth a little sad for the small object. It was completely unlike the other ornate objects in the store and didn't seem like it belonged there, but, rather, somewhere else where it could have its own space. She had placed it on the table beside her bed.

The door swung open softly and Elizabeth heard her mother's step on the carpet. She lay there motionless, trying not to breathe, wondering if her mother knew she was awake. Wind continued to blow the soft, transparent curtains sending the small shards of green light racing across the bedroom walls and ceiling. Elizabeth heard her mother step closer to the bed and she knew that in a second, she would feel a gentle hand on her shoulder and hear her mother's voice. That's how it always was – she would wake to a gentle pressure and calm voice, never as jarring as when her dad or Sean sometimes had to wake her up. She often wondered how long her mother had been standing there, gently prodding her, bidding her to return from sleep, but not entirely wishing to do so.

Elizabeth waited for the familiar hand on her shoulder, but it didn't come. But, she hadn't heard her mother walk out of the room either. Within a few moments, too curious to wait any longer, Elizabeth rolled over and opened her eyes, trying to make them look bleary so that her mother would think she was just waking up.

She was just standing there, next to Elizabeth's bed, looking out the window, seemingly lost deep in thought. Her mother looked tired. Elizabeth had heard the phone in her parents' bedroom ring earlier that morning when it was still dark – she must have been talking for a long time.

"Was that Dad on the phone?" she asked quietly, still lying still in her bed.

Her mother turned at her voice and nodded, but didn't say anything. Elizabeth rolled on to her back and stretched. "Are they done with all the research stuff yet? When are they coming home?"

Elizabeth's mother sat down on the bed.

"Oh, not quite yet. Some things... some unexpected things came up, so they might be there for a while still. Maybe longer than they'd planned," said her mother quietly. She stared into space for a few moments, lost in thought, and began chewing the inside of her cheek. Suddenly noticing the silence and Elizabeth's questioning stare, she turned back to her daughter and smiled.

"I think your father's getting a cold or flu or something – he said he had a terrible headache. He just needs some rest. You know how he likes to stay up late reading. Sean's doing okay though. He's tired too – they've had some pretty late nights already. So much activity..."

Elizabeth watched her mother's gaze drift away again as the phone conversation turned over again and again in her mind. Elizabeth wondered how her brother really was. He always acted so tough at home, even when he was sick or got hurt. She knew that he'd really been a little nervous when their father had told him that he would get to go to Russia. Of course he'd been excited, but she knew he was a little scared about the whole trip. But, Elizabeth knew he'd be okay – somehow, Sean always was. She hoped the meteorite research didn't take too long – she thought it was all pretty silly anyway that all those people would want to travel to the middle of nowhere just to look at a big rock. Elizabeth just wanted both of them to come back home so that her mother would stop worrying so much and everything could get back to normal.

"Why don't you stay home from school today and help me around the house? I've got to get those plants into the garden. We could take a free day – just you and me. Sound good?"

Elizabeth stared at her mother, unsure of how to respond. She must really be missing her father to allow Elizabeth to take a day off from school. But, the twelve-year old knew when to not ask questions. Maybe, she thought to herself, it would be okay if Dad and Sean take a little longer in Russia – this could be fun.

CHAPTER NINE

Sean carefully balanced the tray in his left hand as he fumbled with the key in his right. It hadn't bothered him nearly as much as it had his father that the hotel still used metal keys rather than the otherwise ubiquitous magnetic cards. He just chalked it up as another charming and inexplicable quality of Russia, a country that always seemed poised at the edge of the modern age while still being held back by some elusive and primal force.

Like the city's transportation, he thought. He had seen some very nice cars in Moscow – BMW's, Mercedes – especially around the embassy and sometimes parked in front of the hotel. But, most of the cars on the streets looked like they were at least twenty years old and of such an outdated model and make that Sean wasn't sure that he would be able to recognize them even if he had had any knowledge of Russian automobiles. Most of them looked like they had been on their last leg several thousand miles ago and were only still running because of their owners' sheer stubbornness – tires were cracked and balding, pipes and other parts occasionally dragged underneath and clouds of black smoke shot out of the exhaust pipes every time they accelerated. All of them were covered in a thick layer of grime.

Despite the number of wheeled death traps lumbering down the city streets, there were still scores of pedestrians and public transportation riders. Sean had watched crowds line up and literally fight each other for space on buses and trolley cars. The city had seemed completely dead just a few shorts hours ago. Now, the stream of humanity pouring in and out of the VDNKh metro station across the street never seemed to stop. Like the cars, most of the buses and trolleys appeared to have been built decades ago, with the only update being an additional coat of thick, dull red, yellow or off-white paint each few years since.

The room door swung open and Sean walked in, hunched over as he held the tray of food against his chest. He locked the door behind him and then set the tray on the table over by the window. His dad was talking loudly into the telephone, covering his other ear with his hand. His face was lined with worry – sweat beaded his forehead.

"Garrett? Garrett? Okay, I can't hear you again – hello? Are you – yes, yes, okay, we'll try, but I'm not sure how – hello? Hello – Garrett?" he yelled into the phone.

Finally, he pulled the receiver away from his ear and stared at it for a second as if waiting for it to begin speaking again, his face completely blank. Suddenly, he slammed it down into its cradle, several times until the entire phone fell off the night stand. He reached down to grab the cord when Sean yelled, "Dad!"

Kevin jerked his head up, seeming to notice his son for the first time. His face was red and contorted in a grimace of rage, his eyes jerking wildly from Sean to the phone to the television and back. Sean stared back at his father, watching him slowly straighten up and wipe the spittle from his lips with the back of his hand.

"Did you get cut off again?" Sean asked as he walked over to the phone lying on the floor.

Kevin nodded and looked dazedly around the room. Sean set the phone back on the nightstand and pushed his father into a sitting position on the bed, hands on his shoulders.

"What did he say – what did he say to do?"

Kevin swallowed, trying to slow his breathing and pounding heartbeat. "Leonard's, uh, Administrator Hoffman's dead along with about half the embassy staff. He's there…" Kevin paused, a wave of nausea surging into his head and throat. He strengthened his grip on Sean's arms and continued, "Garrett's at the Embassy now. He's trying to make some calls."

Both father and son glanced over at the television. Images continued to flash across the screen – crowds of families mourning their dead, masses storming airports and bus terminals with all their belongings packed in a few bulging suitcases, mobs running down the streets as they broke windows and pulled out televisions and stereos and set fire to buildings. There was blind panic everywhere.

They had been trying to reach anyone by phone all morning: first home, then the Embassy, but it was almost impossible with the amount of traffic that was pumping through the lines. Sean had finally wandered downstairs in search of something for them to eat when his frustration level began to rise almost as high as his father's. There had only been a few of the hotel staff downstairs – one of the cooks let him in the kitchen to make a couple of sandwiches.

Sean looked now into his dad's eyes as they almost glazed over staring at the screen. It wasn't the jammed phone lines that made Sean frustrated – it was his father's reaction to them. Rather than meeting the difficulty with his usual candid analysis and detached cynicism, his father had become angrier and more irrational each minute. Through the anger in his face and voice, Sean saw fear in his eyes – fear that was gripping him tighter and tighter. He remembered seeing his father that way once before when Elizabeth had been running through the kitchen and tripped on a chair, gouging the back of her head on the corner of the open dishwasher. He'd completely panicked, stammering and yelling, trying to hold her and pacing back and forth at the same time. His mother had been kept just as busy trying to calm her husband as she was in treating her daughter's injury. Sean didn't understand how his father could be so good at astrophysics and managing a whole team of scientists and at the same time be unable to cope with some blood and a screaming girl.

Now, Sean was trying to do exactly what he'd seen his mother do – gripping him by the shoulders and speaking calmly into his face. At the same time, Sean struggled to keep his own fear out of his voice and features, knowing that any hint of weakness would only send his father further into greater hysteria.

"Dad, Dad – what did Garrett say to do? Does he want us to go to the Embassy?"

Kevin turned back to look at Sean, a look of sharp pain etched into his face. "He said to, but how are we going to get there? I don't think we can even get a car! I don't know about the metro, we can't read the signs..." his voice trailed off as he stared down at the floor.

Sean shook his father's shoulders again, forcing him to look up into his face. "Did you get through to the airport? Do they have any flights going back to America?"

Kevin looked sadly at his son and shook his head. Then, with a long, slow breath, he said, "I don't think we're going to be able to get a flight today, we're going to have to wait until things calm down a little. Maybe the government will freeze all flights or something – I don't know, I don't know."

"Did you talk to Mom?" Sean asked carefully, keeping his words low so that the tightness in his throat wouldn't be audible.

"No, I couldn't get through," Kevin replied weakly.

They both looked back at the T.V., its grisly images of widespread death and grief reflected in their faces. The activity out on the street could be plainly heard through the window – cars, buses, loud music from one of the CD kiosks in front of the metro station. From the sound of things, it was a completely ordinary day on the streets of Moscow. The silent images flashing in front of them created a sense of looking down on another world, somewhere completely removed from their present location, another time and place that had been abandoned by all reason and hope. For a moment, none of it seemed real – just some kind of illusion. The pictures on the screen looked as if they were just from the latest iteration in the Hollywood disaster movie genre. The ambulances and police cars would all be returned to some props warehouse at the end of the day. The scores of people lying on stretchers and in the streets were merely actors that at any second would return to their plush trailers to sip imported, bottled water. And, in any minute, the whole thing would end and the audience would stand up and go home.

But, it had to be real. The phone lines were jammed, weren't they, Sean thought. And there had been almost no one downstairs. No, this was all real. Somehow everything on the screen was happening just as they were showing it. People everywhere were waking up to find their mother or their sister or their husband dead, never to wake again. Sean slid his hands up his father's shoulders and around his neck, pulling him close to his chest in a tight hug.

- -

Sean woke to the feeling of being turned over as his father pulled the bedspread down from underneath him. He pulled himself up to a halfway sitting position and looked around the room. The alarm clock on the nightstand said ten o'clock. They'd been in the hotel room all day waiting for word from anywhere or anyone. No one seemed to know what was going on.

"When did I go to sleep?" Sean asked.

"Oh, probably a couple hours ago. I just got off the phone with your mom. They're doing okay. She's... she's been trying not to watch the news, but it just seems like it's everywhere..."

"Do they know what's causing people to die? Have more died today? Any in the U.S.?" Sean asked quickly as he sat up.

Kevin nodded somberly. "No one knows for sure, but they say it could be several hundred thousand, maybe a million or so – just in the U.S. There's bound to be even more around the rest of the world. No one even has time to count – there are just too many. They just can't get a handle on it... sounds like everything's pretty chaotic."

Sean watched his father. He seemed to be doing better than he had earlier that day, but that could be just because he was more tired now and didn't have the energy to get worked up into a panic. The teenage boy wondered what they were going to do – if there was anything they could do. At least, he thought, I'm here with my dad. He'll figure this out, I know he will.

"Mrs. Donaldson next door..." Kevin continued. "She came over and chatted with your mother for a few minutes. Her son in Denver died last night. His wife called – she didn't hear anything during the night, he just didn't wake up this morning... but, Elizabeth's okay, she's doing fine, they're both fine, just a little scared."

Sean slid his feet to the floor. "What are we going to do tomorrow? Are we going to the Embassy?"

"I haven't been able to reach Garrett or anyone else there all day. Phone just rings. I was talking to Bob Quidley earlier. His hotel's a little closer to the Embassy than we are and he heard from some other reporters that a bunch of Russians were trying to break into the compound. The marines had to seal the place off – they're not letting anyone in or out until the mob dissipates. He heard too that the government has shut down the airports and most of the train system. The metro's still running, but it only goes to the edge of the city. He said most of the mob outside the Embassy was probably just trying to get a flight out or something. They always think the Americans have all the answers."

Sean quickly changed into his pajamas and Kevin helped him crawl back into bed and pulled the blankets up over his shoulders. "I'm going to keep in contact with Bob – he's going to call in the morning and let us know if he's heard anything more. We'll probably just lie low tomorrow and ride this out. I bet they'll have the airports back up and running by next week. As long as we stay inside, we'll be fine."

He patted Sean's head as the boy's eyes continued to droop lower and lower until finally settling down for sleep. The streets outside were quiet again. It was as if the whole world had gone home to dig in deeper, seeking refuge from the rising storm of fear.

CHAPTER TEN

No matter how hard Viktor tried to hold the book still, the delicate pages kept quivering, preventing him from reading even a few lines without worsening his already painful headache. He wasn't sure if it was the muscles in his face that were twitching especially badly as they did some mornings, or it if was his left hand at the top of the pages. He sighed and let his rigid hand slip off the book to rest by his side.

Luckily, he hadn't really been enjoying the book anyway. It was an old book that he'd found on one of the shelves in his room. He hadn't counted in a long time, but he thought that he'd probably read at least half of them by now. Many were Soviet romance novels from the sixties; the plots typically centered around some young factory worker falling in love with a dashing minor government official, with the young woman eventually giving her life to save him from some terrible foreign threat. He'd learned by now to pass these over for the more interesting text books on physics, astronomy, history and foreign languages. He realized that most of them were horridly outdated, but he didn't have the opportunity or means to get more recent editions. Once in a while his Aunt Lydia was able to sneak a few books into the apartment for him, but most of these turned out to be young teen adventure novels.

Viktor had woken earlier than usual that morning with a pounding headache. He'd tried to go back to sleep, but the pain had already fully wakened him. He had made his way into the kitchen as quietly as he could, knowing that if he made too much noise he would hear about it later from his mother. He ate breakfast, which helped to temporarily ease the pain in his temples, then had picked up the book. No one else was up yet.

Both his mother and Tatyana had come home early yesterday. They said that some virus was going around and their bosses didn't want anyone else to catch it so they sent everyone home, telling them to take a few days off. Missing a couple days of work didn't bother either of the women. It had already been a couple of months since either of them had been paid, so an additional few days of no pay wouldn't really make much of a difference at this point.

Viktor placed his right foot firmly on the floor beneath his stool and slowly pushed himself up, balancing with his left hand on the table. He slowly hopped around the edge of the table and was halfway to the doorway when he stopped and turned around. After slide-hopping his way back to the table so that he was parallel with it and facing the doorway, he half-squatted down on his good leg and used his left hand to slide the book over to the edge where he could trap it with his right elbow. The cramped fingers on his left hand carefully guided the book toward his armpit until it was tucked under his arm. He then raised himself to a standing position and hopped into the hall.

Halfway down, Viktor noticed that the door to his mother and grandmother's room at the end of the hall was open. Maybe mama's already up, he thought. Since she has the day off, she'll probably want her tea in bed. Probably a better idea to ask her now rather than have her loudly complaining in a few minutes, he said to himself as he slowly shuffled down the hall. Early morning was usually the best time to deal with her – she hadn't yet had the chance to warm up to yelling.

The ancient, paint-peeled doorframe bit into his shoulder as he leaned against it, poking his head around the half open door. He could see his mother lying on her back, her mouth open. Viktor had never seen her mouth open so wide – she usually kept it tightly shut, a habit that she'd developed long ago to hide her extreme under-bite. He could see her dark yellow teeth poking out of nicotine-stained gums and her small, slightly upturned nose. Her covers were pulled tightly up to her chin – she didn't look like she had been up at all yet.

Viktor glanced over at his grandmother on the other side of the room as he was turning to go. She was in roughly the same position with her hands neatly folded on her chest. She was still wearing her rings, four or five large, tarnished brass bands with fake rubies and emeralds. Since either Irina or Tatyana had had to get her dressed and undressed every day for the past several years, they had long ago given up removing her precious rings. If they forgot to put them back on in the morning, she would whine loudly until they did.

He couldn't remember exactly who she'd received the rings from, even though she'd told him the story once when he was a little boy. He recalled that it was someone besides her late husband, possibly a former employer or some close friend. Viktor had always thought that the rings were terribly ostentatious, but who was he to tell old women what to wear on their... he suddenly came to himself and remembered that he'd been standing in the doorway for several minutes. During that whole time, her hands lying on her chest hadn't moved at all.

He glanced quickly over at his sleeping mother, wondering if he should wake her to find out if his grandmother was okay. As he considered this, his eyes locked on to his mother's chest and he slowly counted out each second. After a minute or so he made a couple, quick bent-knee hops over to the side of her bed, taking care not to let his slipper slap on the floor when he landed. Standing above her, Viktor could see that her chest was, in fact, not moving at all. Her mouth hung open motionlessly – not a sound was coming out. She looked perfectly peaceful.

Viktor planted the heel of his left hand firmly on the mattress as he eased himself down to kneel beside her. He strained his neck to get his face as close to hers as possible. After a few seconds of staring at the sun-weathered, waxy skin, he gently turned his head and laid it on her chest.

After half a minute, he slowly raised his head and looked back into his mother's face. She did look peaceful, he thought. The almost constant scowl and look of derision that had adorned her features for as long as Viktor could remember were gone, replaced now by a calm serenity. Viktor continued to stare at her as tears came to his eyes, until, finally, he laid his head back down on her forever silent chest.

CHAPTER ELEVEN

Cold water ran down Svyeta's hands, dropping off her fingers in rivulets before falling down the drain. It was early morning and everything was quiet and still – her favorite time. Her mother was often at work at dawn, either finishing her shift or having just started one, as she had today. Zhenya usually slept later, especially on school days. And her father always slept late, almost until noon when he would habitually rise and begin drinking again to chase away the pain of his hangover. So, she usually had the apartment to herself – time to think, time to gets things done. Because if she didn't who else would?

Svyeta pulled her hands out of the still ice cold water and waved them absently to chase away the somber thoughts and the stab of pain in her head. She'd awoken with a headache, but it had subsided once she got dressed. The pain eased now and she started washing the dishes.

With all that was going on in the world after the meteorite landed she wondered how long the water would last. Her mother didn't like for her and Zhenya to watch television that much, but she'd caught a few minutes of the news yesterday. She'd seen people being pulled out of buildings, ambulances rushing to the hospital, lines stretching outside of stores, crowds of worried faces. Her friend, Elena, who watched much more television than she did, had called after they found out school was cancelled. She said that there was some type of sickness going around and that many people were sick and some were dying. They hadn't found a cure yet, but were going to soon – at least that's what Elena had said. She was much more worked up about it than Svyeta was. That was pretty typical.

After finishing the dishes, Svyeta was sweeping from

underneath the kitchen table when her father emerged slowly from his bedroom. His feet plodded heavily across the wood floor, his slippers scraping dully as he pulled his feet forward. The kitchen table chair creaked as he eased his weight onto it.

"Breakfast?" Svyeta asked as she swept dust into the garbage can.

Her father stared glassy eyed, his elbows resting heavily on the table.

"The usual. Ha!" He smiled at his daughter.

She set a glass in front of him. He pulled an almost empty vodka bottle from the shelf, filled the glass and downed it.

"Ahh," he said, closing his eyes. "That's better. Much better my Svyetochka. Sweet Svyetochka, you're so good to take care of your papa so well."

He jammed the heel of his hand into his eye, rubbing deeply. "Where's your mom?"

"At work. They wanted her to do a double last night, but she had a bad headache so she came home just after midnight to rest for a while. I think she left again at four or five. Hospital was really busy – she said they had so many people coming in with that flu or whatever it is."

Svyeta glanced over at her father, watching him fill his second glass as she wiped off the counter.

"Elena called yesterday. She said her mom's pretty worried about it. They're probably going to just stay indoors for a while to see…"

"Who were those boys yesterday? The ones bothering you on the street?"

Svyeta looked at her father again. He was still staring out the window, his head resting on one hand.

"Nobody, Dad. They were just fooling around. They like to bother kids on their way home. But mostly just the boys, they don't give me any trouble."

"Do you know their names? Who are their parents?"

She paused. Her father had never been interested in her friends before. Why the questions now?

"I only know a couple of them – that tall, older boy is Pyotr and the shorter light-haired one is Ivan. Ivan actually goes to my school. I don't know their last names. I think they live around

here, but I don't know where. They're just idiots anyway. I don't
pay any attention to them."

Her father slid his glass back and forth slowly on the table.
"They were paying attention to you."

Svyeta didn't respond. She was surprised he remembered
anything at all from yesterday.

"You're getting older now. Boys are going to start paying
more attention. So, you'll have to too. You need to watch out for
yourself. You pretty girls have to watch out. Pretty girls always
have it harder. Do you understand?"

"Yes, Dad." She thought she understood – mostly. She
knew she needed to be careful around boys – especially those
Black Scorpion boys. But, she didn't understand why her father
was talking to her about this now – he never had before. Never
had seemed to notice – or care.

"That's my girl, that's my Svyetochka. Be a sweetie and grab
me another little bottle. This one's run dry."

CHAPTER TWELVE

Bob Quidley's call came late in the morning on Tuesday. Both Kevin and Sean had been awake since a little after six, huddled under the covers in their beds because of the cold. The heating had gone off sometime during the night.

"Okay, right, thanks Bob," Kevin said and hung up.

He pulled the blanket tighter around his shoulders, looked at Sean and shook his head.

"No news really. Bob went over to the Embassy this morning, but couldn't find anyone around – he rang at the front gate, but no one answered. It looked like there might have been some kind of riot outside – broken glass and some tear gas canisters. He said the streets are mostly deserted, but it looks like some started looting last night. Smashed windows, some limited fires, that sort of thing. He said we should just sit tight. He'll call again if he finds out anything more."

Sean nodded somberly and looked around the small room where they'd been effectively confined for over a day now. Looking back at his father, he asked, "Does that mean we can turn on the T.V. now?"

Kevin had made Sean turn it off earlier that morning, because it seemed like just the same report over and over – the same grim news from the day before. Now, he nodded quietly to his son and Sean flicked the remote.

A well-dressed British reporter appeared on the screen. He looked like he was under a lot of stress and fumbled through the pages in front of him as he spoke somewhat nervously into the camera. Occasionally, video footage from locations around the world would appear on the screen: weeping families in Vietnam, Australia, India and South Africa watching loved ones being bundled up and carried away.

"Emergency officials report that thousands have died in the United Kingdom since yesterday morning. Today, Tuesday, is shaping up to be about the same, if not worse. U.S. broadcasts indicate that similar scores of people perished yesterday… emergency response personnel across the nation have been entirely, uh, overwhelmed and many callers are being told that they will have to wait for several hours even possibly days before receiving any attention. One paramedic is quoted as saying that 'we are not able to do anything – there's nothing to treat, we're just collecting bodies.' But, experts think that they may have found at least a small clue as to the cause of these unexplained deaths."

The scene switched to an older man in a tweed jacket and glasses sitting in front of a large shelf of books. The subtitle indicated that he was Dr. Sherman Folsom of the St. Thomas Hospital.

"As of yet we are not able to accurately ascertain what distinguishes any of the victims from those still alive. Almost everyone is experiencing headaches – I myself have had a severe, almost migraine level headache since yesterday afternoon. Almost ninety percent of the victims have reported similar headaches the night before they died. We've received a few initial reports from the post mortem examiners. They indicate that nearly half suffered some type of massive stroke, with many of the arteries in the brain squeezed tight. A few of the cases even showed signs of some brain swelling, which is completely incongruous with other signs of stroke. As to the other half not exhibiting these symptoms – we have no idea. Their hearts have just stopped."

Sean jerked his head in his father's direction. Kevin was still bundled up in his blanket, black-rimmed glasses circling his tired eyes, long brown hair pointing every which way. "Didn't you have a headache yesterday?"

"Yeah, I did, but it went away – I… I don't remember when exactly, but I didn't have one this morning when I woke up," Kevin said slowly, then turned to look at his son, more alarmed. "You don't have a headache, do you?"

Sean shook his head. "I feel fine. I'm kind of hungry though."

Dr. Folsom continued, "Until we have something we can go on, we're not able to treat this right now. We just don't have any idea what it is."

Sean and Kevin switched off the T.V. and ventured briefly downstairs. They couldn't find anyone in the restaurants' kitchens, so they just helped themselves. Sean and Kevin weren't sure whether the other guests were all just locked up in their rooms as they were or if they had all fled. If it was the latter, they wondered, where had they all gone? Either way, they didn't see another living soul on their brief trip downstairs.

More people were out on the streets later that afternoon. Kevin and Sean watched in silence from the balcony as small gatherings of tightly bundled Russians poured through the kiosk market surrounding the metro station. They couldn't make out many details from their vantage point across the street, but it looked like a few of the merchants had opened up shop. Old babushkas, young mothers, decorated veterans and thin-faced, young men alike were carrying away cloth sacks packed with loaves of bread and potatoes – stocking up.

Kevin made a few more attempts to get Sean to leave the television off, but was ultimately unsuccessful. The young boy sat on the edge of his bed, staring blankly at the changing images on the screen: ambulances with sirens blaring, racing down the streets only to arrive too late – again. One story reported on the mass exodus of people from densely populated areas to more remote villages and mountain hideaways, further compounding the already growing sense of loneliness and desertion present in the world's largest cities. Some experts estimated that half of London's usual occupants had either succumbed to the mystery plague or had joined relatives in the suburbs or smaller nearby towns.

Mystery plague. Illness. Epidemic. The strange deaths. Sean pondered all the different names for what was going on around the world. He'd half been waiting for the official title of the world's latest disaster to be handed down from the truth-making media. That's how it had always happened before. The war between the United States and Iraq hadn't been just that – it was "America at War" or the military-originated moniker "Operation: Iraqi Freedom." The "events of September 11, 2001" had obviously been too long to fit into the sound-bite-size news reports and had been truncated to "America under Attack" or the more sensational "Terror in the Skies" depending on the television network. But, no such title had yet been given to this latest series of occurrences as far as Sean could tell. The BBC had been airing portions of CNN reports and he couldn't see that the U.S. had decided upon any single tagline to describe what was happening.

What could you call it, he thought: "World Epidemic" or "The Silent Deaths?" Maybe they were all too afraid to name it. Where before news agencies had been able to conveniently contain and package world events for the rapt public into a single delineated and easily definable name, now they were afraid to attempt any name at all. They weren't able to conceive of a single phrase that would encompass the horror of what they were experiencing. Or, maybe, they were just too terrified to call it what they all deep down knew it to be, but were unable to say aloud: "The End of the World."

For the first time since yesterday morning, when it all had started happening, Sean wondered if anyone that he knew had died yet. Like, maybe Mr. Alvarez, his physical science teacher. Sean liked Mr. Alvarez. He wasn't old and grumpy like many of the other teachers. His classes were always informative, challenging and, occasionally, even a little entertaining. What if he wasn't there when they got back to Pasadena? Sean supposed that the school could always pull in Mrs. Gilberts or one of the other science teachers, but that would be really weird. Substitutes only came in when teachers got sick. Teachers weren't supposed to die. No one was.

I'm not afraid to die, he told himself. It doesn't sound like it's really all that painful, you just go to sleep one night with a headache then don't wake up in the morning. Pretty simple, he thought. I guess I would miss out on some things – getting to drive a car, going to MIT, finding out if Jenny Hilton really liked me or if her friends were just lying. He guessed that he would be okay if he missed out on those things if he had to.

Sean looked over at his father. Kevin was sitting at the table by the sliding glass door to the balcony, the blanket wrapped around him again. He had a folded-over magazine in his hands, but he was staring out the window, his eyes glued to something – or nothing – just over the edge of the railing.

As Sean was looking at his father's long, unkempt brown hair and thick glasses hanging on the slight rise of his nose, almost teetering on the brink of slipping down his face, the thought came to him that his father might die. This immediately struck him with a jolt of pain deep in his stomach and a flash of heat spread up into his cheeks. A brief image of his father lying on the bed, cold and unmoving, flashed across his mind and he hurriedly pushed it away with thoughts of them back at home in the living room, waiting for his mother to finish dinner.

And what about Mom, Sean thought. What would happen if we got back and found Elizabeth alone and Mom asleep upstairs, not moving, not talking? As much as the thought of his own death had not really bothered him, the idea of his parents dying struck him forcefully, depriving him of the ability to reason clearly. All he could picture was the two of them, lying side by side in some shallow grave, their eyes closed and arms folded over their chests as he and Elizabeth stood there, holding hands.

Suddenly, Sean realized that he really missed his mother and Elizabeth. More than he ever had while he'd been at Scout camp for a whole week. And more than he'd expected to. Leaving home for a week or so to see the Jerry site in Russia was supposed to have been the pinnacle point in his young life. He'd secretly been a little afraid about being away from home for so long, but he'd convinced himself that it would be okay since his father would be there. But, now, with everyone dying... he just wanted to go back home. He wanted his family to be together and not ever have to go anywhere again.

Sean rose slowly to his feet, the strength in his legs having fled. He treaded softly over to where his father sat and put his hand on his shoulder, trying to see what he was looking at over the balcony. Kevin glanced briefly at his son, feeling the tight grip of his hand through the blanket wrapped around him. He patted his son's hand with his own, then turned back to the gray sky. The wind could be heard blowing against the glass. Sean wrapped his arms around his father's shoulders from behind and squeezed him tightly.

CHAPTER THIRTEEN

Just as it was getting dark, Sean and his father were jolted by a loud boom from across the street. They both jumped up quickly and raced to the balcony window to stare at the flames coming out of one of the kiosks near the metro station. Three or four boys Sean's age were quickly running down the sidewalk toward the field while others in the marketplace snatched at some of the CD's and videos that had fallen to the ground.

There weren't many other people near the metro station, but the few remaining Russians quickly disappeared down the street or onto paths that skirted the market area. The flames quickly engulfed the entire kiosk and burned steadily. The boys that had apparently caused the explosion and those that had stolen the loot were now out of sight. After staring at the fire for a few more minutes, Sean and Kevin turned back to the TV and their magazines.

Kevin called Cindy later that evening, but only talked to her for a few minutes because the lines kept failing. After he hung up he sat down on the bed next to Sean, who was drawing over the faces in one of the Russian magazines, giving everyone black eyes and moustaches.

"Well, they're doing okay, things are pretty much the same for them too. But, it looks like Mrs. Donaldson next door might have died. Your mom went over there early this morning and rang several times, but didn't get any answer. Her car was still in the driveway, but she never goes anywhere anyway, especially at a time like this. She didn't want to try to break in there to have to find her like that. She tried calling 9-1-1, but couldn't ever get through."

He patted Sean on the back absently, drew in a deep breath,

then continued. "Your mom didn't sleep very well most of the night – not surprising. She had Elizabeth sleep in bed with her. She said that CNN early this morning was reporting additional deaths today – even more than yesterday. I told her to be careful, not to go anywhere. I didn't say anything about the looting here – no need to worry her even more."

Sean was tracing lines around a woman's face that was wearing a tight-fitting, gray business suit. Kevin watched as he put the finishing touches on a large bandage around the woman's head to match the cast on her leg and the scars on her neck and cheek. He smiled.

"Sean," Kevin began slowly. "We should probably talk about something – just in case… just in case you might need to, to be able to get somewhere on your own."

"But, you'd be with me. We could figure out the metro stops together."

"Well, in case we were separated, or I had to stay somewhere while you went for help or something."

"We'll just stay together – I'm not going anywhere without you."

"Look, Sean, I know this may not be the easiest thing…"

The phone rang, the odd pulsing tone cutting through the hotel room air. Kevin stood quickly and picked up the receiver.

"Hello, hi, this is Kevin."

"Kevin! Kevin, Kevin, Kevin! Finally! Look, pal, I have been calling every single room in that whole damn building, you know the front desk or the switchboard people or whoever the hell they usually have down there must be out to an all-day lunch, because I have not been able to get a hold of you at all, you're the…"

"Alan Connors? Is this Alan? Where are you?"

"I'm, uh, well, right at this moment, I'm at one of our dear government's safe houses over near the Embassy. Things were getting pretty sticky over there last night, so, we, well, a few of us, thought it might be a good idea to make ourselves scarce."

"Who's with you? What's going on at the Embassy?"

"The Embassy's compromised, my friend. They overran it last night. They flushed us out completely. I got separated from Garrett and most of the others. It's just me, John Rohrstadt, his assistant Kimberley Borland and, uh, Ralph Thompson, one of the state department guys at the Embassy. And I have absolutely no idea where anyone else is."

Kevin didn't respond for a few seconds. He turned around and faced Sean, closed his mouth, then turned back toward the wall. "What, what do you mean about the Embassy? Who got in?"

"About a hundred and fifty angry Russians with some sticks and chains. A couple of them even had machine guns and a few old pistols. They ended up finally getting through the back entrance. We didn't think they knew about it or would try that way – we had all our guys up at the front gate, they kept a crowd there throwing chairs and rocks and everything, but they were just distracting us. They drove a truck through to get into the compound at the back and once they reached the front building, a bunch of us just went out the front, trying to cut through the crowd. We made it – the others were grabbed by people in the crowd. I didn't see what happened, I was just running… anyway, Thompson here knew about this safe house and even had the keys, so we're holed up in here for the time being."

Kevin remained silent. He simply stood with his hand in his pocket, head turned downward.

"Listen, Kevin, you're going to need to get over here. Are you getting the riots outside – the crowds?"

"There's been a little looting, nothing too major," Kevin said quietly.

"Yeah, well, the entire area around the Embassy is like a battle zone or something. There were people out late last night and most of the day breaking into the stores and stealing food and TVs and anything they could grab. I saw a few police cars, but there were no uniforms in sight, everything is completely out of control. The apartment we're in is just about a thirty minute walk from the Embassy. You and your son need to get over here early tomorrow morning."

"Why? We haven't been having as many problems over here, I mean we've just been waiting it out in the room for the past couple days doing…"

"Kevin, if things aren't bad in your area yet, they will be soon. The entire city's going crazy. We heard that some of the crime families are taking advantage of the confusion and are settling old debts – there are gunshots down the street every few minutes. We are in a completely secure apartment, we've got plenty of food, even some weapons. I mean, just for the sake of sticking together, we'd all be safer here. We've got everything we're going to need – we can just hide here and ride this thing out. You are not safe in that hotel."

Kevin looked around the small room and over at Sean. He stepped toward the balcony window, trying to peer out into the darkness, but nothing was visible past the railing, besides a few neon lights in the market across the street.

"Okay, but how are we going to get there? We've hardly seen any cars all day. I don't even know if the metro is still running."

"I wouldn't try to get in a taxi even if you could still find one. I'm not sure about the metro – I haven't seen any of the buses going, so I'd imagine that they're out too. Probably the best idea is for you to grab a car and just try to make it here on your own. But, wait until the morning – early in the morning. Don't try and get over here in the night, that's when things have been the worst."

Kevin nodded grimly. "Alright. Alright, I think we might be able to... to find something. Where are you at?"

CHAPTER FOURTEEN

Svyeta pulled her sister Zhenya close, tugging her collar up higher on her neck against the cool morning wind. The road in front of them was empty, the same as all the other streets they'd walked during the last half hour since they left their apartment... since they left *him* at the apartment.

She shuddered again – a painful physical echo of the shaking her body had started when she'd found Zhenya crouched in her parents' room by the bed only an hour ago. Her six-year-old sister was crying as she repeatedly shook her father's unmoving form. Svyeta had only stood in the doorway, staring at the two of them, instantly realizing that what she had feared was going to happen, what she knew was going to happened, had. She had no idea why she was shaking, where it came from, but she fought instantly to control it, wrapping her arms tightly around her sister as if Zhenya was the one shaking and she could make it stop just by squeezing harder.

Her shaking lessened once she sprang into action. They had to get out, they had to find their mother and tell her, she would know what to do. As she got herself and her sister dressed she pushed the shaking and the rising sense of panic that was causing it to the back of her mind, instead focusing on the immediacy of getting outside and to the hospital.

The streets were too empty. It was still early in the morning, but there should have been more people out – would have been more people out ordinarily. The most disturbing thing to Svyeta was all the signs of recent activity: some smashed shop and car windows, garbage in the streets, odd pieces of broken furniture. The presence of these only emphasized the absence of people as the former couldn't exist without the latter, yet here they were.

As they were approaching the hospital a car sped past them and skidded to a stop in front of the building. Svyeta and Zhenya kept walking and watching as a frantic younger man jumped out of the car, ran to the passenger side and carefully lifted the limp body of a young woman. He ran into the building and the girls heard him shouting, calling out.

When they reached the doors they found him arguing with a stone-faced woman dressed in a dingy white coat. The lobby was filled with people, many of whom looked like they'd been there all night and some of whom looked like they wouldn't ever leave on their own.

The young man sobbed as he begged the nurse desperately. He was trying to hold the young woman's body, but she was slipping to the floor and he slowly sagged down with her like they were both melding into one form. The nurse only shook her head and asked him to please move her to the side of the room out of the way.

"Marina Valeriovna?" Svyeta's question was really two. But one of them she didn't want to ask – she was afraid to know the answer. Is my mother here? Is she alive?

The woman nodded and gestured for them to follow. They walked out of the lobby beyond some swinging double doors and began weaving through dimly lit hallways. There were bodies everywhere – pushed against the walls, a few on gurneys, some curled up in chairs mimicking sleep. Some of the rooms were open and Svyeta saw one with a body in the bed and six more just lying on the floor. A family had checked their grandmother into the hospital only to end up dying there with her.

Every corner they turned there were more bodies. No one alive was with them, tending to them, recording their information – who they were, where they were from, why they died. The building appeared to be overflowing with the dead.

The silence was only disturbed by their steps as they turned another corner into what appeared to be an exact duplicate of all the other hallways they'd come through. Finally the woman stopped at the open door to one of the rooms.

"Marina, your girls are here."

Svyeta's mother was sitting on a chair by the bed where a woman her age lay with a tube hooked to her arm. Marina's head was resting on her arm on the bed, her eyes closed.

Svyeta noticed that she was holding her breath, gripping Zhenya's hand tightly as she stared at her mother. She couldn't see her chest moving at all, couldn't tell if she was breathing. Wake up, wake up, she said silently to mother. Wake up now.

Zhenya walked over and placed her hand gently on her mother's shoulder, staring intently into her face.

"Mama, Mama."

Marina's eyes fluttered open briefly then closed again as she inhaled deeply. Svyeta felt the air rush into her own lungs as if her mother's intake had pushed it there. She walked quickly to her mother and knelt by the chair.

The nurse left the room. Marina rolled her head on her arm and tried opening her eyes again, wincing against the dim light.

"Zhenya? Svyeta? What are you doing here?"

"We found Dad this morning. He was… gone."

Marina lifted her head and leaned back in the chair, her bloodshot, weary eyes filling with tears. She nodded and looked down, her lips held tight.

"You didn't come home last night. We didn't know if you were… we didn't know what to do. What's happening, Mom? Why is everyone dying?"

The girls hugged their mother, all three squeezing each other tightly. None of them spoke for several minutes. Marina gently stroked their backs and smiled sadly. Svyeta stood up and Zhenya crawled into her mother's lap.

"We're not sure what's happening. Everyone comes in with these headaches. But no one's sick, as far as we can tell. There are no fevers, no coughing. Nothing except for the headaches."

She winced again as she said this, holding her hand to her temple.

"Have you girls had any headaches?"

Both nodded. Seeing this, Marina nodded too as she slowly ran her fingers through Zhenya's brown hair.

"This is Lyuba," she said turning to the woman in the bed. "She's one of the only patients still alive. She came in on Monday with a severe headache – more than a migraine she said. We actually went to school together. I haven't seen her in… fifteen years. We were friends, just lost touch after school. So strange –

this is how we meet again."

Marina turned back to her daughters, still smiling sadly. Svyeta touched her mother's shoulder, feeling the exhaustion in her body. She had dark circles under her eyes and her face was thinner than when Svyeta had seen her just a day or so ago. She thought she could almost feel her mother's strength slipping away. This woman who was always so strong, always taking care of everyone else, giving everything and never leaving anything for herself, was fading.

And if – no, once – she faded away entirely, what would they do? Who would they have then? Who would take care of them? Svyeta's lips tightened firmly in resolution as she watched her mother slowly running her fingers through her little sister's hair.

She would take care of them – both of them. As she had been doing for so long already.

CHAPTER FIFTEEN

Sean and his father finally found a set of keys plugged into the ignition of the thirteenth car. Both of them had been quite surprised to find almost twenty cars, most of them taxis, parked out in front of the hotel, completely unattended, most not even locked. They were even more surprised to have found keys. Kevin opened the door of the large, shiny black sedan and started the engine without any trouble.

The sky was just beginning to lighten as Sean put his suitcase in the back seat. There had been no activity in the streets and still no sounds from any of the other hotel occupants or staff. They assumed that they were the last ones left in the building. They'd locked up their room after making a few last-minute sweeps to see if they'd left any belongings, then dropped the keys off at the front desk before walking out the glass front doors.

The large, black vinyl seat was cold, but well-cushioned. Kevin pulled his seatbelt into place and gripped the steering wheel, checking the gas tank. Sean sat expectantly next to him. Despite the early hour, his eyes were open wide and he was leaning forward in his seat.

"I haven't taught you how to drive before, have I?" Kevin asked.

"Not yet."

"Well, we can probably just go over a few basics. Um, once you've turned on the car you might have to give it a little gas to get it started, especially on cold mornings – then, you can just pull it into drive right here."

"I know all that, Dad. I just need practice on the road."

"Huh," Kevin said, glancing at his son as he eased out of the parking spot. "Have you, uh, had any road practice yet?"

Sean didn't say anything. Despite the boy's excitement, Kevin had seen his son wince a couple of times as they were talking. They'd both awoken with pretty painful headaches. Aspirin with breakfast had helped a little, but they were still aware of the pressure pounding in their temples.

"Maybe we'll have to get you out on the road sometime – not today," Kevin said as he pulled out into the deserted street.

It had been a cold night. There was frost on the grass in the field across from the Cosmos Hotel. The tires rolled smoothly across the chilled asphalt. They didn't see any cars or other signs of life as they drove down the multi-lane boulevards.

Connors' directions had been fairly precise, but it was still difficult navigating in a large, foreign city with unreadable street signs. With Sean holding tightly to the notes jotted down by his father yesterday evening and cross-referencing them with a map of Moscow that they had found in the glove box, Kevin drove the large, black car through quiet intersections, past locked department stores and abandoned metro stations.

Once they got onto the Garden Ring road, they saw a couple of men rummaging through garbage bins at the edge of a large, outdoor market. The men raised their heads briefly as they heard the car go by, then went back to their search.

A few minutes later, they noticed something ahead in the road. As they got closer, he could see that it was a person, heavily bundled in a large coat and boots. He slowed down and drove to the left of the body. As they continued, they found more bodies on the sidewalks and in the streets – most appeared to have died of some type of injury, rather than from the mystery plague.

They drove up a small rise and Sean pointed out at a large, dark building rising above the rest of the tenements. "Is that it? One of the seven sisters?"

Kevin studied the immense building closely as they neared. A delicate spire pierced the early morning cloud cover. This was set atop a series of blocks of three or four stories, each one larger than the one above it, until they all rested on a large, square base that looked to be several streets wide and hundreds of yards long. Delicately crafted spires matching the tall main one were set at the corners of each level giving the building a dual quality of both gothic cathedral and industrial skyscraper.

Stalin had ordered these buildings constructed during his thirty year tyrannical rule. Now, seven of these large, dark temples adorned Moscow's skyline, all built in celebration of the new species of Modern Soviet Man: *Homo Sovieticus*. Most had originally served as government agency buildings, but many had been converted after the fall of the Soviet Union for private use – apartments, offices.

"Yes, that has to be it," he said as they continued up the gradually rising street toward the monolith.

The road curved to the left around a high-walled park, then rose quickly past a metro station marked with the familiar "M" that stood directly across from the Seven Sisters building. The smaller apartment buildings around the gothic structure, leaned closely toward its protective walls, hiding in the immense shadow it cast across the city.

Kevin turned right a couple streets later and parked behind a gray car. The street was narrow, sandwiched between a series of ten-story apartment buildings that ran parallel with the huge, Stalin edifice. As Kevin and Sean were unloading their luggage from the back seat, a young man pushing a baby carriage passed them on the sidewalk. He calmly strolled behind it, occasionally reaching in to adjust the blankets around the sleeping baby. His eyes passed over them briefly, but he didn't otherwise acknowledge their presence as he continued walking. The Prochazek's waited, watching him for a few moments before crossing the street and entering a building with a large "164" on the placard outside.

The interior lobby was tiled in polished stone and was lit by several wrought iron lamps hanging from the ceiling. There was a large stairway, built along the wall to the left and a single elevator stood directly ahead. While not exactly fresh, the building smelled much better than they had expected judging from the plain, stone exterior and trash strewn around the entrance.

They waited for the elevator and stepped inside, pressing number nine. Just as the doors were closing, the front door to the building burst open and a large, short-haired man in a heavy, black leather coat shot inside, running straight for them.

Sean's back pressed against the wall behind him and he drew in a quick breath. Kevin stepped forward quickly, his hand hovering above the elevator's control panel, then froze as he watched the large, blond-haired man reach out as the doors continued to close.

His fingers curled into a fist which just barely stopped the doors from closing, then he inserted his other hand to force them open. Both Kevin and Sean stood unmoving as the round-faced giant glared at them. Under his coat he wore a dark-blue exercise outfit and graying sneakers.

The front door swung open again and a smaller man, in a black wool coat that reached his knees, stepped inside. His shiny, black dress shoes clicked hollowly on the stone tile as he crossed the lobby, his head down and one hand in his suit pants pocket as he walked.

An irritating buzzing noise started from the elevator's control panel as the tall, blond man held the door for the latest arrival. The man in the dress shoes was older and had a thin goatee and slicked-back black hair. He nodded at Kevin as he stepped inside, then turned quickly on his heel to face the doors as the blonde brute let them close.

They reached the ninth floor and the older man stepped out first and turned to his right, walking down the short hallway, ignoring the blonde man behind him. The large man exited the elevator in front of Kevin and Sean and walked down the hallway as the older man knocked and responded to a question from someone inside the apartment.

Kevin looked at the apartment number scrawled on the slip of paper in his hand, checked the number above the door in front of him and turned to the left. They reached the door at the end of the hall and knocked as the two men down at the opposite end were being let in. The peephole in the door in front of Kevin and Sean darkened, then they heard a series of locks being turned.

The door, covered with thick, black matting, swung inward and they saw Alan Connors standing in front of them, his face haggard and his eyes darting about nervously.

He ushered them inside quickly without a greeting. The large door swung shut. The interior side of it was made of thick, polished steel with four or five strong locks firmly rooted into its edge. Alan deftly slid all of the locks into place before turning back to Kevin and Sean.

"So, you made it okay? Good, that's good." He walked a few steps into the center of the room and stopped, turning around to face them. His hand smoothed back thinning dark hair as he stood staring at them and their luggage. Kevin and Sean took the chance to look around the apartment. They were standing in a large room with tall windows to their left. A couple of desks and some bookshelves lined the walls, with some couches in the middle. Several computers were on the desks as well as what looked like radio equipment and multiple security televisions. There was a small, but well-stocked kitchen to the right and a hallway leading to a white-tiled bathroom and another door. A set of metal stairs on the right rose to a second level that was open and overlooked the large living room.

A thin middle-aged man with deep-set lines in his face, wearing charcoal suit pants and a dirty dress shirt, emerged in the second-story room. He looked to Connors, then at Kevin and Sean and exhaled loudly. "Hi. I'm Thompson. Ralph Thompson."

"Kevin Prochazek. This is my son, Sean." He turned again to Connors. "Where are John and Kimberley?"

Just as he finished speaking, John Rohrstadt, his large belly stuffed into a tight, crimson sweater, walked out behind Thompson. He looked like he'd been awake all night and was now holding a hand to his head. When he saw Kevin, he smiled.

"Hi, Dr. Prochazek – you made it! Well, guys," he said glancing at Connors and Thompson, "looks like the day's already taken a turn for the better!"

Kevin set his suitcase down on the floor and looked at Connors. "What's going on?"

Connors, his hand on the back of his neck, turned to look up at Thompson and Rohrstadt and said, "We found Kimberley this morning..."

CHAPTER SIXTEEN

"We're estimating that probably as much as half of Moscow has died in the last three days," John Rohrstadt said. He was hunched over, sitting on the edge of his chair, elbows on his knees and hands together in front of his tightly tethered stomach. The warm pullover he was wearing looked to be three sizes too small.

"And probably most of the ones who are left have left for the dacha – country cottages," added Thompson. He looked every bit a man employed by the state, from his delicately pressed but cheap dark slacks and manicured fingernails to his short, non-descript haircut and clear, waxy skin. He rubbed his eyes as he spoke. He'd been keeping them closed for the past twenty minutes – he said the light made his headache worse.

Kevin stood, leaning against the marble kitchen countertop, sipping a cup of real American coffee. The bitter taste filled his throat and chest, warming him. He was surprised at how much he'd missed it after only a few days away from home.

"But, Moscow has – had – over ten million inhabitants. That's five million people – how are you estimating that?" Kevin asked.

"I spoke with a doctor yesterday when we went out to survey the neighborhood," said Thompson, his back to the large windows that looked out on a narrow alley below. "He'd been driving around to hospitals throughout the city to try to find out some news – how the illness is spreading, how to treat or prevent it. Nobody had any answers, but he got a rough poll on how many had died. John, here, did some extrapolating and came up with the fifty percent figure."

"It seems about right with what we've been seeing on the

BBC and CNN," muttered Connors. He was sitting with his legs crossed on one of the plush couches, staring out the window. His voice was a steady monotone, the words sliding out without emphasis or emotion.

"You get CNN?" Sean asked. He was sitting on one of the high stools at the counter next to his father, busily munching on a toasted bagel with cream cheese.

John nodded. "Yeah, this place has a pretty great satellite hook-up. But, we were just getting the color bars for a few hours last night. Our equipment's working fine, but they must not be continuously broadcasting right now. It was on earlier this morning."

The five of them remained silent, rolling the last spoken words over and over in their minds. A deep, resonating techno beat throbbed dully from the direction of the front door. Sean remembered that it had started shortly after they had arrived. He assumed it was the two men that they'd ridden up in the elevator with – there was only one other apartment on this floor and he hadn't heard or seen any signs of life there as they'd passed.

"Dr. Rohrstadt," Kevin said, "theories?"

John peered up at him, rubbing his hands together. He seemed about to say something, then sat up straight and started pacing the floor back and forth with his eyes as if searching for a lost contact.

"The facts: deaths began sometime between Sunday night and Monday morning. They typically occur while the victim is asleep. Some report headaches beforehand, some do not. Autopsies show some hemorrhaging in the brain…"

John paused. His thumbs rolled over and over each other as his large, round eyes continued to roam aimlessly back and forth across the hardwood floor. "As far as we can tell, the first wave of deaths occurred in Russia and the Middle East. After that, they seem to have spread fairly uniformly, irrespective of geography. No signs whether or not the disease or condition is communicable or how it is transmitted in general. All the victims are adults, with no discernable concentration in…"

"What do you mean – adults?" Kevin asked.

"They're all adults – no children have died yet as far as we can tell," replied John, looking up at Kevin. "Didn't you see any bodies at the hotel or on the streets on your way here?"

"Just a few, but I didn't, I didn't really notice..." his voice trailed off as he looked from John to Connors.

"But, I've had the headaches too, same as my dad," Sean said.

"Remember we don't know if the headaches are actually a symptom – some have them, some don't. I haven't talked to any other kids, so I don't know if any of them have been having headaches either, but I'd say it's a good possibility," John replied.

"Aren't you forgetting the big one, John? The primo, grando fact of them all?" Connors said as he smiled out the window. His chin was resting on his hand as he leaned into the armrest. "Everyone started dying the day after Jerry hit – ignoring, of course, the six Russian airmen that died right when the thing landed."

"Could it be some type of radiation that it brought? I think we'd have detected such a lethal level before it got here," John queried.

"Radiation poisoning has other symptoms, unless it's some type we've never come across before," Kevin said.

"A virus maybe. Some organism that can survive in space that destroys any life it comes into contact with?" John said.

"We didn't see any dead cats or dogs. Did you?" Sean asked as he licked cream cheese off his fingers. Kevin looked down at his son with an unreadable expression on his face. Sean glanced up at him and stopped licking his fingers.

"Not that we noticed. Of course, we weren't looking for that kind of thing, but you'd think that if that many dogs and cats were dying, they'd be everywhere. There are thousands of stray dogs in Moscow," said Thompson.

"Okay," John said in mock excitement, beginning to count with his fingers, "we've got radiation, deadly virus or possibly even some kind of, I don't know, high frequency sonic boom that only kills humans eighteen and over."

"How could a giant rock generate any sound?" asked Thompson, entirely missing the sarcasm.

John was about to launch into a highly detailed explanation that he was carefully constructing right on the spot, when Connors switched the television on with the remote.

Everyone looked up at the sound of the news correspondent's voice. Sean saw that it was an older man, in his late forties. His hair was graying and he didn't speak as fast as the British guy who had been doing the reports on the BBC for the past couple of days. This guy seemed to pause and stumble a little more also, seemingly unsure of what to say next or how to properly lead into a story. Sean wondered if the regular newscaster had left town, or if he was just gone like so many others.

They had all forgotten Thompson's last question, their tired minds and aching heads totally enraptured by the calming voice coming out at them from across the miles. Many of the video clips were the same ones that had been broadcast for the past couple of days. Sean was beginning to recognize some of the people as they crowded around ambulances and loved ones.

"We received a report this morning on the status of the fire on Manhattan Island – it continues to rage out of control as the understaffed fire departments have been unable to gain any footing. Traffic out of the city had been at a standstill for the three hours leading up to the sending of this communication and many motorists have reportedly abandoned their vehicles."

The gray-haired man shuffled through several loose papers in front of him, before choosing one as if at random. "We've also just received a video feed from the crash site of the Jerry meteorite. We, uh, it was sent here late last night – here it is."

Sean and Kevin drifted over to stand behind the couch as a still image of a couple men in white protective suits and glass-faced helmets stood beside some trees coated in a light layer of snow. John hopped over and slid a video tape into the VCR below the TV and pushed the red "record" button.

A distant voice, partially muffled by the protective helmet and speaking in Russian, began as one of the men gestured behind him. A translator's voice came in a couple of moments later. "Here we are at the crash site, at approximately sixty degrees north longitude, sixty-two and a half degrees west latitude, six-hundred and forty-two kilometers north of Yekaterinburg. The meteorite has come to rest here at the base of a hill after bouncing and scraping along the landscape for roughly seventy kilometers."

The video cut to a shot of the two men's backs as they approached a small hill a few hundred yards away. The image bounced as the cameraman apparently trudged through the snow and mud that rested between the low-lying brush and trees in the area. As they neared the hill, a long shape at its base began to take form, about a hundred and fifty meters across and thirty meters high.

The video cut again and the two men were now standing in front of a craggy, rock wall facing the camera. "This is the base of the meteorite. As far as we have been able to determine, it is largely intact with no pieces lying anywhere nearby. Some of our other team members are currently investigating the initial touch-down site and the meteorite's trail. We should hear more from them by this evening."

"The outer layer appears to be slightly porous and we are detecting strong iron readings that seem to be rather evenly distributed throughout the meteorite. We have as yet detected no abnormal radiation readings, but are still wearing protective clothing as a precaution. Already one third of our crew has died. We still have not been able to discover the cause."

The image switched abruptly back to the newscaster who was still conferring with someone off-screen to his left. He quickly turned back to the camera and glanced nervously down at the sheet of paper in his hand. "That is all that we have at the moment, we are hoping to receive more footage later in the day. Until then, though, we will only be offering a minimal broadcast, featuring some special reports on North Sea Whaling and foreign adoption procedures that were taped last year. Thank you."

John leaned forward from his kneeling position on the floor, pressed the stop button on the VCR, then pulled out the video cassette and set it on the shelf. Leaning back on his haunches, he let out a low whistle and said, "Intact. Completely intact. Man, I'd give anything to be there. Wouldn't you, Dr. Prochazek?"

Kevin nodded wordlessly.

"The Russians had a different name for the meteorite," Alan Connors said tiredly as he stared out the window. "They called it Ilya, or Elijah in English. 'Jerry' was probably just a little too American for them. Ilya, or Saint Ilya, is the prophet Elijah from the Bible. When Russia adopted Christianity a thousand years ago

81

or so, many of their old pagan gods didn't die out. Rather, their legends and attributes were just passed on and became attached to the new saints and characters of the Bible. The Russians stopped worshipping Perun, the god of thunder and lightning, and instead passed on his powers and characteristics to Ilya, or Elijah, probably because Elijah rides a chariot of fire up into heaven at the end of his life."

"There's an old Russian legend," continued Alan, "about how God called on Ilya to rid the heavens of some pesky devils by attacking them with a terrible storm of thunder, lightning and rain. Ilya sent the storm at them for forty days and nights, creating so much rain that it washed all the devils away down to Earth. That's actually the explanation for where meteorites or shooting stars come from – they're just these little devils being swept out of heaven by Ilya's storm. Maybe that's what this all is – God's punishing us for our wicked ways by sending Elijah and his fiery chariot full of little devils... I'd say he overdid it."

Kevin looked grimly at Alan. "We probably all need some rest. Let's figure out some sort of plan afterward. I don't think any of us want to be stuck in here forever."

CHAPTER SEVENTEEN

Sean's fingers closed tightly around the headphones over his ears. The soft foam squeezed under his grip and he strained to understand the words that were intermixed with the static. The slanted rays of cold, winter sunlight danced over hundreds of steel-colored buildings, around wind-blown deserted street corners and through the window's reinforced glass into Sean's eyes as he stared out across the city.

The efficient and well-mannered Thompson had shown him a couple of hours ago how to operate the shortwave radio that sat on one of the desks near the computer equipment. Sean was fascinated right from the start. The only people that he'd been able to find so far didn't speak any English, but their voices sounded friendly enough. After a while, he'd given up trying to contact anyone and just sat listening, slowly rotating the dial through all the frequencies, picking up on various tones of static.

The sun was going down. Kevin was asleep on the couch, having taken four Advil to fight his headache. John Rohrstadt was sitting on one of the kitchen stools reading. Thompson and Connors had taken Kimberley's body outside earlier in the day. Sean assumed they were napping upstairs.

Suddenly, a couple words of what sounded like English barked through the headphones. Sean reached for the dial to make the signal clearer, sitting up straighter and turning some of the instruments on the radio that Thompson had shown him.

"This is Gremlin Seven, repeat, Gremlin Seven. Can you hear me?" Sean said into the microphone. He held the headphones securely to his head with both hands. The voice was still there, just faintly. It sounded like singing or crying. He closed his eyes, trying to figure out if it was saying anything when it suddenly stopped.

"Oh, oh, you're, somebody's there, oh somebody can – can you understand me? You, viy govoritye po-angliskiy? Can you understand me?"

Sean's eyes popped open as soon as he heard the woman's voice coming in clearly through the headphones. His hand jumped for the button and he responded, "Yes, I can understand you. Where are..."

"Oh, thank God, I've been trying to call out to anyone, anyone out there for... for a long time, since last night, maybe? I don't know, there's, there's just no one else here, I haven't been able to find anyone else. They're all dead..."

Sean paused, unsure of how to reply. She sounded like she was crying, her words coming out between big gulps and sniffles. She wasn't making a lot of sense.

"My name's Sean. I'm from Pasadena, California. I'm in Moscow with my dad on business. What's your name?"

Soft laughter filled his ears. "Hello Sean from Pasadena. I'm Pamela from... I don't know where I'm from. Not from here, that's for sure. Not anywhere near here ..."

"Are you alone Pamela? Where are you at?"

There was no response – just a soft crackling sound across the airwaves. Sean was about to readjust the dial when her voice came back on.

"Uh, I don't know, not sure where, Sean from Pasadena. Not sure where, not sure how long I've been here. They chased me in here... maybe yesterday some time? I ran across the big courtyard and came in here and now there's a shelf and a desk in front of the door and I'm keeping the lights off, but I know that really it's just a matter of time..."

"Who chased you?" Sean asked.

"A bunch of kids. A bunch of filthy, ugly bleeding Russian street kids. I saw them outside the hotel and they just looked at me walking down the street. I wanted to find a taxi, but I couldn't... somewhere... far away somewhere, I couldn't get there. Then they started running after me, they were yelling something at me, I couldn't understand. I threw my money at them, dropped my purse, but they kept running, I don't know what they wanted..."

Sean held onto the microphone firmly. He took in a couple of breaths, but let it out slowly each time, unsure of what to say. Finally, he said, "It's okay, Pamela, everything's going to be okay. We can come get you and, and then we'll bring you back here, it's safe here…"

He heard the soft laughter again. The volume gradually increased until she began to cry. Her whimpers came clearly through the headphones into his ears and her voice began to rise into a loud wail. Then, the mournful sound immediately stopped and he heard the faint catches of laughter in her voice.

"Oh, Sean, oh, Sean from Pasadena, it's not safe there. It's not safe anywhere. Sean?"

"Yeah?"

"Sean – we're going to die, honey. We're all going to die."

The last words were hissed out so loudly that Sean had to tear the headphones off his head. He threw them onto the desk and sat staring for several moments, only listening to his own quick, short breathing. Finally, he pulled the black earpieces back on.

"Pamela? Hello?"

There was no response. He tried several more times, but was unable to get anything more from her. Maybe she had to go out, he thought. Maybe her radio stopped working or something.

He sat there for several minutes, leaning back in the chair, the headphones still on his head relaying the occasional burst of brief static. Sean stared out at the dark windows in the apartment building across the street. The fading sunlight was casting long shadows on the asphalt and the chunks of dirty, melting snow in the gutters.

Staring intently at the darkened window only a street away from him, Sean wondered who lived in that apartment. He wondered if last week at this time the window had been lit from a kitchen or bedroom light of the family that lived there. He wondered where they'd gone. Had they stayed in their apartment, in their own beds right up until the end? Or, had they left the city for their summer cottage or gone to find relatives somewhere? He wondered if that light would turn back on again sometime, if anyone would ever look out of that window again.

CHAPTER EIGHTEEN

Sean was roused from his doze by a soft tap on his shoulder. He must have only been asleep for a couple minutes – the sun was only a little farther down in the sky. His father was standing behind him, bleary-eyed, rubbing a hand over his face.

"I thought I heard voices – did you get somebody on the radio?"

Sean shook his head. "She's gone. I tried to find out... she's not answering."

"Well, who was it? Did she speak English?" Kevin said as he stretched his arms wide and yawned.

Sean continued to stare out the window. "Dad – what's going to happen?"

Quick pounding echoed through the hall outside the thickly padded front door. Then, a deep voice shouted something in Russian.

Kevin turned at the sound. John Rohrstadt put his magazine down on the counter and walked over to the door to peer through the peep hole.

"No one there," John said. "Must be someone at the apartment down the hall."

Kevin turned back to Sean and put his hand carefully on his shoulder. "We're going to be okay, son. We're going to get back home."

The shouting in the hall resumed – louder. John started unlocking it – going down the row of five locks.

"Don't open that door," said Connors from upstairs. John had his hand on the knob and turned toward Connors as the man walked quickly down the stairs.

John pulled the door open slightly, as far as the chain would

allow. "We could try to talk with them – maybe they know
something. Thompson speaks great..."

His words were cut off by deafening cracks of gunfire from
the hallway. Connors nearly tripped down the stairs and John
leapt back from the door, leaving it still slightly ajar. Kevin
gripped Sean's shoulders tightly and started pulling him away
from the desk, behind the couch.

Alan Connors slammed the front door and quickly
refastened all the locks before ducking down and backing far
away from the apartment entrance. Thompson emerged into the
loft area above the living room carrying a handgun.

They heard more shouting from the hallway, then the sound
of running feet on the stairs. They all quickly moved toward the
kitchen, ducking behind the counters and eyeing the door.

A thunderous blast ripped through the corridor. The walls
seemed to heave and the window panes rattled so violently that it
sounded as if they were about to shatter into pieces. All the men
immediately dropped to the floor as debris struck the outside of
the front door.

Peering at the door from his position facedown on the floor
in front of the refrigerator, John said, "They didn't get through –
the door held!"

"They weren't blowing our door, dummy. Looks like our
neighbors have company," Connors said.

Again, the sound of feet running on the stairs and down the
hallway, along with shouting, came through the thick black
matting of the front door. This was quickly followed by more
chainsaw-like machinegun fire, punctuated by screaming Russian
voices.

"Who are they?" Sean asked. He was sitting on the floor,
leaning back against the cabinets with his father's arm cradled
protectively around his head and shoulders.

"Mafia probably," Thompson said. "This is a fairly nice
building. Most of our neighbors are rather wealthy. Many of
them probably have some kind of mob connection."

"Do we have any other weapons?" Connors asked
Thompson.

"Plenty – front closet. Rounds are in the boxes at the back."

Alan Connors stood up and walked toward the closet a few

feet down the hall from the front door. Machinegun bursts and the occasional single-fire pistol shots could still be heard clearly, echoing through the building.

Connors shouldered a couple of M-16 assault rifles and a sub-machinegun. He grabbed handfuls of ammunition boxes and stuffed them in a duffle bag, then tiptoed back to the kitchen.

He crouched down by the cabinets and passed one of the assault rifles over to Thompson, then handed the sub-machinegun to Rohrstadt. "Okay, Ralph, how do these things work?"

Thompson's response was cut off by another deafening explosion, which sent them all back to the floor, hands over their ears as the walls shook. Dust was coming into the room at the edges of the door.

"That one sounded a little further away," Sean said.

"They're in that apartment. Are those things grenades?" Connors said to Thompson.

"Possibly. But, I've only heard grenades go off at a practice range. They sound a lot different outside," Thompson said as he began loading the M-16.

There were a few more machinegun bursts down the hallway, then a calm silence descended on the building as dust settled onto the living room furniture in the fading light.

Everyone looked up, training their ears toward the front door, as if this new position would help them hear better into the apartment down the hall.

"They've stopped," John said into the silence. "Are they coming here next?"

Connors shook his head, still staring at the front door. "I'm not sure that they know anyone's here. It might be a good idea to keep it that way."

The five of them sat huddled on the kitchen floor, clutching the firearms closely to their chests, straining to hear anything. A steady hum of muffled voices had been bouncing down the corridor for the past ten minutes, but they weren't sure if it was the home assault team or a television or radio left on. The cadence and volume of the speech was a little too regular for casual post-massacre conversation.

Finally, they heard what sounded like a few pairs of feet

shuffling through debris in the hallway. The elevator pinged, then there was silence. A couple minutes later, they heard an engine starting outside, which then slowly faded away down the street. The sun had gone down and the Embassy apartment was quite dark with only a little light from outside street lamps streaming in through the windows.

They all lay on the kitchen floor, trying to control the sound of their breathing in the relative silence. The only thing they could hear was the steady hum of those same muffled voices from the other end of the hallway.

"Are they gone?" asked Rohrstadt softly.

"Can't be sure," Thompson replied.

"Do we go check it out?" Rohrstadt whispered.

"Go ahead – you first," said Connors.

Silence again fell on the small group of men huddled together in the dark. Twenty minutes later, Kevin sat up straight, leaning his back against one of the cupboards and stretching.

"How long are we going to wait?" he asked.

"We're doing fine in here, aren't we?" Connors replied.

"We'll have to leave the apartment eventually – shouldn't we know for sure?" Kevin said.

Ralph Thompson stood up slowly, his hands gripping the rifle tightly. He stepped quietly across the wood floor towards the hallway, stopped and listened. After a few seconds, he turned back and shook his head.

Connors, a doubtful grimace on his face and his M-16 held ready, walked slowly to the front door and looked out through the peep hole. "It's too dark," he whispered back to the others still in the kitchen.

Thompson tiptoed over to stand beside Connors as he slowly unlocked the front door. Connors pulled it open a crack and peered out. The door to the apartment at the opposite end of the hallway was gone and chunks of plaster and dust were scattered everywhere.

The two glanced at each other, whispering, and Thompson nodded. He flattened his back against the wall and squared the rifle in his hands with the muzzle pointing in the air. Connors pulled the front door open slightly and stepped out into the hallway, M-16 held out in front of him.

He picked his way carefully down the hall, stepping over the occasional piece of concrete or wood splinter from the destroyed door frame in front of him. Lamplight poured into the corridor from a window above the stairwell opposite the elevator. Connors made his way carefully to this midpoint and tried to look out the window onto the street below. The sound of a television continued from the blasted apartment at the opposite end.

Suddenly, a figure stepped casually into the doorway. Connors froze and turned quickly toward the young man dressed in a blue jogging suit. The thin, pale-skinned, buzz-haired young man looked in surprise at Connors. A cigarette hung from his lips. A sub-machinegun was resting in his right hand.

Both of them stood motionless for a split second, staring at one another. The young man glanced down at the M-16 in Connors' hands. He began to raise his own weapon as he stepped through the doorway. Connors spun around and began running for the open doorway.

The young man brought the sub-machinegun up to his shoulder and fired a quick burst at Connors' back as he was reaching out to push open the apartment door. The force pushed him forward into the door. It swung open, banging against a table and swung back as Connors crumpled into a heap on the living room floor.

Thompson kicked the door back open and swung himself into the doorway, M-16 at his shoulder. He fired down the hallway, riddling the walls and the young man. The pale-skinned youth grunted in surprise as he fell backward, the cigarette slipping from his lips and scattering ashes down the front of his blue warm-up jacket.

Thompson stepped back into the apartment and slammed the front door, quickly locking it. John and Kevin rushed over to Connors who was lying facedown on the floor. They carefully rolled him over and John cradled his head, trying to make him comfortable.

Sean stood by the refrigerator, watching Connors coughing and sputtering as Thompson flicked on the light and started rifling through the front closet for a first aid kit.

"Left one behind," Connors croaked. "Left one to clean

up." He coughed and blood shot out of his mouth onto his shirt.

"Don't speak Alan, we've got to stop the bleeding," Kevin whispered.

Thompson brought over a first aid box and started pulling out white gauze bandages. Kevin glanced from him to the exit wounds in Connors' chest and then to Sean who stood silently by – watching.

"No matter," Connors rasped. "We'd all have been dead by morning anyway. I just beat the rest of you by a few hours." He coughed again, flecks of blood spattering from his nose and mouth. "You know, it's kind of funny. This is my first time to Russia."

Thompson pressed the white gauze against the oozing holes in his chest – his shirt was mostly soaked. Ten seconds later, Connors' chest stopped moving.

The three men knelt in silence for a few more minutes. Thompson glanced at the front door. "No more shots. No voices," he said. "He probably was the last one. Otherwise, someone would have come."

John carefully laid Connors' head on the floor and closed his eyes. Kevin stared at the body as he tried to wipe some of the blood off his hands.

"Okay, what now?" Thompson asked quietly, his rifle slung over his left shoulder. "Stay or go?"

"Why would we go? They don't even know we're here," John said.

Kevin shook his head. "When they come back and find their man dead, they might start looking around. We can't hide out here forever, especially if they brought more explosives."

"Can't we just keep the door locked? You said that was reinforced steel." John asked, his loose jowls hanging open in fear.

"We don't know what kind of firepower they have. With us trapped in here, they could wait out there all day just trying different things to see what would finally work. They'd eventually get in – or just wait for us to come out," said Thompson.

"If we go, we have to go now. They could be back any minute," Kevin added.

"Let's load up and be out of here in five minutes,"

Thompson said. He turned to grab the duffle bag and began loading boxes of ammunition.

Kevin and John quickly joined him, stuffing weapons, clothing, food and first aid supplies into bags. Sean remained standing in the kitchen, staring at Connors' body. He'd never seen anyone die before. It all had happened so fast: one minute, Connors was talking and walking around the apartment. Now, he was lying on the floor, not moving. It was like it wasn't even him anymore. Like the man before had been someone else entirely.

Thompson quickly unlocked the front door and pushed his rifle's muzzle through the opening. He took a quick glance outside, then nodded back to the others.

Kevin pulled Sean to the door, carefully stepping over Connors' body. John suddenly turned and ran to the VCR to grab the tape. He stuffed it in his bag and followed the others out the front door.

The rest of the building was deserted as was the street. They quickly loaded their things into the car that Kevin and Sean had arrived in and sped away.

CHAPTER NINETEEN

The large key rattled in the lock as it sought to take hold. It always stuck right when it was almost all the way in, almost to the point where it could be turned to open the thickly padded door. The key sawed back and forth viciously a couple of times before it fell into place and turned the lock.

Tatyana stepped into the dark apartment, set down the bag of groceries and shook her bleach-blonde hair out of the black lamb's wool shopka. She plucked the canned nuts from one of the bags, slid her feet into the worn slippers on the floor and shuffled quickly to the end of the hall. A faint light was coming from the cracks between the door and its frame – the only light in the apartment. She swung open her mother's bedroom door and walked in.

Viktor sat on a stool at the edge of his mother's bed, his chin resting on his chest which rose and fell with small, steady breaths. A thick book lay in his lap.

Tatyana walked over to the edge of the bed and stood right in front of Viktor, staring down at the top of his head. She paused, canned nuts in hand, and glanced from him to her mother, lying silently in the bed. The old blankets were pulled up over her face. A faint smile tugged at the corner of Tatyana's mouth. Even through the blanket, she could see her mother's determined little grimace, the strong jut of chin clamping tightly over a mouthful of wayward teeth.

She knelt down in front of Viktor and smoothed the hair out of his eyes. He raised his head up quickly and looked around, unsure of where he was. Tatyana put her hand on his shoulder to steady him as he got his bearings. Viktor finally relaxed and leaned back against the wall, staring at his mother's form as he blinked away sleep.

"I couldn't find the teriyaki flavor, but they did have some smoked hickory left," she said as she held the canned nuts in front of him.

He looked at the can and nodded, then pulled it toward himself with his left arm and cradled it against his chest before turning his head again to his mother. Tatyana followed his gaze and then looked into his face.

"Viktor, you know I'm going to have to take them out tomorrow. It's already been more than a day," she said softly, still looking into his face. "They'll start to stink."

"Ehy don't 'tink!" Viktor said forcefully, not taking his gaze from his mother.

Tatyana stood up and walked toward the door.

"Aunt 'ydia? 'id you find her?" he asked insistently.

Tatyana stopped and paused for a moment before turning to answer him. "There wasn't any answer when I rang the doorbell. She wasn't there."

He turned back to his mother, pulling the book and canned nuts closer to himself. Tatyana watched him for another couple of seconds from the doorway before walking out into the hall.

CHAPTER TWENTY

"He's heavy," Zhenya said, her voice quivering. "Why is he so heavy?"

"He's always been heavy," Svyeta replied. She gathered the tablecloth edge in her cramped fingers again and leaned back with all her weight. Her father's body slid another couple of feet down the hallway toward an open apartment door.

After the girls had returned home late that afternoon they noticed the smell. It was faint, but given the odor they'd caught from some of the hallways in their apartment building, it was only a matter of time before it got worse. They'd knocked on all the doors on their floor, but no one had answered. Luckily they had a key to the Frolovs' apartment, a couple doors down. The families had exchanged keys a few years ago in case anyone ever got locked out. Svyeta had found the older couple's bodies in their bed. It seemed as good a spot as any for her father's final resting place.

Immediately the image came again to her mind, unbidden, unwanted. A lone form lying on a hospital bed in an otherwise empty room, the sheet pulled up over the face. It would be a lonely and forlorn picture no matter who lay there. That it was her last memory of her mother transformed the image into something else entirely – a concept with a weight and finality so deep that she had no sense of it. It stretched long and darkly into all directions. It was larger than her. It began before her and seemed like it would far outlast her. Not even the idea of her own eventual death felt as vast and empty.

Their mother's headaches had worsened throughout the morning until finally the nurse had freed up a bed in a nearby room and they'd led their mother there to rest. She'd slept,

95

awaking briefly only a couple of times before falling silent later that afternoon. Zhenya had cried, but Svyeta couldn't. Not even on the long walk home.

"You have to push. Keep pushing!" Svyeta said.

"My hands hurt – he's so heavy!" Zhenya whined.

Svyeta looked down at her sister. She hadn't realized she'd spoken aloud. Poor Zhenya. Svyeta couldn't imagine what this was like for her, for a six-year-old to lose both her parents on the same day. She shook off her previous thoughts, pushing the image of her mother's body to the back of her mind where she knew it would lurk waiting until later to parade out again.

"It's okay, only a few more meters, we can do it. On three! One, two, three!"

It took another fifteen minutes of tugging on the tablecloth holding her father's body to get it into the Frolovs' bedroom. They left him on the floor, next to the couple's bed and covered him with a blanket. It was the best they could do. They were exhausted.

The girls dragged themselves back to their apartment, locked the door then plopped down at the kitchen table for a quick dinner.

"I want another slice," Zhenya mumbled, her mouth still full of bread.

"We need to save it. It's the last loaf."

Svyeta chewed the last of her slice slowly, then finished and swept the food away into the cupboard. She glanced through the remaining items.

"We have some noodles and some cans of soup, but probably only enough for three or four days. We'll have to go out to get more, but I want to wait as long as we can. It could be… it's safer if we stay here for a while."

Zhenya nodded sadly, her eyelids starting to droop.

"Svyeta, are we going to die too? Like Mama and Papa?"

Svyeta stared at her sister as she sat quietly waiting for the answer. She seemed so small perched delicately on her chair. Too small for all of this.

"Are you afraid?"

Zhenya shook her head. "I don't think so. You said Mama and Papa are in Heaven, didn't you?"

Svyeta nodded.

"Just like Grandma?"

"Yes. They're all together."

Zhenya folded her arms and blinked slowly.

"That doesn't sound so bad. I'm not afraid."

Svyeta nodded slowly, still watching her sister as the image of her mother in the hospital room filled her vision again.

CHAPTER TWENTY-ONE

Sean dropped his suitcase onto the bed and stood silently, taking a look around the room. It was just as they'd left it – everything. The wadded up sheets and garbage in the trash can, towels on the floor in the bathroom. He hadn't really been expecting to come back to their hotel room and find that the cleaning staff had taken care of everything as they normally did at a hotel, but all the same, it was a little weird. Nothing had changed, everything was exactly the same.

Sean plopped down onto the bed and stretched out, staring at the ceiling. No one had said much on the trip back. After their initial fear of mafia thugs following them had faded, they had just settled into the drive, passing through empty intersection after empty intersection, flying along the mostly deserted avenues. Along the Garden Ring road, they had seen something large burning in the distance – buildings or factories possibly. Passing through the endless streets, Rohrstadt had thought he'd seen a group of people standing outside of a school, throwing things at the windows. He wasn't sure how many there'd been or what else they'd been doing. No one suggested that they stop and go back for a closer look.

John Rohrstadt and Ralph Thompson walked into the room and set their bags down by the door. John moved around the room with an exaggerated swagger. "Nice place you've got here. Huge building, isn't it! Looks like a big shiny magnet that's been bent out of shape. It's a lot better than the hotel we'd been staying in near the Embassy," he said jovially.

"Yeah, it's, it's not bad, not too bad of a place…" Kevin replied, his voice trailing off.

A thick silence descended onto the room. The heating still

didn't seem to be working, but at least it was warmer inside now than it was outside. The three men stood there for a few moments, glancing absently around the room. Sean lay quietly on the bed, his eyes starting to droop.

"Well, I don't know if anyone else is hungry, but I think I'll go downstairs and see if there's anything in the kitchen. Anyone want anything?" John asked, pointing his fingers at the group like he was taking a survey. No one said anything, just a couple shakes of the head.

"Okay, I'll see what I can bring up. Eat it later or something."

"I'll go with you," Thompson said as John walked out the door. The Embassy man adjusted the strap on his M-16 and followed him out into the hallway.

An hour later, John sat at the edge of Sean's bed in front of the television. Thompson relaxed in a chair in the corner by the balcony door. Sean was curled up on his pillows, watching the TV and listening to his father's repeated attempts to get through on the phone.

Kevin placed the receiver back down and picked it up again and re-dialed.

"No luck?" John asked as he popped a chip into his mouth.

"I'm finally getting the line to ring on the other end for more than a couple times, but it keeps cutting off," Kevin said. He pressed the heel of his hand to his temple and held it there for a few moments, closing his eyes against the headache.

The weary looking newscaster on the television was new. The guy that had replaced the original guy was gone. This one was a lot younger – he looked like a college student in his father's old suit. The charcoal gray lapels were a little larger than was recently fashionable and the white shirt hung loosely around his neck. The paper that he was reading from was shaking in his hands and he was only able to look into the camera lens briefly every few seconds before glancing down at the page to find his place again.

He'd been repeating the same message for the last few minutes. The BBC was going off the air. They weren't sure for how long, weren't sure when they'd be back broadcasting. The young man said that the deaths worldwide were too many to calculate – they weren't even able to reach the experts any more who had previously been hazarding guesses.

"Hello? Hello – Elizabeth? Is that you? Are you okay? Let me talk to your mother!" Kevin shouted suddenly into the phone. He held his left hand clamped against his other ear, squinting as he strained to hear.

"What? What – where is she? What time is it there? Isn't it morning? She's still asleep?" Kevin laughed loudly. "Oh, Elizabeth, that's okay, that's okay. Could you go wake her up for me, I need to talk to her quickly."

John turned the television down and all three of them watched Kevin as he listened to Elizabeth. His smile started to fade.

"Well, try again. Are you in our room? Yes, just shake her gently on the shoulder, okay? Hello? She won't? Okay, maybe I'll try – just put the phone up to her ear so she can hear," Kevin said urgently.

"Hello? Hi, Cindy? Hi, honey, good morning… can you hear me? Hello? Elizabeth! Elizabeth – hi, try shaking her again."

Kevin hunched over, putting his elbows on his knees then quickly straightened up again. His lips started tightening and he tried to swallow. "She won't? Not even when you yell?"

John looked down at the floor and gripped his hands together tightly. Sean remained lying on the bed, his arms folded together, hugging his chest.

"No, Elizabeth, that's okay, that's okay…" Kevin said the last couple of words in a whisper. He put his hand over his mouth and squeezed tightly as his shoulders began to shake.

He swallowed once and then said, "Honey, I… I'm going to need you to do something for me. Could you put your hand on her neck, below her chin? Is it warm? Okay, feel down around her throat, to the side of her esophagus – yes, where the food goes down. Okay, press your fingers there lightly to the side of that – what do you feel …? Okay, that's okay."

Kevin sat silently at the edge of the bed, hand over his mouth again, staring at the floor for what seemed like several minutes. "Yes, honey, I'm still here. I'm okay. Listen… how did you sleep last night? Yeah? That must have been cozy, yes I like our bed too. I like it too."

Rohrstadt motioned to Thompson, then both of them left the room. Kevin talked with her for another ten minutes before the connection failed. He tried to call her back for another half hour or so before finally setting the phone back down. Kevin then shuffled slowly over to Sean's bed and put his arms around his son's shoulders.

CHAPTER TWENTY-TWO

A distant crash brought Sean to a sitting position in his bed. At least, that's what it sounded like. He sat blinking, slowly turning his head from side to side, trying to wake up. There it was again! It sounded very far away and muffled, from somewhere below him. Daylight shone in through the window – the curtains had not been drawn the night before.

Sean pushed the blanket off and swung his legs to the floor. He was still dressed. In fact, he didn't remember falling asleep last night. The last thing he could recall was his father lying next to him, whispering something about Elizabeth. But, what had he been talking about? And where were Thompson and Rohrstadt? Had they –

Then, suddenly, it all came rushing back to him: his father's phone conversation and trying to get through on the quickly deteriorating phone lines – the image of Elizabeth lying on his parents' bed, next to the still form of his mother, her face cold and white.

Was it a dream? His still sleep-blurred eyes rested on his father's face, asleep in the opposite bed. His glasses were in his hand, the blanket half-drawn over his chest. His light-brown curly hair delicately framed his head lying on the pillow. He was absolutely motionless.

Sean sat at the edge of the bed, staring at his father, afraid to move. He wanted his father's eyes to flicker open, for him to wake up and say something. He didn't want to have to lean over to check if he was still warm and breathing – he wanted his father to get up and let him know that he was still there, still alive and that everything was going to be fine, that they were going to get on a plane and fly back home and that Mom and Elizabeth would both be there waiting to greet them.

Suddenly, Sean jumped up from the edge of the bed and grabbed his father's shoulder, shaking him violently. Kevin's eyes shot open and he yelled out "Wha...?"

Sean quickly recovered from his surprise and wrapped his arms around his father. Kevin rubbed at his eyes and patted Sean's shoulder in confusion. "What's wrong, what happened?"

Sean said nothing, but continued holding on to his father.

- -

His knuckles hit the door harder the second time. He paused and listened, looking up at the room number on the door – he didn't hear any movement from inside. "Dad," he called through the open doorway to his right, "still no answer."

"Is it locked?" came his father's reply over the buzzing of an electric razor.

Sean tried the door handle – it turned smoothly and he pushed the door open just a crack. He peered through the gap, listening again for any sound, but still nothing. He hadn't heard anymore crashes that morning either and was starting to think that he may have just been dreaming.

Sean found himself pushing the door open wider and stepping carefully into the room, the thick mauve carpet crushing lightly under his white-socked feet. The curtains were open too, bounteous daylight streaming in. The sky was a pale blue, the first one that Sean could remember since arriving in Moscow only five days before. Only five days... it seemed like so much longer.

John was lying on his back on one of the beds, his shoes still on and a blanket pulled over most of him. Ralph Thompson was curled up in the armchair in the corner, one of his feet resting on a stool in front of him. He cradled a pad of graph paper in his arm and a black pen lay on the floor next to the chair.

Sean walked slowly over to stand beside John's large, inert form. His eyes were closed, his mouth open, his chest motionless. Sean stared, waiting for the chest to rise, knowing in his heart that it wouldn't. Finally, he turned toward Thompson near the window.

There was a pot of cold coffee on the table next to the

window, with several mugs mostly drained. Thompson's hair was
wet at the temples and his collar was unbuttoned down to the
middle of his chest. His lips looked blue and cold.

He carefully pulled the pad out of Thompson's grip. The
first page was a brief will, leaving everything to his sister in
Illinois. The next page contained a log – entries running down
the page with the times next to them. Sean's eyes quickly scanned
over them – most were about how his headache felt, how he was
trying to stay awake, how many cups of coffee he'd drank. The
last was at 3:08 a.m. and was very brief: "Tired. Head's worse.
Coffee's making me sick." Higher on the page at 12:53 a.m. was
an entry in different handwriting: "Hi, this is John Rohrstadt,
guest writer and special invitee to Ralph's all-nighter. I'm very
tired. I'm going to bed. See you in the morning!"

Sean laid the pad on Thompson's lap and left the room.
Kevin was just splashing some after shave on when the thirteen-
year old walked back into the room and stopped in the bathroom
doorway.

"Are they in the room?" Kevin asked as he glanced at his
son in the mirror.

Sean nodded, without looking back at him. Kevin paused
and opened his mouth to ask, but Sean glanced up quickly, then
looked away again.

Kevin turned back to the mirror, twisted the cap back on his
after-shave lotion, smoothed his hair down in the back. "You
ready?"

"For what?" Sean asked morosely.

"I thought we'd go out and get some breakfast, walk around
a bit. Looks like it's going to be a nice day. A little cold, but still
nice."

Sean nodded and walked out to put his shoes on.

- -

Bundled up in their coats and scarves, they walked through
the large, empty lobby. Just as they reached the midpoint of the
lobby, one of the large glass doors that led to the street swung
open. A small, middle-aged man with a black fur hat entered the
hotel, an olive-green knapsack slung over one shoulder. He was

staring at the floor as he walked, but lifted his head and stopped when he saw them. His mouth fell open for a brief instant as they stopped, staring in turn. Then, without a word, he walked past them as if they'd never been there. Sean and Kevin stood and watched him make his way around the large armchairs and couches scattered around the lobby and head down one of the spacious hallways that led further into the hotel. Kevin looked at Sean and shrugged, before pushing open the heavy glass door onto the street.

The sun had melted most of the morning frost on the grass in front of the large statue across the street. The silver-colored statue was of a young man and woman striding forward, side by side, holding a hammer and sickle. Their youthful faces were full of hope and strength, entirely heedless of the fall of the soviet empire they symbolized, and equally as unaware of the devastation that their country was currently undergoing. Sean thought they looked very lonely perched high above the world – entirely untouched and unconnected to anything but each other.

Kevin and Sean stopped at a convenience store near the metro station. Kevin calmly strode behind the counter and pulled a couple of boxes of Swedish Muesli off the shelf and retrieved a liter-size box of milk from one of the freezers. They found some plastic bowls and spoons in another kiosk – luckily the door was open and they were able to help themselves. They walked around the empty outdoor market, peering at other kiosks full of foreign CD's, stereos, clothing and videos. They dropped off their bowls and utensils in a garbage can when they were finished.

Both father and son walked in silence for several minutes, keeping their hands buried deep in their pockets and their heads turned toward the ground to prevent the cold air from sliding up over their zippered collars and reaching their necks and chests. Sean wasn't sure where they were going, but assumed they were probably just walking. He'd been on a few long walks with his father before. He'd usually ask Sean to take a walk with him when he wanted to talk to him alone, away from Elizabeth's inquisitiveness or his mother's helpful suggestions. Sean remembered that they'd taken a long walk one winter evening in Pasadena when he was trying to decide whether to play soccer or baseball. Another time, when Sean had been sent to the principal's office for fighting with a couple of other boys during the third grade, they'd walked through the entire neighborhood and into the next. His father had begun that time by talking about young male aggression and the need for winning peer acceptance. His calm and reassuring, but ambiguous tone kept Sean confused for most of the time as to who his father was referring to exactly – him or the couple of boys with whom he'd been fighting. Sean finally had to say that they were just fooling around when one of the boys had accidentally kicked the other too hard, which started off the whole brawl. That had seemed to pacify his father.

They were approaching an upward slope as the road turned into a bridge over a thin waterway that ran through the neighborhood. Sean noticed again how dirty the streets were in Moscow, especially with all the piles of snow collecting mud in the gutters. He wondered if all cities that had snow were that dirty during the winter, or just cities in Russia.

His father suddenly started speaking. "When I was getting ready to ask your mother to marry me, I had to walk around the block about five times before going to knock on her door – I was so nervous. Walking always calms me down, it helps me think better. Talk more candidly. She didn't know I was coming over that night, I'd told her I had to work on some things late. She was surprised when she answered the door and I told her I just wanted to go on a short walk. We ended up walking around the block another five or six times before I drove her to our favorite park. "

He smiled, looking at the river under the bridge as they walked. "But, when we were walking, I kept running out of things to say, I was so nervous. All I could think about was the ring in my pocket and what I was going to say to her and how she was going to react. I hoped she didn't notice how nervous I was – she did most of the talking." Kevin looked over at Sean and smiled.

"It ended up turning out okay though. She told me later she could tell I was nervous and that she knew why. But, she didn't say anything about it then. She just let us walk and waited for me to do what I had to do."

They crossed over the bridge and continued past a couple apartment buildings, their dark brown brick corners towering a couple hundred feet above the road. Kevin was clapping his gloved hands together, trying to keep the circulation going. The air was sharp as it came into their nostrils and over their chapped lips. It was much colder than it had been since they'd arrived in Moscow.

"I think on our way back, we should load up on some food from that market and take it back to the room. We might grab some more clothes and coats for you too. I saw some that would probably fit you back there."

Sean didn't reply, just kept walking beside his father down the street, leaning slightly into the soft wind, trying to stay warm. "Maybe we can find some flashlights and matches and stuff like that. Maybe some camping type equipment – sleeping bags, tents. I'm not sure what kind of stuff they have here, but we should be able to put something together for you. I'm thinking your best bet is going to be to get out of the city as soon as possible, maybe find a small town and set up camp in some nice, warm house. Wait a month or so – however long it takes this place to warm up before you try going farther."

Sean still didn't look at his father. He wasn't sure if it was the cold wind blowing in his eyes or thinking about waiting out the spring chill in some Moscow suburb that was making him tear up. He already knew the answer to his next question, but he had to ask it anyway. Not because he wanted his father to console him, but because he just wanted to say it, wanted to express the fear and the loneliness he already felt as they walked around the empty streets.

The aching feeling in his throat got worse for a second when he first tried to speak, but he finally forced it out. "Where are you going to be?"

"Oh..." said his father in a long, slow exhale of breath that formed a cloud in front of his face. "I'll be around, you know." Kevin continued strolling, his gaze fixed on some distant point ahead.

"I think this is probably just going to have to be your own adventure, Sean. I think you're ready for it, we've taught you some good stuff, I think you can handle yourself on this one," said his father casually.

Sean stopped walking, staring intently at his father. Kevin

halted after a few paces and turned back to look at his son. The boy could feel the anger and grief filling his throat and head, threatening to spill over at any moment and erupt from him in a pitiful wail of tears. As he clenched his mouth tightly shut to prevent any sound from escaping, he looked into his father's eyes. And there he saw the same tears, the same anger and pain at what they both knew was coming, but that neither could prevent. But, in his father's eyes, Sean also saw the acceptance – Kevin's resignation to the knowledge of what was going to happen. And, he saw his father begging him to understand and to be strong – strong enough for the both of them.

Sean swallowed hard, then looked away trying to gain control of the trembling he could feel in his chest. Finally, he asked, "What do I do when summer gets here?"

Kevin smiled faintly at his son. "I know it's a lot to ask, but I'm going to need you to find a way to get to your sister. I'm not sure if you're going to be able to find a lot of pilots waiting around that still take Visa or MasterCard, but you should be able to figure out a way."

The faint wind had quieted down and the street was completely silent now. Kevin looked into Sean's face, at his red cheeks and the bright green eyes staring back at him.

"It doesn't matter how long it takes you, you make sure you can get there safely, if at all possible and you give it your best shot to find her, okay? You've just got to do whatever it takes for you two to be together, okay?"

"I will, Dad."

CHAPTER TWENTY-THREE

Sean and his father spent the rest of the morning and most of the afternoon hauling boxes and cans of food back to the hotel. Kevin put most of it in the trunk and backseat of the car, along with some extra coats, boots and shirts that they'd found in one of the walk-in clothing stores at the marketplace. None of the stores had any sleeping bags or cots – Sean hoped that he wouldn't need them on his journey.

During most of the time that they were carrying supplies to the car and hotel, Kevin told Sean stories. Stories about his college and graduate school days, how he hated high school, all of his favorite professors and some of his best classmates. He told him about some of the trips to Las Vegas and San Francisco and New York that he'd been on with roommates and friends, the different hotels he'd been to and the shows he'd seen. Before and during dinner, they played chess with a portable set they'd found at the marketplace. In between moves, Kevin talked a lot about the first few years of his and Cindy's marriage, what it was like living with a woman compared to male roommates and how the heating and electricity in one of their earlier apartments had kept going out one winter.

He also talked at length about the months before Sean's birth, how his mother had been so calm and reassuring the entire time while Kevin ferociously read every book about childbirth and early childhood development that he could find. He wanted to do it all right, he said, to make sure that Sean was raised and taught properly from the beginning so that he would have every opportunity in life. Kevin talked about Sean's reactions to Elizabeth when she was first born, how he had to learn not to play roughly with her, how he couldn't say her name for the first year or so and just called her "Izbet."

Many of the stories Sean had heard before, especially those about his upbringing and Elizabeth. But throughout his father's telling of his many life experiences, Sean was aware of a difference in tone and style than had been used previously. His father was telling them less as he would to a thirteen-year old, but more as he would to someone his own age. Kevin talked for hours as he would to an observer or biographer, sparing most of the more intimate details, but highlighting several amusing anecdotes of which Sean suspected his mother would not have entirely approved.

Sean found the entire story time very funny, listening to his dad describe the first time he'd ever been drunk at a party, certainly something he'd never mentioned before. He found himself wondering exactly why his father was doing it – was it so that Sean would remember him and his life as they really were, as he had lived it all? Or, was he recounting his life experiences just as a way of remembering them himself, a last review of everything he'd ever done, the good and the bad. Finally, Sean stopped wondering and just listened to his father, watching his eyes light up at memories of his first Christmas with Cindy and laughing with him about how he learned to fasten diapers securely.

By ten o'clock, they had both quieted down and were quite exhausted from the day's activities. They'd played several games of chess – Kevin had won almost every time, except for a couple in which Sean suspected he'd made errors on purpose. They were both lying on their backs on Sean's bed. Kevin reached over to the nightstand and picked up a couple sheets of handwritten paper. He laid them on the bedspread between them.

"I wrote this out last night. I've already told you most of it, today and probably a hundred times before, but, you know, I wasn't sure when everything was going to happen. So, I just thought I'd put it on paper. You can have it to read or look at, whatever. Whenever you want. Just my thoughts on life and such."

Sean nodded and patted the pages.

"I'm not sure when my time will come, but probably soon. There doesn't seem to be many people my age left around. Plus,"

Kevin said, looking out the window into the cold night, "I had this dream last night. About your mother. I don't know where we were, I wasn't aware of anything else going on around us, but I saw her standing there, just looking at me. She didn't say anything, just stood there kind of smiling at me, like everything was all right."

Sean fumbled with the blanket corner in his lap, folding it over his hands and unrolling it again. "Was it like Heaven or something?"

"Your mother believed in Heaven. I suppose that if it's there, then she... then that would be the kind of place where she'd end up."

Both father and son sat for a few minutes in silence. Kevin brought his hand up to his forehead and massaged his aching head. "I've always kind of wanted a Viking funeral," he said with a small smile. "Like in that one movie we saw – what was it? You know, where they send the grandpa's body out on the boat in the ocean and shoot an arrow that lights the little boat on fire. That would be going out in style – noble, manly and everything."

Sean nodded. His eyelids were starting to get heavy. He'd had a headache earlier that afternoon, but it had gone away by the time they were ready to eat dinner. He leaned against his father's shoulder.

"Sean?" Kevin whispered.

"Yeah?"

"I – I always did what I thought was best for you. Your whole life, I just wanted the best for you. And for your mother and Elizabeth. Anything I did, whether good or bad, was for you guys," he said softly.

"I know Dad," Sean said as he scooted closer to his father and closed his eyes.

- -

Sean didn't remember what time he awoke during the night, but he'd found that he was lying in his bed, his head resting on his father's arm. Even with the blanket over him, he was a little cold, so he moved closer to his dad. As he lay there in the darkness, he could tell that his father was cold and still. Sean pressed his head against his silent chest and held it there for a long time, past when the tears came and long after they had dried. He finally fell asleep again holding his father's body in his small arms.

- -

Sean awoke late the next morning with a splitting headache. They'd forgotten to close the curtains again and diffused sunlight filtered into the room stabbing his eyes. He pulled the blanket up over his head and managed to sleep for a while more before getting up to look for some aspirin and a glass of water.

He pulled a box of crackers out of the stash that they had amassed the day before and sat at the foot of his bed, looking at his father's body. The eyes were closed, he lay on his back. He looked as though he were asleep, but there was no shine from his face or movement from his chest. Not even the occasional twitch or muscle spasm. That's not really him, Sean thought. He left during the night. He left to find Mom.

Sean dragged in some of the supplies from Thompson and Rohrstadt's room, including the firearms and ammunition. He arranged everything in a large pile in the corner near the window. He wanted to move it all downstairs and put it in the car for his trip, but every few minutes the waves of pain in his head grew so bad that he couldn't see. He lay down on the floor a couple of times as he was walking around the room and curled up until the flashing spots went away.

He slept again for what felt like a long time, but when he awoke the sun streaming through the window made it look like it was only a few hours later. Checking the date on his watch, Sean was surprised to discover that it was Saturday already – he'd slept for more than twenty-four hours straight.

The light coming in the window was a different color, more red and orange. He could hear the wind blowing against the building outside and wondered if it would snow that night. His mind reached back to Pasadena, how warm it was during April there, how spring was real and actually happened. Nothing here in Moscow seemed real to him. It wasn't supposed to snow in April. The airport wasn't supposed to close and people weren't supposed to die and leave the streets empty and quiet for days. And your father wasn't supposed to call home and find out that your mom had died.

Elizabeth! Sean thought. He crawled out of the bed and reached for the phone on the nightstand. He dialed the number with the country code that his father had written down for him. The line was a little weak, but he managed to get it to ring steadily after a few tries. There was no answer. He wasn't sure what time it was in California, but he thought that, no matter what, Elizabeth should still be at home. But, she never picked up. How am I ever going to find her, he thought, if she's left the house and gone somewhere? How long is it going to take me to get to America?

He lay back down on the bed and pulled the blanket over himself. The presence of his father's body so close comforted him, but he didn't look at it. He told himself again that it wasn't his father, that he'd gone somewhere else. Sean closed his eyes tightly and relaxed his head back into the pillow, wishing the dull aching away and trying to clear his mind of all thoughts of Pasadena and his house and the cold and rifles and boxes of food.

CHAPTER TWENTY-FOUR

On Sunday morning, Sean awoke early. The clock on the nightstand said 6:15 a.m., but he thought it must be wrong. He felt completely rested – he never felt that way when he had to wake up that early in the morning. Propping himself up on his elbows, Sean looked around the room, trying to recall when he'd fallen asleep and what he'd done the day before. Vague memories of his headache came rushing back, along with the recollection of the stale crackers he'd eaten. Suddenly, he realized that he was very hungry.

The clear cellophane of the package came away easily and he pulled out a triangular shaped, flaky, fruit-filled pastry. He washed it down with a few gulps from a carton of milk as he sat on the bed, taking a brief mental inventory of the supplies in the corner and the food that they'd loaded into the car downstairs. They'd estimated that he should be able to last for a month or so on what they'd collected. His father had said that that should be more than enough time to find somewhere safe to stay for a few weeks while the weather warmed up.

He glanced over at his father's body on the bed beside him. It was so still. It didn't even really look like him as the face was turned away. Sean stared for several minutes at the body, picturing his father's animated gestures once again, the excitement and laughter in his voice on his last day as he was relating his life stories. That's who he was, Sean thought, as he wiped the tears from his eyes. That's who he was to us and that's who he'll always be.

Sean pulled the blanket up over his father's head, tucking it in all around the body. As he collected the letter that his father had written for him, his eyes raced over the first few lines before they began again to fill with warm tears. He placed the letter on top of his clothes in his suitcase.

It didn't take him long to move everything into the car downstairs. They'd only put enough food in the room to last for a few more days. The food, medical supplies from the Embassy safe house, his suitcase and the extra clothing filled up the trunk and much of the backseat. He carried the rifles and handguns with their ammunition down and put them in the front seat. Sean wasn't exactly sure what he'd need them for – he assumed that all of the Mafia guys they'd run into had also died or would in the next few days. But, his dad had wanted him to take everything "just in case." He'd been sure that Sean would be able to handle the weapons safely mostly because of his Rifle and Shotgun merit badge training, but also because of the quick, impromptu lesson on the dangers of firearms while they'd been carrying supplies over from the market. Sean tucked a handgun into the inside pocket of his coat – just in case.

Sean slammed the black car door shut. Just as he did, he thought he heard a car engine somewhere further up the street. He looked out of the carport area in front of the hotel, to the market and metro station across the street. Nothing stirred. He waited for half a minute before turning to go upstairs for one last check to make sure that he'd grabbed everything – and to say goodbye to his father one last time.

Halfway through the lobby of empty armchairs, plush couches and coffee tables filled with magazines, he heard a crash of glass from further back in the hotel. Sean froze next to a tall, skinny white lamp, trying to hold his breath in order to catch any other sounds. His heart leapt when he heard the second crash. This one was a little louder than the first – the sound of glass exploding against something.

There was a long hallway leading straight back into the hotel to the left of the elevators. It was fairly wide and had thick carpet and large plants in ornate brass pots between the several sets of double doors.

Sean stood unmoving, staring down the hallway. He was fairly certain that the sound had come from one of the sets of doors. Maybe it's that guy we saw a couple of days ago, he thought. Maybe he dropped something. Or threw it.

He continued toward the elevators and pressed the call button, eyeing the entrance to the hallway as he waited. The elevator doors opened, but Sean didn't step inside. He was leaning back so that he could see further down the hall. Finally, he walked over to the hallway entrance and peered carefully to the doors at the end. It was well lit – a lamp was fastened to the wall every few feet.

Suddenly, he heard what sounded like metal utensils banging together from one of the rooms ahead. He walked quickly to the next set of doors, put his hand on the large, brass handle and paused – there weren't any more sounds coming from inside. Sean took a deep breath and slowly turned the handle and pushed the door inward.

The room was smaller than he thought it would be. There were padded chairs stacked against the walls and a couple of intricate chandeliers hanging overhead. Light came from only one of the chandeliers – half of the room was hidden in shadow.

Again he heard the chinking of glasses from further down the hall. After another quick glance, he closed the door and hurried down to the next set of doors. Hand on the handle, he sucked in a deep breath and pushed the door open.

This room's layout was much the same – chairs, chandeliers. Except all the lights were on, shining down on a large table, set up in the middle of the room. Chairs were arranged around the table which was covered with a thick white linen tablecloth. Plates, utensils and glasses were set at each place, but only a few of the seats were occupied. Sean quickly counted three people sitting on the side closest to him, their backs to him and maybe three or four more on the other side.

They were all slumped down in their chairs or hunched over on the table, their faces and hands on the plates, curled around glasses or clutching at some piece of food. In fact, the table was loaded with food spread out on white porcelain dishes and large, shiny metal saucers. There were candlesticks, some still burning, and at least a dozen bottles of wine and other types of alcohol. Most of the food didn't look very fancy – mostly the frozen type of stuff that he and his father had been able to find in the market across the street. But, there were the remains of a chicken or turkey on a large, intricately decorated saucer in the center of the table.

Sean, still standing at the door with his head poking inside, jumped at the sound of a dull butter knife being dragged across the linen tablecloth. He didn't see any of the three people in front of him moving, but he wasn't sure about the others on the opposite side of the table. With a quick glance over his shoulder he stepped into the room.

As he walked closer to the table, he could see that the faces of the people on the other side of the table were pale. Some of their mouths hung open, their frozen eyes wide. He recognized the man who had come through the lobby a couple days before, but he wasn't wearing his black rabbit fur hat anymore. His hair was thin and gray, collecting mostly at the sides of his head which was cradled in his plate.

Sean saw a small hand clutching a silver butter knife jab at something on the table. He put his hands on the back of one of the large wooden chairs and looked past the bodies closest to him to see a toddler sitting in the lap of a woman. The woman had graying blonde hair and was dressed in dark, drab clothing, a dark red scarf wrapped tightly around her neck. Her head was resting gently on one shoulder, swaying with the motion of the young child sitting at her lap.

Estimating his age at two or three, Sean watched as the boy stretched forward with the knife trying to reach a pastry that sat on a plate in the middle of the table. It was the last one left, the crumbs of its companions littering the face of the white porcelain plate. The boy's large blue eyes turned toward him and he opened his mouth to grunt as he made another lunge toward the pastry.

Sean stood at the edge of the table staring at the six adult bodies still in their chairs. He could see a pile of suitcases against the wall on the other side of the table. There were some blankets and pillows spread out on the carpet around the room. Each of the people, four men and two women, were wearing a suit or dress. One of the older men had a row of old war medals pinned to the lapel of his jacket. Their plates had scraps of food, remains of their feast. Several glasses half-drained of wine and vodka sat around each person's plate. One of the men on Sean's side of the table clutched a large bottle of pills in his calloused hand.

The little boy threw the butter knife across the table where it hit an empty glass bottle before thudding onto the carpeted floor. The toddler cried out in frustration, pounding his little fists on the table. His hair was blond and curly at the ends. He was dressed in a little, buttoned-up shirt and dark pants.

Sean stood still glancing around at the six bodies as the boy wiggled in his seat. It looked like he was caught between his mother's legs and the table. He made an angry whining sound before reaching out his hand again toward the pastry.

His little fingers expanded and contracted, spreading away from his chubby palm as he tried to reach the flaky, buttery treat. The pastry sat on the edge of the plate closest to the boy, only five or six inches away. Suddenly, Sean felt a pressure building inside his head and an intense rushing of blood in his ears. All of his attention was immediately brought into focus on the boy's outstretched fingers, the pastry and the short distance between them. The pressure increased, concentrating at the front of his skull and behind his eyes, to the point where his knees started to shake and he had to grip the chair in front of him for support. It felt and sounded like a powerful wind was rushing through his head and he felt a pulling sensation as if everything around him was being expanded and contracted at once. He was staring helplessly at the little boy reaching out across the table, when he saw the pastry move.

One corner of it turned toward the little boy. For a split second the pressure in his head and the deafening rushing sound in his ears abated. The toddler continued to stretch his hand out to the pastry, grunts of frustration coming out of his tightened mouth and tears collecting at the corners of his eyes. Then, the wall of pressure, like a compact boulder leaning on the inside of his forehead, resumed forcefully and Sean watched as the pastry flipped over off the plate and slid over four inches of tablecloth into the boy's outstretched hand.

As suddenly as it had started, the pressure in his head and rushing in his ears were gone. Sean exhaled sharply, his lungs feeling like they'd been about to burst. He stared in disbelief as the blond boy quickly pulled the pastry to his mouth and took a large bite. He stared back at Sean, smiling as dark, red jelly ran down the side of his cheek.

Sean looked around the room, blinking to make sure that he was fully awake, wondering if he was about to die, wondering if this is how it was for his father, for his mother right before they'd finally gone. But, his head didn't hurt at all. There was no residual pain left from what he'd experienced. In fact, it hadn't been painful at all – just the most extreme and concentrated sensation he'd ever had. It reminded him of what he'd felt in the RKA control room when Jerry had hit, but it was much more intense this time, and, somehow, more focused.

The toddler was halfway through the pastry when both he and Sean jumped at the sound of a thundering crash from down the hall. Sean ran toward the double doors that he'd left ajar as sounds of shattering glass, splintering wood and the gunning of a car engine echoed through the hotel.

Sean stepped out into the hallway to see a black BMW slam into one of the couches in the lobby. The pink couch flipped onto its back, sending cushions flying out onto the floor. The large front doors to the hotel were completely gone and the entire lobby was covered in tiny chunks of glass and pieces of wood from the tables and chairs through which the car had just plowed.

The car reversed to the left, then shot forward to the right, smashing through a long, glass coffee table in front of another set of chairs. Sean had trouble seeing who was driving the vehicle because of the tinted windows, but it looked as though there were several people inside. He slipped back into the room and shut the doors securely behind him.

The little blond boy had finished the pastry and was licking jelly off his fingers. Sean ran around to his side of the table and lifted him off the dead woman's lap. The car engine revved again, but was quickly cut short by a loud crunch. Sean thought he heard excited yells from the car.

He carried the boy a few feet toward the back of the room and set him down on the floor. Sean quickly gathered up a pile of blankets and dumped them behind some chairs that were sitting a few feet away from the wall. He pulled some of the suitcases in front of the chairs and then picked up the boy again and took him behind the makeshift hiding place. Sean ducked under the blanket, covering himself and the toddler, lay down on the floor and listened.

The car backed up, switched gears, then sped forward again, racing over the carpet. Sean heard it tearing down the hallway, the engine's hum sounding very strange as it bounced off the wood walls. There was a dull ripping sound as the driver slammed on the brakes. The car doors opened and boyish cries and screams echoed through the hallway.

Sean pulled the little boy close to his chest, but he squirmed and fidgeted. He kept trying to push the blanket away from his face, but Sean kept it securely over the both of them. Laughing voices were talking loudly just outside the doors. They sounded young. Sean couldn't tell how many there were.

Another smash of glass cut through the air immediately followed by a dull thud against the wall. Hysterical laughter followed amid several exuberant exclamations in Russian. The toddler jumped at the sound and immediately began to cry. His mouth opened wide and a tearful scream poured out.

The voices outside quieted abruptly. Sean tried quietly shushing the little boy, stroked his head and rocked him back and forth. He felt the little lungs fill up with air and then the boy let out another loud scream. Sean heard the door handle turn and then the bottom of the door sweep across the carpet.

A young male voice said something in surprise. Sean heard feet entering the room – he still couldn't tell how many there were. Despite his efforts, the toddler kept screaming, hot tears pouring down his red cheeks. Sean put his hand over the little boy's mouth and squeezed gently, still rocking him back and forth.

The chairs in front of them toppled over and the blanket was yanked away. A thin boy, about twelve or thirteen, was standing over them, staring in surprise with a large sledge hammer in his hands. There were three other boys, two roughly the same age and one a little older standing a few feet behind him. They were all dressed warmly, some of the black leather jackets hanging loosely around their shoulders. One of them also had a large hammer and the other two carried thick lead pipes.

The boy standing above him said something harshly. The toddler was still struggling to get up, so Sean let him go and then sat up. The four of them ignored the toddler as he waddled back

120

to the table and tried to climb up onto the woman's lap. The boy didn't lower his heavy hammer and repeated the phrase, more insistently.

Sean shrugged his shoulders, pushed the blanket off and stood up. The oldest of the four boys, about fourteen or fifteen, stepped forward and slammed his hand into Sean's chest, knocking him against the wall. He held him pinned there and screamed something into his face, gesturing at the table behind them.

"I don't understand! I don't speak Russian!" Sean yelled back at him. The boy had black hair and dark brown eyes, was several inches taller and smelled strongly of onions and garlic. Short, dark hairs dotted his upper lip, which was twisted into a threatening snarl.

Sean let the boy hold him against the wall. The other boys were stepping nervously from foot to foot, looking at each other and their ill-tempered leader. He could hear the ridicule and scorn in the boy's voice as he spoke quietly into his face, occasionally turning to his cronies behind him. Sean thought of his fight with Kyle and Paul only a week or so before. Kyle had had that same look in his eye as he held Sean against the tree. It didn't look like hate or evil or anything like that. Both this Russian kid and Kyle just had a mean, mischievous look in their eye, a readiness to get into trouble, to give other people a hard time. More than the feeling of the hand against his chest and the taunts and jeers, Sean hated the presumption and attitude that went along with this behavior – the desire to hurt and intimidate others, to assert your will above theirs, just because you can.

Sean watched the boy carefully as he continued to mutter cruelly at him, looking into the boy's eyes and leaving his face expressionless. He waited until the boy turned briefly to the pale kid beside him to laugh at some joke. Then, he grabbed the dark-haired boy's hips and brought his knee up into his groin, pulling the kid toward him as he did so.

The Russian boy gasped and doubled over, tripping over the blanket as he hastily backed away. Sean immediately turned to the pale boy next to him. The boy dropped his heavy hammer and raised his arms in front of his face. Sean fumbled quickly for the handgun in his coat as the other boys stood dumbly, watching their friend moaning on the floor.

He gripped the weapon with both hands, keeping the short barrel pointed straight at their feet. Sean was shaking so hard that he was afraid that he was going to accidentally pull the trigger and didn't want to shoot at anyone if he didn't have to. He motioned with the handgun and began backing away from the now frightened boys. The toddler had made his way back to the table and was trying to climb back up to his dead mother's lap. He paid no attention to Sean or the others as the American boy ran quickly through the double doors to the hall.

The black BMW sat right in front of the doors, pointing away from the lobby. Behind him, Sean heard a shout and then the rapid shuffling of coats and running feet. Right before he turned to run toward the lobby, he briefly considered the possibility that they'd left the keys in the ignition – not likely, he thought. Besides, he was betting he could make it out of the building before the four of them could get the car turned around through all the couches and other debris.

Angry, pubescent Russian voices echoed through the empty hotel as Sean sprinted over the soft carpet toward the daylight ahead. He heard car doors slamming and the engine roaring to life as he reached the lobby. The tires spun, quickly tearing the carpet, as the oldest of the boys slammed on the pedal in reverse. Sean didn't even turn to look back as his feet bounded lightly over the scraps of destroyed furniture and shattered lamps.

He ran straight for where the front doors used to be, carefully stepping over the large, jagged shards of glass that littered the area in front of the check-in desk. He dared a brief glance over his shoulder as he reached the carport. The car was quickly turning around in the lobby, the dark-haired boy at the wheel, pointing the hood straight at him.

Sean fumbled in his pocket for the car keys as he darted to the left, sprinting past the row of empty cars parked in front of the hotel. Just as he reached his black sedan full of supplies, the BMW shot out of the hotel about thirty feet behind him.

The car's tires hit the pavement with a screech as the boy tried to turn the vehicle to the left. But, the car quickly reached the other side of the carport and plowed into a waist-high concrete wall.

Sean paused halfway into his car to watch the BMW bounce off the concrete wall and the four boys inside being thrown toward the right side of the vehicle. He jumped into the driver's seat and started the engine, quickly buckling his seat belt before pulling out of the parking spot. He sped past the BMW, seeing the four boys groping around inside, dazed from their collision.

Sean's foot slammed onto the brakes and he jerked the wheel to the left unsteadily as he barely made the turn down the ramp that led to the street. After seeing no signs of pursuit in his rear-view mirror, Sean pressed on the gas pedal and drove away from the hotel.

CHAPTER TWENTY-FIVE

The grime-coated window fogged up as Viktor held his face against the glass, peering down into the sunlit street below. Their apartment was in a long, gray five-story building, one of the thousands built during the Khrushchev regime. City ordinances required that any building with six or more floors have an elevator. Hence, all the tenements in this older section of the city only had five floors – Soviet efficiency.

Viktor could make out the monolithic shapes of more recently built, fourteen-story buildings in the distance. The day was clear and the bright sun shone on the dull colors of the buildings' exteriors – yellows, muted reds and browns – all tones from late sixties and early seventies construction. The combination of colors and varying building heights made the apartments look like a super-sized Lego village. The out-of-place splashes of cheap paint had been a poor attempt to distract the people from the oppression of the times – Brezhnev's policy of cultural stagnation and isolationism.

He rubbed his sleeve against the pane to wipe away the moisture from his breath. The stool beneath him creaked as he adjusted his weight. Viktor had been there for the past hour, staring down at the street, trying to find out what was going on. So far, he hadn't seen a soul. There was nothing but static on the television in the kitchen and the radio wasn't picking up anything either. As far as he could tell the rest of the world had just disappeared.

After his sister hadn't responded to the knocks at her door the morning before, Viktor had quietly entered, only to confirm what he already knew deep inside. Her room was even a little smaller than his, but minus all the clutter. The bed was crammed into the corner beside a chest of drawers. Dog-eared rock star posters covered the walls and piles of clothes covered most of the floor and chair at the end of the bed. She had laid still there, covers pulled up close to her chin. Viktor hadn't touched her – just looked into her face to see that she was gone.

Tatyana had been planning to do something with the bodies of his mother and grandmother that morning. She'd said that they were starting to stink, that they need to be buried or at least taken somewhere else, but Viktor didn't want them to leave. He knew they were already gone, but just having them lying peacefully in their beds made him feel like they were still all at home, as long as he didn't walk into the room. He'd left Tatyana's body undisturbed, closing the door quietly behind him.

Viktor leaned back against the table. He wasn't sure that he'd really expected to see anyone walking around outside, but he'd hoped that he would. His mind had been trying to avoid thinking about much of anything going on outside his small, confined world of the apartment for the past few days since his mother had died. He'd cried himself to sleep most nights, despite his attempts to dredge up all his memories of his mother's abuse – all the slaps and taunting, the way she would sneer at him sometimes as she stared. Viktor knew the thoughts flickering through her eyes – why didn't she have a normal son, what had she done to deserve this? But, with each painful memory he harvested, one more tender and kind had popped up, robbing him of the solace from grief that he had hoped resentment would bring.

His aching fingers twitched reflexively as he stared at the window, imagining his mother's presence behind him. His ears could almost hear the chink of dishes as she worked at the sink, the slap and scrape of her slippers as her quiet mass moved through the apartment. Suddenly, her smell came flooding back to him, momentarily overwhelming his senses. It was the scent of her skin lotion and a trace of perfume, the odor of the laundry detergent she used on her clothes – the smell of domesticity and comfort.

The image of a birthday card came into his mind – one that she had given him the day he'd turned six. It was miniscule and the colors were faded. She had probably found it in one of the boxes piled in her room, an unused card from years before. There was a round snowman on the front and a couple of enormous snowflakes. The note inside had been short, the handwriting blockish and uneven. He still remembered it: "Viktor, happy sixth birthday. I'm glad you're my boy – Mama." The card was tucked away in one of his books. He'd saved it, but hadn't looked at it or even thought about it in years.

Suddenly, he saw a form dart out of the building across the street and disappear below his line of vision. Viktor lurched forward, reaching for the window sill with his left hand. His right arm also shot out feebly, his elbow emitting a dull crack as the unused joint flared painfully into action. The stool underneath him tilted forward on two of its four legs. Just as he reached the window, one of the wooden legs snapped underneath his weight. For the split second that he hung in mid-air, he saw a young girl, maybe ten years old, in an oversized coat and boots, run to his side of the street and start around the building.

His tailbone crunched into the floor first, followed by his shoulder blades, then the back of his skull. Viktor lay silent for a moment looking at the dull white ceiling above him as he tried to slow his breathing, with both his legs twisted beneath him. His mind began to race, quickly focusing on each part of his body separately, beginning at his toes and then running up his legs and into his back, checking for painful spots, trying to quickly assess any injuries.

It wasn't the worst fall he'd ever had – nothing seemed to be broken, just bruised a little. He lifted his left arm to roll onto his right side, his right arm tucking beneath him, the palm flat on the floor. He slowly pushed himself into a sitting position and looked around dazedly as the blood pounding in his head slowed. His legs were still tucked carefully beneath him and he looked down at his right hand, planted firmly on the floor with the arm extended, delicately supporting his weight.

Viktor blinked his eyes in confusion. But there it was – his right arm: fully extended, no longer tucked in a useless ball at his side. The elbow was beginning to ache terribly and his arm was starting to shake under the strain. Ignoring his trembling limb, he pulled his left hand up to his face, almost to confirm that it wasn't the one supporting his body. The fingers were still locked in their usual cramped position, the middle finger slightly extended. Still holding the hand in front of his face, he concentrated on wiggling the aching fingers, willing the locked joints to move. Usually when he did this, he was only able to get a limited degree of movement from the fingers, but it was often enough to ease some of the pain. Wiggling them now made it feel as if metal pins were being slowly pushed into the knuckles. He grimaced and continued flexing the fingers, working them gradually until all of them were almost fully extended. Then, he curled them into a weak fist and opened it again.

Viktor leaned forward to take the strain off his right arm and sat on the floor, opening and closing both his hands in front of his face, watching the fingers curl in upon themselves then shoot out straight like ten perfect arrows.

CHAPTER TWENTY-SIX

The tires hummed ominously as the car glided across the asphalt streets interrupted only occasionally by large puddles or patches of slush. Sean gripped the black steering wheel tightly, his hands spaced as far apart as his shoulders, as he stared intently at the empty road disappearing underneath the vehicle.

He leaned slightly forward on the wooden box underneath him and adjusted the volume knob on the dashboard radio. Soft static floated through the air, interrupted only as Sean punched through the various frequencies. Shaking his head, he turned the volume back down and returned his eyes to their duty of scanning the empty road.

Despite the numerous street signs and the Seven Sister landmarks looming in the distance, he had no idea where he was. The thought that it might have been a good idea to plot a course before driving off into a large unknown city had briefly crossed his mind, but he'd quickly dismissed it because it dredged up thoughts of his father. He'd tried so hard to prepare Sean in every way he could think of before he died – he couldn't have considered everything. Besides, Sean had decided to stick to the strategy he'd arrived upon a few minutes after leaving the Russian boys at the hotel: just go in a straight line until you get there. Since it didn't matter where "there" was, then it didn't matter how he got there. Any one direction was as good as another to get him outside the city and to a smaller town away from more bullies where he could stay for a while and make his plans, just as his father had told him.

His only problem right now, besides the painful grumbling in his belly, was that he'd been driving for almost an hour and still didn't seem to be getting anywhere near the edge of the city.

The gray buildings and empty streets seemed to stretch on forever and, soon, Sean was unable to tell if he was actually driving in circles and had already been through this particular neighborhood before. The only thing he knew was that he'd made no turns unless he'd had to and that if he just kept on a straight course he should eventually leave Moscow.

It was a clear morning with only a few clouds in the sky. The temperature had risen sharply and Sean now wore only a light jacket as he drove, watching sunlight bounce off the occasional chunk of melting ice on the side of the road. He was driving high on the bank along a large river in what appeared to be one of the warehouse districts. The river has to lead somewhere, he thought to himself.

Above the buildings in the distance, Sean saw a plume of billowing black smoke rising into the sky. Two voices inside his head chimed simultaneously. The first, which, as always, sounded very much like his mother's, hinted that smoke could mean trouble and that he should avoid it. The second voice, which usually sounded like his own when he did his Gollum imitation, suggested that a closer look wouldn't hurt and might even turn up something that he could use later. As the car's engine purred along, Sean wrestled with these voices and finally decided that since the road he was on was headed toward the smoke anyway, then it probably wouldn't hurt to continue on in that direction.

A tall, walled compound appeared along the bank on the opposite side of the river. Sean could see the roofs and windows of several buildings behind the wall and he noticed that a bridge was coming up that led to the other side – to the source of the smoke.

Stretching his legs to depress the brake pedal, Sean kept his eyes on the smoke as the car slowed. The smoke was thick and poured out of one of the buildings at the edge of the compound. As he approached, he could see that the building had multiple towers with onion-shaped domes at the top. St. Basil's Cathedral – he remembered the name from one of the hotel guidebooks he'd read. He was approaching Red Square.

Nearing the bridge, he could see that the cathedral wasn't inside the compound at all, but just outside it at the edge of the large, cobble-stoned square. He slowed the vehicle almost to a crawl as he turned onto the bridge – he still wasn't very adept at turning the sedan's large black steering wheel.

There were a few cars on the bridge, mostly lining its edges. Their sides were smashed in, apparently with great force. A body lay face down beside one of the cars, its ankles crossed casually one over the other as if the person had just been taking a nap in the middle of the bridge. Sean tightened his grip on the steering wheel and drove on.

St. Basil's Cathedral was burning on the opposite side from where Sean was. Smoke was still pouring out of the building, but no flames were visible. A large green truck, its open bed blackened, was parked at the base of the building, its front grill pressed firmly against the bottom of one of the towers.

There were more cars parked on the road on the other side of the bridge, some with damage matching that of the other vehicles. Sean carefully made his way along the crowded street until he was about parallel with the cathedral before he had to stop the car. Many of the cars were burned, the seats inside reduced to blackened metal frames with the tires looking as though they'd melted into the road.

Sean had been able to smell the smoke as he'd neared the square, but it was nothing compared to the stench that met him when he opened the door. A wave of burned rubber assaulted him, forcing him to cough several times as he stepped out of the car.

He still couldn't see much of the square from where he was – almost directly behind the smoking cathedral. Pocketing his handgun, Sean placed a scarf over his nose and mouth, then began winding through the parked cars toward the large cathedral.

At least a dozen dark tanks and a few other large trucks were strewn about in front of the Kremlin walls. A couple of the vehicles were tipped over and several were charred and still smoking slightly. Sean could see a few dozen bodies lying around the immense doors that lead to the interior. Some wore uniforms, but many did not. Many were still clutching rifles, machine guns, sticks and rocks.

The remaining shell of an exploded tank was parked in front of St. Basil's Cathedral. There were words spray-painted on the front doors and along the cathedral's base. A woman with a dark green shawl covering her head lay in front of the doors, a can of spray paint still clutched in her hand.

A cool spring breeze pushed against Sean's jacket as he stood staring down at the destruction all around him. For a moment, he imagined the crowds amassing on Red Square, could almost hear their angry chants as they demanded protection and answers from government leaders who were able to provide none. It didn't look like anyone had made it through the gates. They'd tried to get into the Kremlin walls, had probably started pushing against the soldiers, throwing rocks and burning torches or bottles. The young men in uniform had probably started firing in fear and self-defense, but there were just too many.

Sean was filled with an overwhelming sadness as he looked at the scores of dead. So many people had died afraid, unable to understand what was happening to them or their world, not knowing whether or not they would wake the next day or, if they did, who would be left alive with them. Everything must have happened within the last two or three days. Both the soldiers and the people must have assumed that they would be dying soon anyway, neither group really having anything to lose. Dying in the streets or in bed at home – what did it matter? It was all such a terrible and futile waste.

Sean felt the grief begin in his stomach, spreading quickly into his throat, filling him and causing his shoulders to shake. He sank to his knees on the dark gray cobblestones that were stained with blood and fire, as tears poured from his eyes and a whimper escaped from his now uncovered mouth. A deep sense of loneliness seeped into him as his mind attempted to wrap around actually how many people in the world had died. So many fathers and mothers and sons who would never wake again, would never be able to simply walk away from this nightmare, but would lie in the open for years until the wind and rain finally washed them away forever.

He thought of his father lying cold and alone in the bed back at the hotel and wondered why he hadn't been able to do anything to stop this. Nothing had ever seemed to get in his way before, there was nothing that his father couldn't overcome. Why couldn't he stop this? Why couldn't he figure this out? A brief memory flashed through Sean's mind – the look in his father's eyes once he'd hung up the phone with Elizabeth, after finding out that his wife was dead. That's when it happened, Sean thought as he stared down through tears at the rough stones beneath his feet. That's when he gave up – when he stopped caring and resigned himself to the fate he knew he couldn't escape. What was the use of fighting to live in a world where she was no more?

And what about the rest of us, Sean asked himself. What happens to us now that they're all gone? What is left for us? A dead world full of used up bodies and the orphans they left behind? No way to communicate with anyone far away, no way to get anywhere really – especially across an ocean. Elizabeth's long hair came into his mind – an image of her running through the house, checking all the doors and windows like she always did when their parents went out for the night. How long will she keep the doors closed, Sean wondered. How long can she keep herself safe?

CHAPTER TWENTY-SEVEN

Sean didn't remember how long he'd been kneeling there on the cobblestones of Red Square when his eyes finally stopped letting out tears. They felt dry, unable to cry anymore. His hands resting helplessly in his lap, he looked around the square again at the silent vehicles and faces everywhere.

A flicker of movement at the opposite side of the Square caught his eye. He strained to see what it was, but could only make out some type of frantic flapping – maybe it was a bird. Sean hoped that the scavengers hadn't started already.

Pushing himself to his feet, he trained his eyes on the figure or object that appeared to be getting closer. The figure's arms were discernable now – they were pumping wildly, as were the legs as it sped across the ground. Several others were following quickly behind – all of them headed in Sean's direction.

His fingers fastened around the nine millimeter handgun in his pocket and his feet began to back up, his eyes still locked on the figures in the distance. Whoever was coming was getting closer as Sean started into a small jog back toward his car, craning his neck over his shoulder as he moved. There were three boys running toward the cathedral, the first one he saw was in the lead, his white, oversized sweatshirt sleeves flapping around him as he ran. Sean counted three additional figures in pursuit, wielding weapons of some kind, possibly rifles.

Now, Sean focused all his attention on running back to the car-packed street. He heard a series of fast gun shots and glanced back in time to see that the boy closest to the pursuers had stopped to return fire with what looked like a handgun. The three pursuers scattered and hugged the ground temporarily, until he turned and began running again. The boy with the handgun had gone only a few steps before one of the chasers paused and fired a couple rifles shots at him. Sean saw the boy clutch at his back and trip, falling quickly to the ground.

For a split second after reaching the street, Sean stared in confusion at the silent traffic jam of vehicles – which car was his? They all looked the same! Feeling panic beginning to rise in the back of his mind, Sean quickly scanned the area, his eyes sweeping to the right where he spotted the large black sedan at the back of the line. He ducked around an old compact car and started running up the street toward his vehicle.

Suddenly, he heard a loud blast from the direction of the boys. He stopped and crouched behind a gray car to peer through its windows at the boy in the white sweatshirt running past the cathedral. His pursuers rose quickly from their positions of cover and began running again.

Feet slapping against the ground to his left alerted Sean in time for him to turn and see a boy about his age dart around a fender two cars away. The boy's eyes were wide as he stared at the group moving closer toward him. He was several inches taller than Sean and unusually thin. His head jerked to the right and his gaze locked immediately on Sean. They both paused for a split second in shock and surprise, before Sean glanced down at the black handgun in the boy's hands. The boy noted Sean's hands by his side, checked the advance of his pursuers as they drew closer, then looked back at Sean. A split second later, three distinct pops sounded across the square and both boys jumped as a car window exploded a few feet behind Sean.

Sean was the first to move. He dodged around the car to his left and began running across the street away from the square, weaving between the motionless vehicles. The thin boy stared for a second at the approaching group now only a few dozen yards away, then ran across the street in the same direction as Sean.

Sean could feel the heavy weight of the pistol bouncing against his side as his legs and arms pumped wildly. His breath had already been coming in ragged gasps even before he'd started running, but now Sean felt as though a giant machine was sitting on his chest, squeezing his lungs open and shut. His mind turned back briefly to his car, but then quickly focused on the ground in front of him. I would have never made it, he thought. And I can't go back now. Feet pounding on the sidewalk, he rounded a corner onto an empty street between some shorter buildings.

Sean's eyes raced over colorful displays in shop window fronts and blockish Cyrillic signs plastered above doors. The street was narrow and strewn with yellowed newspapers and continued straight for several more blocks. There were numerous side streets branching off from the main one and Sean stopped briefly at an intersection, ducking around the corner of a building to try to catch his breath.

Five seconds later, the taller, skinny kid came running up the street, his white face held high as his arms and legs pumped wildly. His shoe caught on the rough pavement and he went down, his outstretched hands skidding out in front of him. He bounced up a second later, drops of blood and bits of gravel falling from his palms, and continued running. The boy made it another few yards, up until the side street that Sean had turned down, then tripped again, this time landing heavily on his side before rolling over onto his back, his chest heaving.

Sean shoved his hand into his jacket pocket and gripped the handgun. The boy lying panting on his back hadn't seen him yet. Sean paused, crouched by the building, unsure of what to do. Had they lost their pursuers? Had any of them even seen Sean? He wondered if he should continue down one of the side streets and try to double back to his vehicle. His head turned in the direction from which they'd come, straining to detect any sign of the rifle-wielding chasers.

A door on the other side of the silent street creaked open. Two girls, huddling together, crept out and down the steps to the cracked pavement. The taller one was about twelve years old – her younger companion was probably five or six. Both wore faded dark blue coats and scarves wrapped around their heads in a peasant woman fashion that Sean remembered his father had found charmingly quaint. The older girl held the younger to her side as they made it halfway into the street before stopping suddenly at the sight of the boy lying there.

The older of the two girls gasped at the sight of the thin boy's bleeding hands. Her frightened eyes jumped up to see Sean crouching in the side street, hand in his pocket. Before either the girls or Sean had a chance to move or speak, the boy in the large, white sweatshirt rounded the corner, his long sleeves turning like tiny windmills as he ran.

His eyes were fastened on the ground in front of him, so he didn't see the two scared girls until he was about six feet away. His feet skidded to a halt and he fell onto his butt as he gaped in confusion at the girls. Right at that moment, a tall, grim-faced, dark haired teenager sprinted around the corner, a compact machine gun clutched in his hands. Two other younger, armed boys, one with a thick neck and broad shoulders and the other smaller with white, spiked hair, came running right behind him.

The tall, dark-haired lead teenager, or Dark-hair as Sean thought of him, halted when he saw the four youngsters in the middle of the street, two girls staring at him in fright and the two boys on the ground trying to scramble to their feet.

"Svyeta!" yelled the armed boy with white, spiked hair. He was staring intently at the twelve-year old girl who was still clutching the younger one by her side.

The girl blinked in confusion at the boy. "Ivan?"

Sean felt a rushing in his ears and what seemed like a hand or something brushing in front of his face, very similar to the sensation that he'd experienced back at the hotel with the young toddler reaching for the pastry. Dark-hair looked quickly into the faces of all four kids in the street, pausing for a brief moment on each, before glancing away, a hint of confusion flashing across his face. His dark hair was close-cropped and his eyes were brown, set deeply in a wide, strong face. A black wool military coat trailed down to his knees, resting on bony shoulders framed by a tight-fitting black t-shirt.

The strong, brown eyes scanned the street and store fronts as the armed boy with the thick neck and broad shoulders, or Muscles, ran past him toward the group in the middle. Suddenly, Dark-hair jerked his head toward Sean, still huddling at the edge of the building.

Sean leaned into the wall as his head began to swim with different shades of color and light. He felt as if he were plunging headfirst down the constantly expanding tube of an enormous kaleidoscope, thousands of rainbows and intricate patterns colliding before his eyes. At the edge of his vision, he saw Dark-hair start toward him.

Both the boys on the ground were having difficulty getting to their feet, the thin one because of his scraped and bleeding hands, the other in the white-sweatshirt because he was caught between two girls and his pursuers and was unsure of which way to start moving. The younger girl was crying and the older, Svyeta, started to scream in fright as Muscles advanced quickly toward them, his assault rifle leveled.

The swirling colors behind Sean's eyes stopped moving and began to dissipate just as Svyeta started screaming. Her voice carried through the street, echoing off the squat buildings and reverberating against the windows. Sean suddenly felt that same rushing sensation, only this time it felt like a river was slamming into his head and ears and his entire being was filled with the sound of her voice. He stared, helplessly fascinated, covering his ears with his hands as her piercing voice began to crescendo higher and higher. The younger girl by her side covered her ears, as did both boys on the ground.

Muscles, who was running toward her, was just beginning to slow and bring his hands up to his ears when her voice rocketed upward in a sharp spike, splitting the air in front of her with a high-pitched crack. Sean watched in amazement as what appeared to be circular waves of energy rippling through the air shot out of her mouth and struck Muscles, now about ten yards away. The force took him off his feet and slammed him into the ground on his back.

The high-pitched screech forced everyone to wince and groan as the sound tore through their ears. A couple of store front windows to the girl's left quivered briefly before shattering, sending tiny shards of glass all over the sidewalk. Finally, she ran out of breath and the ear-splitting scream died on her quivering lips as she clutched the younger girl tightly to her side.

Muscles, still lying on his back, shook his head dazedly and began wiping the blood from his ears away with his coat sleeve. Just as the boy in the oversized white sweatshirt was attempting to pull himself to his feet, Dark-hair rushed forward and slammed his boot into the smaller boy's side.

With tears still running down her face, Svyeta stared in horror at Dark-hair and began to open her mouth. Just as she did so, he clamped a large, long-fingered hand over it and hissed

"Molchi, Svyeta!"

Sean leaned heavily against the wall feeling as though his knees were about to buckle, the strength slowly draining from him. He sagged down to a kneeling position and placed his hands on the rough curb trying to keep himself from sinking further. Ivan, the armed boy with the white, spiky hair, ran over to the skinny boy whose palms were still bloodied and embedded with bits of gravel. His face twisted into a scowl as he raised his rifle, threatening the boy on the ground with its butt. He shouted some orders at the helpless youth and kicked him in the back, gesturing in the direction of the two girls and the white-sweatshirt boy.

"Idi syuda!" shouted Dark-hair as he pointed his snub-nosed sub-machine gun at Sean. He waved it menacingly as he approached, eyeing the young American carefully.

Sean watched helplessly as Dark-hair advanced on him. He could feel his strength returning, but was unable to even consider expending effort to stand and run the other direction. Dark-hair reached him and hauled him to his feet by his jacket collar and pushed him in the direction of the four other captives.

As the pounding of blood in his ears began to slow, Sean staggered over to the middle of the street, dragging his feet as he went. Muscles jumped to his feet, trying to hide a bitter scowl of embarrassment as he wiped the few remaining drops of blood from his ears with his sleeve. He was a couple years older than Sean, with a potato-shaped face. He began pushing the two girls and two other boys into a line, shoulder to shoulder, cuffing the older girl on the side of the head to get her to move.

His hand still on Sean's collar, Dark-hair guided the skinny boy over to stand with the others next to the boy in the white sweatshirt. All five of them were quickly patted down by Dark-hair's two cronies as the latter paced slowly back and forth in front of the line of frightened faces, his weapon resting calmly on his shoulder.

From under the white sweatshirt came two grenades and a couple of cigarette lighters along with a pack of half empty cigarettes. Muscles stuffed the lighters and cigarette pack into his own pocket and handed the grenades to Dark-hair. The thin boy, his mouth slightly open, but still staring straight ahead, stood frozen as Ivan emptied his pockets – a couple cigarette packs and a few unspent rounds of ammunition.

Sean felt his fists clench as Ivan walked up to him, his rifle strap resting calmly on his shoulder. A worn leather coat hung loosely over his small, bony shoulders. The rest of his clothing was equally as ragged, his thin pants a crusty mottled mixture of black and brown stains. Dirt and grime was caked on his hands as well as around the corners of his mouth and ears. His dark eyes scanned Sean's face as he thrust his hands into his pockets. He pulled out the handgun, weighed it for a moment in his hand, then turned to hand it to Dark-hair.

Ivan and Muscles gripped their weapons menacingly as they stepped behind Dark-hair who stood silently watching. A light wind blew through the street and a few clouds moved in front of the bright sun hanging overhead.

After a few more tense minutes of staring at the five forlorn faces in front of him, Dark-hair handed his machinegun to Ivan and pulled Sean's nine millimeter from the pocket where he'd placed it earlier. He walked slowly over to the thin boy at the other end of the line, his over-sized boots thudding softly on the pavement.

Sean could feel the boy in the huge, white sweatshirt next to him trembling. He chanced a glance out of the corner of his eye and saw the kid's lip quivering as he bit it, trying to keep in a whimper that finally escaped in a muffled moan. Sean's eyes turned to Ivan and Muscles as they looked on the five helpless children with smug grins on their dirty faces.

Dark-hair began walking down the line, pausing for ten or fifteen seconds in front of each person, looking intently into their eyes. Sean thought for a brief second that the cool spring wind had picked up as what sounded like a powerful gust whistled through his ears. But, no – wait. It was the rushing sensation he'd felt earlier, a source-less sound that filled his ears and mind, like a great waterfall spilling over a sharp precipice. Although, this time it was more focused – it seemed to be coming from Dark-hair.

Colors began to swirl in front of Sean's eyes again, rotating like various shades on a palette wheel. Yet, the colors weren't exactly in front of his face – he wasn't seeing them with his eyes – but, rather, they were in his mind, as if he was trying to imagine what blue or red looked like.

Sean turned his head to watch as Dark-hair stared into Svyeta's eyes. He was saying something to her, half smiling. She was no longer crying, but her gaunt cheeks were red and her shoulders trembling – from cold or fear, Sean couldn't tell. As both Sean and Dark-hair stared at Svyeta, Sean could sense a specific color coalescing around and over her, a mix of pale blue with darker brown staining the edges. The sensation confused him at first, but then he began to feel something seeping from the color that was infused with her face. He felt fear.

Svyeta was afraid. Suddenly, it made complete sense – Sean's attention shifted from the color to the emotion he could feel pouring out of her. It was terrible. Fear mixed with helplessness and resignation washed over him suddenly and he looked away quickly, but the sensation didn't cease. He opened his mouth as if trying to suck in a breath of fresh air, but the emotion wouldn't dissipate. More clouds gathered around the sun, casting the city street in a subdued gray as a quiet wind blew past the children.

Sean began slowly turning his head, trying to shake the sensation, the overpowering emotion that was filling his mind and chest. Dark-hair, handgun gripped calmly at his side, paused briefly in front of the younger girl before moving on to the boy in the white sweatshirt. Sean focused on Dark-hair's face, tracing the strong lines and thick dark eyebrows that hung over his large brown eyes. Now, Sean began to see a different color, a deep, deep pink that almost seemed to seethe and bubble. It filled the space around the tall boy's head and appeared to permeate his features. The fear that had been gripping him only moments before faded as something more calm and pleasant filled his mind – amusement. Sean could almost see the older boy smiling inwardly as he walked down the line of terrified youngsters, waving his gun in their faces. He was enjoying this.

Dark-hair began muttering a few words to the frightened kid quivering beside him. His words were soft and calm, but Sean was almost sure he could detect some type of threat or grim promise underlying the innocent-sounding tone. Sean saw a tear escape from the corner of the kid's eye and heard a hiccough squeak through his trembling lips.

His face splitting into a wide smile, Dark-hair placed the

muzzle of the handgun against the scared kid's forehead. He began to laugh as the younger boy tried to stammer something, but the words wouldn't come out through his shaking lips and he began to sob, tears pouring down his face and a pitiful whine coming up through his choked throat.

Sean felt a pressure building at the base of his skull and the rushing sensation returned, quietly at first, but then gradually building in strength. He watched in confusion as the three armed teens laughed at the terrified boy in the white sweatshirt. The pressure continued to build until his forehead seemed like it was about to burst. As his face crinkled in pain, the young boy gave up attempting to answer whatever question had been posed to him and just tried to clamp his mouth shut over the whimpers that were scrambling up his constricting throat.

Just as Sean thought he was about to sink to his knees again with the intensity of the weight pressing against his skull from the inside, the boy's mouth burst open in a gush of water. Both Sean and Dark-hair thought at first that the kid was vomiting, but they quickly realized the fluid pouring out of his face was clear – and it kept coming. Suddenly, the front and back of his pants were soaked, liquid pouring out over his dirty, worn shoes.

Dark-hair stopped laughing and stepped back, his face contorted in surprise, the handgun raised defensively in front of his face. Two other gun barrels were leveled at the leaking boy as the other teens pointed their weapons. Water began to pour out of the boy's fingertips, coming out in steady streams like from a faucet. He stared down at his own body in horror as water continued to pour out of his open mouth, down the front of his pants and onto the street. Sean couldn't help feeling an intense sensation of relief as the pressure in his head slowly drained away.

A chuckle started deep in Dark-hair's chest and all at once exploded from his face as he doubled over, waving the gun at the frightened children and half-turning to the two boys behind him. All three were laughing hysterically as a steady stream of water ran over the pavement, soaking the bottoms of their boots like a running hose left out on the street. Both the two girls and the other boy at the opposite end of the line stared at the white sweatshirt boy in horror as the water continued to pour out of him.

As suddenly as it had started, the water ceased – like someone had just turned it off. A few last dribbles escaped the boy's lips and fingertips as he continued to stare at himself in confusion and fright. Finally, it stopped altogether and a little hiccough snuck out of his mouth.

The three other boys continued laughing for several moments before Dark-hair took a few steps over the wet pavement and patted the kid on his soaked shoulder. He flung a few drops of water off his hand and turned back to Ivan and Muscles as the laughter briefly resumed. The scared kid stared haplessly forward, his tear ducts even having suddenly run dry.

All at once Dark-hair stopped laughing and began speaking quickly and forcefully to the youth, gesturing threateningly with the handgun. He held the muzzle right against the boy's forehead and repeated the same phrase a couple times, staring menacingly into the boy's terrified face. He's going to shoot him, Sean thought. Right here in the street. He's going to blow his brains out and there's nothing I can do about it.

Suddenly, Dark-hair stepped back, pointed to the street behind him and shouted "Idi!"

The soaking youth blinked in confusion as the older boy shouted at him repeatedly. He glanced at Sean and the others, before taking a few steps forward past Dark-hair. His feet began to move faster, his wet shoes slapping against the pavement. He broke into a jog, still glancing over his shoulder, then began to sprint away as fast as he could. Dark-hair continued to shout after him, gesturing at his own chest with the handgun. Sean watched as the soaked sleeves of the long white sweatshirt turned around the corner of a building and disappeared.

Dark-hair turned back to the group and barked out a few orders, gesturing to the remaining four prisoners. A strong blast of warm air blew into their backs, stirring the trash lying in the gutters, as the two armed boys came around behind them and started pushing lightly in the direction of Red Square.

Sean began to walk forward as he was prodded in the back with a rifle muzzle. A large hand gripped him by the shoulder and Dark-hair said something with a smile as he walked beside Sean. The thirteen-year old looked up in confusion and shook his head.

The teenager repeated himself, his smile fading.

"I don't speak Russian – nyet po-russkiy. I'm an American."

The older boy stopped him and asked another question. Sean shrugged his shoulders, then Dark-hair said, "You – American?"

The words were slow and heavily accented. Sean assumed that this phrase comprised a majority of the street youth's English skills. "Yes. Da."

With the amusement in his dark eyes clearly visible, the boy smiled widely and laughed, clapping has large hand onto Sean's shoulder again. He yelled something to the other Russian kids walking slowly down the street.

Svyeta, still holding her sister close to her side, looked up and responded to the dark-haired boy's question. He then began speaking to her as he gestured toward Sean.

Her face full of sadness and despair, Svyeta turned to Sean and in heavily accented English said, "He say his name Pyotr. He, his people is Black… I not know how to say…" She then said a word that sounded like "scorpion".

She continued speaking slowly. "They Black Skorpioniy – Chyorniye Skorpioniy. All they own this," she gestured all around her, "part of city. Now, he own us too. He own you."

Dark-hair, or Pyotr, waited until she'd finished, then looked at Sean intently and poked him in the chest and said one word forcefully.

Svyeta translated again, "Remember."

Sean stared at the tall, dark-haired boy just a few years older than him. He could clearly see or at least sense somehow a new color that filled the air around the boy's face – black with dark red at the edges. Just as he had with the other colors, he instantly sensed its meaning: hatred with some kind of intent to harm.

The young, American boy nodded and was prodded back in to line with the other children as they continued walking back toward Red Square.

CHAPTER TWENTY-EIGHT

The thin boards that lined the hallway floor in a basic diagonal fishbone pattern creaked in protest as Viktor limped slowly toward the kitchen. His left elbow dragged along the wall, pausing in support every time he placed some of his weight on his left leg. He was still unable to step normally – the ankle was still refusing to cooperate and wouldn't make his foot parallel with the floor as he lifted it up and moved the leg forward. His right hand clutched at his pants just above the knee, helping to guide the weak limb into place. The toes of his left foot touched the floor first, then the heel as he leaned forward, steadying himself with his left forearm planted against the wall. He applied pressure on the left foot gingerly, still unsure how much weight it could take.

He'd immediately started trying to use it three days before when he'd discovered that the cramping and lack of control in his arms had miraculously faded. But, control of his hands came faster than to his withered left leg. Although any type of delicate finger movements were still impossible for him, he was able to grasp things much better than he ever had before as long as he moved slowly and concentrated. During that first night after he'd gained extra movement in his limbs, he'd woken up several times to wiggle his fingers and slowly rotate his wrists. He wanted to keep moving his limbs so that they wouldn't tighten and become useless again. And also to make sure that the whole experience hadn't been a dream.

Despite the slow progress, his leg was coming along nicely, he thought. After all, he was trying to get it to support his entire weight – something that it had never done once in his entire fifteen years of life. His hands had been improving, increasing in strength, and so should his leg, he thought. He'd pulled down an old anatomy book that he'd found high on the shelf in his room and had been studying some of the muscles of the body. Viktor thought that he'd pinpointed all the muscles in his legs, back and hips which were required for basic walking and had been attempting to concentrate his efforts on building those slowly. His nose wrinkled instinctively as he passed by his sister's room. He hadn't ventured into either of the other two bedrooms for the past couple of days – the smell was strong enough in the hallway and he was afraid it was starting to seep into his own bedroom during the night. After a quick, sideways glance at the door, he pushed on slowly.

As he limped toward the kitchen, he ran a few quick equations in his head and determined that if his progress continued at the same rate as during the past three days, then he should be able to achieve fairly normal movement within another seven days, fifteen hours and thirty-seven minutes. But, what if his rate of healing increased – maybe doubled? No, he said to himself as he lifted his left leg carefully, that's too much to hope for – maybe increase it by just a factor of 1.5 or so. Within a minute, he'd arrived at the solution, but then another thought struck him: what if he hit some kind of plateau in his muscle development, or what if the rate of improvement began to decrease rapidly as he used his limbs more? He could probably use differentials to figure out a few scenarios for his healing time.

A couple days ago, when he'd been trying to reach the anatomy book on the shelf, he'd come across one of Tatyana's old high school calculus textbooks. It was pretty thick and dusty, so he'd usually just passed it over the thousands of times that he'd perused the shelf before, but this time it had seemed to almost jump out at him. He'd opened the large cover and began reading through a few chapters, skimming mostly since the concepts toward the front were usually just the basic ones. He'd never been able to do much math in the few years of school that he'd had, but numbers had always seemed to come naturally to him. Before he'd realized it, he'd read through most of the text – he'd gone to bed fairly late that night. And he'd heard his mother's voice in his head, repeating one of her favorite phrases, "You read all night and your eyes'll pop out!" He smiled to himself at the image of her shaking her pudgy finger at him.

By the time he'd reached the kitchen counter, he'd constructed about nine different scenarios for his projected healing time. As he leaned against the cabinets, stabilizing himself with sweaty palms on the dull white counter, he quickly took a weighted average of the nine different times, balancing each according to its respective degree of likelihood. And he ended up with the same answer as he originally had with his first calculation – that made him happy.

Viktor pulled the cupboard door open and scanned the shelf – empty. The next cupboard was the same. He shuffled and limped over to the refrigerator and pulled out a plastic container of rice that he'd saved from yesterday's lunch.

His foot tapped rhythmically against the table leg as he sat, scooping mouthfuls of cold rice into his mouth. The sun was slowly beginning to sink below the roof of the apartment building across the street, casting long shadows on the skinny trees that were just starting to sprout new leaves.

Suddenly, Viktor froze, staring at the spoon in his hand. It hung there, in front of his face, completely still, poised and ready to be scooped into his mouth. All at once, he willed his hand to do so and the utensil came up, delivering the rice into his eagerly waiting mouth. Just a few days ago, this simple action was nearly impossible, he thought. For all my life, up until now, I've been a helpless cripple, Viktor thought as he chewed. But, not now. And never again. He dipped his spoon into the bowl and took another mouthful.

Staring out the window at the setting sun, Viktor knew he was almost out of food – he'd have to leave the apartment soon, try and buy something at the market. He thought he remembered one a couple blocks away – it had been so long since he'd been outside and able to explore his own neighborhood.

The last time was probably with Aunt Lydia in the fall. She'd stopped by, unannounced, and had taken him out for a quick hamburger before his mother got home. She'd steadied him as he hopped along, crunching the big, burnt orange leaves under his foot. After she said goodbye at the door, she'd rushed back down to the street quickly, and waved at him as he watched her from the window, right before she hurried to the bus stop, afraid that his mother would discover her.

Viktor stared at the scarred, white tabletop, the fork paused halfway out of his mouth, hanging on his lower lip. He hadn't thought of Aunt Lydia in several days. He'd been so worried about his mother and grandmother, then Tatyana, that he'd almost forgotten her. Or, was that really it? He felt the truth lurking unacknowledged in the back of his mind, like a gaping mouthed specter waiting to pounce. No, he hadn't wanted to think of her for these past few days – because thinking of her would lead him to the painful, but unavoidable conclusion that he mostly believed to be true.

The fork dropped down into the plastic container with a dull clatter. Viktor continued to stare in thought at the tabletop, rubbing his hands over one another to increase the circulation. They'd all died – Tatyana, his mother, grandmother. All within a few days. And everything on the television before the broadcasts had stopped seemed to indicate that the same thing was happening all over the city – all over the world. She couldn't have escaped it, he thought. Then, he realized that at the same time that he'd been focusing energy on avoiding thoughts of her for the past few days, he'd secretly been building up a small reserve of hope that somehow she had survived, found a way to beat whatever it was and was coming to rescue him.

That hope began to drain away as he allowed himself to examine the situation fully, the frightful events of the past week and a half turning over quickly in his brain. No, he finally said, she couldn't have survived – she would have come already. Or called at least. But, there hadn't been any phone call.

There was one way that he could tell for sure, he thought. He could make it over to her apartment somehow and see for himself. The thought of walking up to her door and smelling the smell that now permeated the air around him filled him with sadness. He wouldn't be able to go in and look, even if he got there, he thought. Seeing her like that, the last time he would see her, would be too much. That's not how he wanted to remember her.

As the weight of this realization began to sink into his mind, Viktor, for the first time, saw his future stretched out before him. It wasn't something that he'd ever thought much about. As he'd grown up, the fact that he was different from other children and would never be able to live the life that they led or even that his family members led, had slowly been ingrained in him and had become a permanent fixture. He'd always assumed, for one thing, that his mother would take care of him as long as she could and then he'd most likely go to live with Aunt Lydia or maybe even Tatyana. But, now with all of them gone, the question of his future arose like a burning road in his mind. He saw it as an empty highway that stretched forward infinitely, with no turn-offs or intersections – and no one else there. He was completely and utterly alone in a world that he'd never understood and probably understood even less now that most of everyone in the world had died. His head sunk down to his thin hands and he continued to tap his foot against the table leg as the last light of day slowly sunk away.

CHAPTER TWENTY-NINE

Shockwaves of pain raced up Sean's thin arms all the way into his shoulders and he staggered back from the force. The heavy, iron mallet dropped unnoticed from his hands as he stared through the dull, dust-filled afternoon light at the obstinate door.

Beside him, Sergey, the muscular fifteen year-old boy who'd been among the group that had captured him near Red Square three or four days before, yelled something and gestured toward the apartment door. Sean wasn't sure if he was yelling because he was angry at him or if he still couldn't hear very well from having his eardrums burst in the brief street struggle.

"You go again or want help?" said Svyeta, the girl with the powerful scream who had been captured with him that day. She, her younger sister, Zhenya and a couple other young girls stood further down the hallway, calmly waiting as the boys worked at breaking in the door.

Sean dropped his shoulders in exhaustion and, in Russian, said, "Help."

Sergey gestured to Alyosha, a wiry-thin boy of about sixteen, urging him to pick up the heavy mallet that Sean had dropped. The thin boy spaced his hands evenly on the wooden handle and squared his feet as he stared at the door. Giving Sean a brief smile and wink over his shoulder, he swung the mallet at the lock on the right side of the door. There was a heavy thud, the door shuddered briefly, then the hallway was still again.

This routine had been going on for the entire time that Sean had been a prisoner of the Black Scorpions. That first day they had brought him back to a hotel near Red Square and locked him in one of the large conference rooms with a bunch of other bewildered Russian kids. Having only a few scraps of food between them, they were all left there until the next morning when Pyotr, the dark-haired leader of the street gang, and his two cronies, Sergey and Ivan, the smaller spiky, white-haired kid, took them out to a nearby apartment building and ordered them to start breaking into apartments. The boys started on the heavy work of breaking down the doors, then the girls would go in and quickly gather up any jewelry, weapons and canned food that they could find. They collected the loot in a truck in front of the apartment building, then drove the load back to the hotel at the end of the day. They'd already amassed quite a horde, but still Pyotr ordered them to keep going back. Through Svyeta, Sean had learned Pyotr intended to have them gathering the supplies "until they had enough." Sean's wearied body knew that it definitely didn't like the sound of that.

Alyosha took another over-the-shoulder swing at the difficult lock. He'd already smashed through one, but this door had several and they still clung tenaciously to the door frame. The boy was trying to stay cheerful, even joking occasionally between swings, but he was growing visibly tired. This was the twentieth apartment that day and they were down to what they hoped would be the last one before heading back to the hotel and dinner.

Sean leaned heavily against the wall and hung his head in despair. Nothing about this trip has turned out like I thought it would, he whispered to himself. First, there had been all those weird things happening at the time that Jerry had landed: the vision or dream of the forest and the light, the Russian air force pilots dying. Then, the deaths happening all around the world, his mother, his father...

Sean coughed, pretending to try to clear dust from his throat as he fought the rising wave of grief that threatened to overtake him. He'd had the dream again last night, just as he had the morning Jerry landed, only this time he was actually asleep. It was mostly the same: a dark, thick forest – running through the trees, an almost oppressive smell of dense vegetation all around him. But, last night, he'd dreamed that he was heading toward some type of clearing and there was someone behind him. Not chasing necessarily, but just there – some type of presence. He hadn't been afraid during the dream, but had felt an almost overwhelming sense of urgency as he moved toward the light in the clearing.

He suddenly recalled his thoughts as he'd sat in the control room of the Russian Space Agency a week-and-a-half ago, right before he'd had the dream or vision. Had it only been a week-and-a-half? It seemed like months or even years. Sean remembered his excitement, the sheer thrill of anticipation that had been coursing through him as he watched the scientists gathering around the monitors, tracking Jerry's progress. He recalled in almost perfect clarity how he had been imagining the events of the coming days: flying out to the site, searching for meteorite fragments, being with his father and watching him in his work. None of that happened, Sean thought again. None of that came true. And, now, it never will. I'll never feel that kind of excitement or wonder again. And I'll never be that stupid, naïve boy… ever again.

Sean was jolted from his memories by a sharp shout from the stairs below. Ivan, who seemed to be Pyotr's second in command, came bounding up the stairs, a sub-machine gun hanging casually from his shoulder. He muttered something to the three boys gathered around the door, throwing his hands up in apparent irritation.

"He wants… faster. Boys in next building finished. Why we slow, he says," Svyeta said quietly to Sean. He'd definitely recognized the words for fast and slow – they'd been repeated often to him over the past few days. The rest of the language was still a mystery to him – he'd only learned a few other words, just barely enough to get by. He wondered how long he'd have to be in Moscow hanging out with Russian kids before he became fluent with the language. He hoped he didn't ever have to find out.

Sean turned his head slowly toward Zhenya, Svyeta's little sister. She had messy brown hair down to her shoulders and always wore a pair of pink leggings with little boots that came up just past her ankles. Even though she was only six years old, she reminded Sean of his sister Elizabeth. Maybe because it was when Elizabeth had been that age, that they'd seemed to get along so well, Sean thought. It seemed that they'd fought more over the past couple of years. All those hormonal changes, his mother always said. It didn't make Sean sad when he thought of his sister like it did when he remembered his parents. It only made him impatient and anxious to get going so that he could make it back to California somehow and find her. He'd made a promise to his father, but more than that, he knew that she needed him now in this strange, lonely world. And now he definitely needed her.

Ivan was talking rapidly, in quick, guttural bursts as he stared in agitation at the three boys. Sergey was occasionally yelling back at him, but it was clear who wielded more authority despite the difference in the two boys' physical sizes. Svyeta and the other girls just stared at the two of them in fear and resignation, knowing that yelling didn't get the work done any faster.

Sean stared at both of them, a deep anger starting to fill his chest. Here two of his captors were arguing about bashing in some stupid door for weapons and useless jewelry while his sister was alone on the other side of the world, waiting for him. The futility and senselessness of the entire situation started pressing down on Sean and he clenched his fists, trying to keep himself from screaming out loud.

Both the boys were yelling now – Alyosha was trying to calm them both down, smiling reassuringly as he moved to stand between them. Sean turned his eyes away from the three of them, looking for something else to focus his anger on so that he wouldn't lash out and get himself shot. He looked at the silly, black-matting covered door that was just like all the others in the building – the source of all their frustrations. Stupid door, he thought, stupid, useless door that's keeping me away from rest and dinner and my sister and the rest of my pointless life!

As he stared at the door, imagining kicking it in and crunching it to a million twisted pieces, the boys' yelling all the while raging beside him, he felt his hands beginning to swell. At least that's what it felt like at first. The sensation quickly became so powerful that he lifted them up to look more closely, half expecting to see his fingers grown to the size of sausages. But, there was no visible change in size, just a very powerful feeling of expansion and force.

Suddenly, the door began to shake. It scared him at first, making him think that there was someone inside making it rattle on its hinges back and forth like that, but then the shaking grew stronger and faster like there was some kind of powerful, vibrating machine behind it.

Ivan, Sergey and Alyosha all quieted down and stared in confusion at the door that was trembling like it was a leaf caught in a hurricane. Sean stood still, his legs locked in place and his hands held in front of him. The swelling sensation hadn't dissipated, but seemed to be growing stronger. Suddenly, a brief image of billions and billions of tiny particles flashed through his mind. He saw the particles moving and jumbling together in a shapeless cloud, then two distinct groups of particles forming and beginning to move away from each other.

Sean became aware of some type of connection between his hands and the shaking door, like an invisible force field of some kind. The pressure continued to mount and spread quickly up his arms, through his shoulders and into his mind. He could feel strength gathering in his hands and the rattling door at the same time and, all at once, the pressure seemed to spike, to grow so strong that he felt like his entire body would explode. In fear and desperation, he threw his hands out in front of him to avoid being torn apart.

The door caved right in half like a dented aluminum can, tearing the locks and the hinges from both sides as it flew backward into the hallway of the apartment. The sound was like some kind of horrifying explosion of wood and metal. At the same time, the tension and pressure in Sean's hands was released and he fell backward onto the floor, staring in shock at the destruction in front of him.

CHAPTER THIRTY

The folded piece of paper lay on the floor next to the bag from where it had just fallen. Viktor stared at the note, almost afraid to touch it. He'd just been about to unlock the door and go outside when he'd accidentally bumped his sister's shoulder bag that she'd left in the hall when she'd last come home. It wasn't the note itself that caused the creeping feeling that was beginning in the back of his throat – it was the handwriting: his aunt Lydia's – "To my dear family."

Viktor bent over carefully, delicately balancing his weight between his right leg and the old crutch that he'd dug out of the hall closet. It was the one that he'd used occasionally as a little boy, when his body had still been light enough to move around with the gray, rubber grip tucked tightly under his cramped arm. It was a little small now, but helped him balance well enough. He'd been practicing for the past day or so, building up his strength – and courage – to go out on the street.

His nose crinkled at the smell of decay hanging heavily in the air of the apartment hallway. He straightened up, the handwritten note still unopened in his hand. Lydia must have given Tatyana this when they saw each other last week – what, on Thursday or Friday? He unfolded the note, drew in a deep breath and quickly read through the looping characters. There were only a few, brief lines – she said goodbye, that she loved them, that she hoped they would never find the note, that they would find happiness in "this terrible sleep."

Viktor imagined his sister knocking on Aunt Lydia's front door and waiting several minutes before using the extra key they kept at home in case she ever got locked out. He could see her stepping carefully into the brightly lit apartment, calling Lydia's name. Tatyana would have found her in her bed, just like mother and grandmother, lying there looking as if she were still asleep, the note positioned carefully on the nightstand by her bed. He folded the note slowly as tears flooded his eyes and a whimper escaped from his tightened lips.

He'd told himself not to hope, that there was no way that she could still be alive. But, hoped he had. In the back of his mind, he'd been holding and nurturing a dream that someday Aunt Lydia would come knocking frantically at the door, then rush in to take him away to be with her, to be safe. Now, he knew that would never happen – the note confirmed it. Tatyana knew that the last time she'd spoken to him. She'd known that they were the only two in the family left. She'd probably been hoping that by the next morning, they'd both be gone too.

He tucked the note into an inner pocket of his dark wool coat. Wiping the tears from his eyes Viktor pulled the zipper up higher over his scarf, checked the keys in his pocket and unlocked the front door.

It was warmer outside than he'd expected. He'd been watching the last remaining patches of snow melt as he'd tried to fill the empty, lonely hours, but hadn't assumed that the change in seasons would be coming so quickly. Moscow springs didn't usually.

Although he'd been making significant progress with his left leg over the past few days, roughly in line with his calculations, it was still not ready for full use and the crutch was absolutely vital as he shuffled down the stairs. And even though his arms and hands had also been gaining strength and coordination rapidly, he knew they were still vastly underdeveloped and would be no help in a real emergency.

Viktor's mind had been occupied recently with exercising his wasted limbs and his other preparations to go out and forage on the street. He hadn't devoted much time to wondering how or why his body was suddenly starting to work, but he was fairly certain that it had something to do with what had killed his family – possibly a virus that he was somehow immune to, that, while killing others who lacked the immunity, bestowed some type of brain healing or regenerative powers on those that survived.

It was these thoughts that began to take control of his mind now, occupying most of his faculties as he carefully made his way down the darkened stairs of his apartment building. He'd read about how diseases could spread – he knew that both his mother and sister would have had regular contact with people as they ventured on the street. Either one or both could have easily contracted something and brought it home. If that was true, that some strange mutated virus had swept the city, then it was quite possible that he was only one of a few remaining survivors who had somehow developed an immunity. Viktor gently pushed the squeaky front door open out onto the deserted street.

The large, indoor market was only a few minutes away. He had been afraid that he wouldn't be able to remember how to get there, but the location and direction were suddenly clear to him as he hobbled around puddles of melted snow and ice. Viktor had wrapped a kitchen towel around the rubber pad that jutted into his armpit, but the constant strain was already beginning to wear on him. He knew that he would be sore by the time he got home, probably even more so the next day, but he pushed on, stubbornly dragging his weak left leg behind him.

After rounding the corner of an apartment building similar to his, he reached the main street that led to the market. A dirty white car was parked several yards ahead – he could see the outline of someone's head resting against the seat behind the steering wheel. He approached the vehicle cautiously, slowing as he passed by the driver's window, and only dared a quick glance at the figure out of the corner of his eye. It was a man, but he almost didn't look real, more like a department store mannequin. Viktor continued quickly onward.

Although the sky had clouded over again, the air was still warmer than it had been for weeks. Viktor paused to loosen his scarf and unfastened a few buttons on his coat. Immediately after doing so, he stared down at his fingers – they had just nimbly performed the delicate task, without him really thinking about it. Suddenly, Viktor wasn't sure if he'd ever actually buttoned or unbuttoned his own coat or shirt or anything before – his mother or Tatyana had always been around for that. He'd watched them both thousands of times as they helped him pull on his clothing, tie his shoes, quickly brush through his hair. Strange, he thought, now that they're gone, I suddenly don't need them anymore.

The market was housed in a large, one-story building, a warehouse sitting on the corner of a large intersection. There was a tall church on the opposite corner, its gold-leafed towers shining dully on the street below. Viktor remembered the throngs of people that had streamed through this area whenever he'd been here before. Often, there were so many that traffic was backed up constantly as shoppers and worshippers alike clogged the sidewalks and side streets carrying armfuls of groceries or candles to burn for their patron saints and dead ancestors.

The only thing on the street now was dirt and a few plastic sacks floating along slowly in the wind. Viktor stopped before crossing the street and noted the blanket of silence that had descended over the entire city. Gone were the sounds of car engines and honking, the shouts of swarthy, mustached young men as they haggled with gray-haired babushkas. The entire city was asleep. Viktor wondered if it would ever awaken again.

Garbage littered the pock-marked stone floors of the market. Spilled, crushed nuts, squashed and rotting tomatoes, dirty heads of lettuce and splintered chunks of wood filled the narrow lanes between the islands of crate-topped tables. The smell of rotting produce, and something worse, filled the stagnant air.

Viktor slowly shuffled through the ransacked remains and decaying vegetable matter as his eyes scanned the mostly empty crates and bare table tops. The market had always been overflowing with buckets of fresh strawberries and large radishes, trucked in from various parts of the former Soviet Union. Patient booth clerks of mixed nationalities had always stood calmly by as shoppers picked through the selection, each one using their own secret method for finding the tastiest melon, the banana of the perfect ripeness. Nothing around Viktor seemed alive anymore – even all the food was dying.

He sifted through a pile of mismatched seeds, dumping a fistful into a clean plastic sack that he'd found. Viktor added a handful of thin carrots that might be saved if used within the next day or so. Before moving on down the row of tables, he paused and looked around – there was no one there to count his items, weigh the vegetables and take his money. He looked down at the scant food in his plastic bag, then reached his hand into an inner pocket of his coat, counted out a few bills and placed them carefully on the table.

As he was examining a dented cardboard juice box, Viktor heard the sound of ripping coming from a back corner of the large, empty room. He stood still, staring toward the corner and listening as the tearing sound continued. Viktor turned and looked back at the door he'd come through from the street – he hadn't seen or heard anything when he'd entered.

He made his way through the aisles, his feet and crutch occasionally squishing through the remains of some tomato or pile of broken eggs. Viktor moved toward the meat section against the wall, the exit a few dozen yards to his left. Most of the sides of beef and skinned chickens that had previously hung in the open air were gone now, their only remains being caked blood stains on the floors and the yellowed tiles of the walls. This was where the smell was the strongest – warm flesh slowly rotting.

Viktor rounded the corner of a large crate covered table and spotted a mangy dog gnawing at what looked like a pig's head. The eyes were gone and the pointed ears were stiff, poking in different directions, almost playfully so as the gray, scraggly dog steadily chewed on the side that faced away from Viktor. Its eyes turned up at him, but continued working, brownish blood caking its nose and the hair around its mouth.

As Viktor stood there watching, another dog with long, black hair trotted silently around the corner and barked at him. The gray mutt raised its head from the grisly work on the floor and began to emit a low growl from its throat. The larger black dog crouched low on its thickly muscled haunches and barked louder at the strange, three-legged boy.

Viktor tried backing away slowly, but had difficulty with his crutch on the slippery floor. Both dogs stood their ground, the gray still growling as the bull-headed black filled the market building with its deep bark. Viktor turned and hobbled toward the door, trying not to hurry or make any other quick movements. He could feel the dogs' eyes on his back as he neared the open doorway, late afternoon light streaming through it into the cold interior.

As he reached the door, he heard the clicking of nails on stone and turned his head to see the two dogs trotting quickly toward him. He ducked through the door and onto the street just as the two beasts began to jog.

As Viktor reached the sidewalk on the opposite side of the street, the two dogs ran out of the market, their eyes intently focused on him, tongues hanging out over large, yellowed teeth. The dogs stopped in the middle of the street, watching Viktor's retreating figure limp down the sidewalk, as the larger black continued barking, louder.

Viktor had given up any attempt at hiding his intent to leave quickly and was now hurrying as fast as he could down the sidewalk, not daring to glance over his shoulder, afraid to show the canines the fear in his eyes. His right arm swung wildly for balance as his left gripped the crutch that supported him. In the quiet, spring afternoon, he heard more barking in the distance, coming closer. Before rounding the corner onto another street, he looked back. The two dogs still stood in the middle of the street, watching him.

He had to get inside somewhere, he thought, as he pumped his legs and arms down the street, they wouldn't be able to get to him if he was inside a building, protected by walls. Viktor paused briefly to check a door to his left, shaking the handle frantically before continuing on down the sidewalk. Most of the doors on this street appeared to be shops – they would all most likely be locked. Suddenly Viktor realized, that in his haste, he had walked down the wrong street and wasn't sure exactly where he was or what direction he had to go to get back home. The barking was now coming from multiple directions. And it was getting louder.

As he neared the end of the street which met a larger boulevard, he heard the distinct clicking of long nails on the pavement and the grating of gravel beneath paws. Turning, Viktor's jaw dropped as he spotted nine or ten dogs of various breeds trotting hurriedly, but calmly, down the street toward him, the gray and black ones from the market in the lead.

A wave of fear hit him, like a punch in the stomach, and he gasped, struggling for air. It finally came in a ragged gulp and he tore around the corner, trying to put distance between himself and the approaching pack of feral street dogs. Viktor could feel the sobs coming up from his chest, but he didn't fight them, trying to focus all his energy on getting his body to move forward, faster.

He could hear the entire group barking now, moving toward him. His right leg was beginning to shake, the muscles twitching spasmodically, unaccustomed to the exertion. Tears were streaming down his face and he could hear his heart pounding in his ears and the hot warmth spreading up his neck into his face as he limped on down the sidewalk.

The group of dogs rounded the corner in a full run, their mouths spread open widely, barking and snarling. Viktor heard a desperate whimper from his own mouth as he felt the panic beginning to take over, driving him forward, raking the buildings with his eyes in search of an open door.

A few feet ahead he saw one slightly ajar, leading into the stairway of an apartment building. He lunged for the opening, dropping his crutch on the ground and hopping entirely on his right leg. Viktor was mostly through when he felt the first set of teeth clamp onto his dangling left foot.

He pivoted behind the door so that he could face the gray mutt that was holding onto his leg, closing the door enough so that there was only space for his foot to fit through. The other dogs were barking and leaping at the door and around the other dog in a frenzy, trying to get their own piece of the escaping meat.

Viktor stared into the eyes of the scraggly haired gray dog, his teeth sunk into the tip of the boot, not yet breaking through to any flesh. He saw the desperation in those eyes and the stubbornness born of years living off the fruits of the street, the undesirables that were left to him. The dog tried to step backward in order to pull Viktor out of his hiding place and into the mouths of the other snarling dogs.

The cool, inky spaciousness of the empty stairwell behind him beckoned, a cold draft tickling his neck. Deep barking and the creaking of the front door against the weight of the dogs pressing forward echoed off the concrete walls. Viktor could feel his leg inching forward, his foot trapped in the drooling maw of the scraggly gray dog. The creatures' hunger was almost palpable – he began to wonder how soon he would start to feel the bites sinking into the rest of his leg, his sides, his face.

With a savage screech, Viktor jerked his left hip, pulling his leg, and the gray dog, a few inches forward. At the same moment, he edged the door open slightly to allow the mutt's head to fit in the space. The long fingers of both his hands wrapped around the handle and he shoved, crunching the dog's head between the set of double doors. The animal immediately released the foot from its mouth and pulled back just enough for Viktor to slam the door shut.

Throwing his weight against the door, he panted and choked down new sobs. The hounds complained furiously on the opposite side, their heavy bodies beating the wood in anger. Viktor leaned, hunched over, listening to the commotion outside and the sound of his own whimpering in the darkness.

Within several minutes, the dogs quieted somewhat, but Viktor could still feel their paws padding slowly over the pavement on the other side of the door. Just as he began to wonder how long he would have to stand there holding the door shut before the dogs eventually tired of the game and wandered off, he heard the deep rumble of a truck motor coming up the street. Some of the pack turned away from their trapped prey and started yipping at the approaching vehicle. The deep hum of the diesel motor passed by the apartment building, but stopped a little ways down the street.

Viktor quickly searched for any cracks between the doors or the ceiling, but was unable to find any way to peer out at the activity in the street. Suddenly, the air was split apart by the sound of thunderous explosions coming from the direction of the stopped truck. Forgetting his duty of holding the doors securely shut, Viktor flung himself toward the stairs behind him, banging his knee on the concrete floor as he came down.

The sound of machine gun fire was punctuated by the panicked yipping of dogs as bullets peppered the sidewalk and walls outside. Viktor kept his head tucked under his arms, praying for the terrifying noise to stop.

The gunfire quickly subsided, with the ensuing silence only being disturbed by a couple additional shots. Viktor thought he could hear the ragged panting of a dog right outside the door, but was unsure with the sound of the truck motor still echoing off the walls. Booted footsteps marched up to the door and suddenly orange, afternoon light burst into the dank stairwell.

"Holy hell, it's a kid! We didn't get you, did we?" yelped Viktor's rescuer – a boy roughly his own age.

Viktor stared at him wordlessly from the floor, trying to allow his eyes to adjust to the light and the quick change in circumstances. Furry bodies littered the sidewalk at the boy's feet. The scraggly gray dog was still alive – barely. Its eyes stared ahead, flickering distantly as it counted the few remaining heartbeats pounding in its chest.

The boy's face was dirty and he wore an oversized military jacket and matching army-issue black boots. He held a large machine gun casually in his hands as he stared down at Viktor still cowering on the floor.

"Hey – you hurt? You're not any good to us hurt."

Viktor shook his head and began to arrange his limbs to stand.

"Looks like we got another one!" the boy yelled toward the truck. The teen, who turned out to be a few inches shorter than Viktor, but obviously much more sure on his feet, grabbed him under the arm and pulled him out into the street.

One dog was feebly limping away past the large military vehicle. The back was covered by a thick wrapping of green canvas with a dark opening large enough for only a couple of people. The boy pulled Viktor over to the step, which came about to his stomach.

"Come on, move it!"

Viktor's eyes were still locked on the pile of canine bodies in front of the apartment building doors. "They're all dead ..."

"Yeah, we've started having quite a problem with wild packs lately. All their masters are dead – no one left to feed 'em."

He helped Viktor stretch his right foot up onto the step. Small hands from inside the truck reached out and grasped onto his outstretched wrists, hauling him up. The interior was dark, the only light coming from the opening. Two benches lined the length of the truck bed, on which sat roughly twenty children of all ages and sexes, staring numbly at Viktor. He stared back in wonder, before being forced down in between a couple of ten-year old, thin-faced boys. None of the children said anything to him, but just stared back at his questioning face. The boy with the machine gun climbed in behind Viktor and plopped down on the end of the bench just as the truck started forward.

CHAPTER THIRTY-ONE

Sean lay staring at the ornately decorated ceiling and multiple chandeliers hanging above him in one of the conference rooms of the National Hotel. The faces of the figures inhabiting the numerous Renaissance-style frescoes covering the walls stared back at the boy in the bright yellow light from the dozens of tiny chandelier light bulbs. He wondered how long the electricity that powered them would last – with no one tending the power plants anymore, the lights would have to eventually go out. Sean wondered how long they had before night would truly become a dark time again. Currently, there were so many street, store and apartment lights that had been left on that it often looked as though the city was still largely inhabited. The strange silence that hung over the streets everyday as the children trudged from building to building, searching for secret treasures to add to Pyotr's horde helped to remind them that Moscow was largely a dead city. Except for their ever-growing Black Scorpions and a few other rival gangs that mostly avoided them, they were alone – completely and utterly alone in a strange, foreign city…

Sean forcibly shook himself to chase away the gloomy thoughts. He concentrated on the voices of the children playing around them. It was the end of another grueling day and the kids were using the last bursts of energy that they had to enjoy themselves before they finally collapsed in exhaustion on their army-issue cots that Pyotr and Ivan had placed in the hotel conference room. There were probably twenty or so kids here, most younger than Sean's thirteen years. Too young to be forced to work like this, he thought to himself.

Things should have become easier over the past couple of days since he discovered that he was able to knock down doors just by thinking about it. Ivan had assigned him as the official "door opener" – the crews would wait in the hallway as he went door to door, tearing apart the locks and hinges with his mind. He'd started to be able to actually unfasten some of the locks rather than destroying them if he concentrated hard enough, but it was often difficult because he couldn't see them from his side of the door and wasn't sure what pieces needed to be moved where. After several doors, he still found himself tiring, not from the previous exertion of physically smashing them in, but from the extreme concentration and force of will that the process required. And now that Pyotr and Ivan knew of his newfound ability, they expected the work crews to operate a lot faster.

A large, rubber ball rolled across the room and bounced into the base of Sean's cot. He glanced down at it, then to the happily approaching face of Zhenya, Svyeta's six-year-old sister. She stopped several feet away and held up her hands expectantly, her long, unkempt brown hair swaying with her nervous excitement. Sean picked up the ball and was about to toss it to her, but then stopped. Instead, he concentrated on the ball and Zhenya's hands just a few feet away. He imagined the billions of tiny particles that made up both objects and began to concentrate on slowly attracting the two together. Even though he'd done it dozens of times now, he still wasn't entirely sure how it worked. Slowly, the ball drifted out of Sean's hands and floated gently through the air toward Zhenya until she reached out and grabbed it with a squeal of delight.

Seeing the gleeful, young girl run back over to her older sister to continue the game of catch reminded Sean again of Elizabeth. What was she doing right now, he wondered. Was she still at home, living off the limited supply of food that their mother had stockpiled for emergencies? Had she ventured out into the city to look for other people just to confirm the terrible truth that she must by now have realized? What if she'd been hurt or become sick somehow or had been captured by some Pasadena gang similar to the Black Scorpions? How would he be able to help her from so far away?

Again, Sean had to chase away the disturbing thoughts to keep himself from becoming overwhelmingly sad. It seemed so easy to do that nowadays – life had changed so quickly. Before he could help Elizabeth, he knew he had to find a way to escape from Pyotr, Ivan and the other gang members.

Sean began to review the strange phenomena that he'd witnessed since leaving his hotel room, hoping to find something that would help him find a way out. First, there was the toddler in the hotel who'd made the pastry slide across the table. Sean suspected that this was somehow related to his own ability to move things in a similar manner with his mind. And then there was that strange rushing or flowing sensation he'd experienced when the toddler had done it. He'd felt the same thing when Svyeta had used her powerful scream in the street to knock down Sergey and shatter the windows. And also when Pyotr had been reading everyone's emotions by seeing the colors around them – and when the boy began leaking water all over the place. In fact, Sean recalled the same rushing sound or sensation each time one of the other kids had exhibited another strange and amazing ability.

He lay back down on the cot and exhaled slowly. He didn't feel like he was ready to actually test any hypotheses yet – he was still in the initial observation stage of the Scientific Method, just as his father had taught him. Wondering about his strange recurring dream with the forest and the light that had plagued him almost every night since he began witnessing the other children's strange powers, Sean's thoughts drifted back again to Jerry. That had to be the answer, he thought. Jerry landed, all the adults started dying, we had the headaches, these strange powers started happening – it all has to be related. He quickly reviewed a mental list of theories about Jerry that he'd been making as they worked over the past several days. So far he had: interstellar radiation, sonic boom, poisonous gas, giant electro-magnet and alien bomb. He didn't really have much confidence in the last one, but he'd added it just because everything that had happened was just so weird.

The double doors to the conference room opened and Ivan walked in, sub-machinegun slung over his shoulder, and made a quick glance around before motioning to the other gang members behind him. The rough-looking boys led in a group of about fifteen new children that Sean had never seen before. They all looked frightened, glancing around nervously as they filed into the large conference room. The gang members gestured at some of the empty cots, barking commands in their guttural tongue.

They were all ages, just as varied as the group of kids with whom Sean had been working for the past several days. Alyosha, the thin kid who was usually assigned to the same work crew as Sean, smiled at the group of youngsters and started talking happily, showing them where to place their few meager possessions and helping them take off their coats.

Sean noticed one boy a few years older than him with dark brown hair and bushy eyebrows who limped heavily over to a cot and sat down quietly. As he watched the boy's large, brown eyes quickly taking in everything from the room, the now familiar rushing sensation began to fill Sean's mind and he relaxed, allowing the powerful river of mental energy to wash over him, forcing out every other thought. Within a few seconds, it ended and Sean again became aware of the sound of children's voices all around him.

Ivan and the other gang members carried in some boxes and began distributing packages of crackers and tins of salted meat to the kids. Quickly, there was a mob of children grabbing at the food, hungrily beginning to stuff it into their mouths. Ivan shouted something to the group, rattling his gun for effect. They quieted down and waited more patiently as Sergey and the others slowly doled out the rations.

Sean walked over and picked up a couple cans and a few packets of crackers, then glanced over at the new boy with the limp. He sat motionless on the cot, still watching everything happening around him. Sean picked out a few extra crackers and made his way over to the boy.

"Mozhno?" Sean said, using the word for "may I" as he gestured at a spot on the cot beside the boy.

The dark-haired boy of roughly fifteen years nodded and moved over to make space. Sean handed him a tin of meat and a packet of crackers and they both began to eat.

Sean patted his own chest, "Sean."

The boy nodded, finished chewing his food, then said, "Viktor," followed by a phrase that Sean didn't understand at all.

"Ya... Amerikanetz... nyet po-Russkiy," he said haltingly.

Viktor blinked twice, then repeated the phase that Sean had

just said, but with a few extra words. Sean nodded, then smiled.

"Shto eto takoye?" he said, saying the phase for "what is this" and holding up the can of meat.

"Myaso," Viktor said, staring intently at the boy. Sean repeated the word slowly, then took another bite.

"Meat," Sean said in English, then repeated the word again. Viktor paused, then slowly formed the word – it came out more or less correct. Sean wasn't sure, but he thought he detected some kind of speech impediment. Viktor's words sounded just a little different than the other kids', like his tongue or mouth didn't move in exactly the same way.

"Pleased to meet you," Sean said slowly.

"Pleezt too meeth choo," Viktor responded.

"Ochen' priyatno," Sean translated. Viktor smiled and nodded.

CHAPTER THIRTY-TWO

"Quiet down – everyone listen, I'm not going to repeat this," Ivan barked. The white-haired, grim-faced boy stood in front of a set of glass double doors in an underground passageway that led to a shopping mall adjacent to Red Square. On either side of him stood several other Black Scorpion gang members, each armed and busily staring down the group of roughly forty children who waited calmly for Ivan to finish.

"We're taking a break from the apartment raids today to pick up some things from the mall. You've got three hours to clean this place out of all jewelry, nice coats, tools and weapons. Then, we'll move on to the shops along Tverskaya. There's a prize for the first person to find..." Ivan quickly glanced down at a slip of paper in his hand, "a diamond-encrusted platinum locket for Pyotr's girl. Any questions?"

Sean leaned in front of Svyeta to whisper in Russian to Viktor who stood to her left, "Encrusted?"

Viktor's eyes flicked up toward the ceiling for a moment, then turned back to Sean, and translated into English, "Encrusted – means, filled or embedded."

Sean nodded and repeated the word silently in Russian.

"I'm just impressed that you already knew 'platinum,'" Svyeta said with a smirk, her eyes not leaving Ivan who was answering a series of questions from one of the younger children.

Sean smiled and responded in Russian. "Viktor and I went over the Periodic Table of the Elements last night. I think my favorites in Russian are Neon and Sodium."

"In English, mine are probably Tungsten and Phosphorus," Viktor added, saying the element names in English and drawing out the 's's.

"You two are nerds," Svyeta giggled, "in Russian and in English!"

Both boys smiled and faced forward, waiting for Ivan to finish. It had been almost an entire month since Viktor was rescued by the Black Scorpions. Rescued then immediately made a prisoner. Ever since the first day Sean met him, the Russian language had been much easier for the American boy, even to the point where he was now able to converse rather easily about most topics. Viktor, in turn, had picked up English rather easily as well, although he'd never even heard a word of the language before meeting Sean. But, Svyeta's English hadn't improved much at all since meeting Sean and especially now that he didn't need her to translate for him anymore.

"Okay, that's enough – we've got to get to work. Remember – no fooling around. Load everything in the truck outside. Sean – open it up," Ivan ordered.

Sean's smile disappeared and he made his way forward through the crowd of children until he stood just a few feet from the glass doors. Clenching his hands together tightly behind his back, Sean stared at the lock. A low hum began in his throat, sending minute vibrations through his chest and down to his toes. He caused his voice to grow louder, but still kept the tone in the lowest register he could manage. Directing the sound right at the metal lock on the door, he could see the metal mechanism starting to vibrate. As it began to shake more violently, he caused his voice to crescendo quickly into a sharp stab of sound, focusing all the undulating sound waves into a forceful bark. The metal lock cracked into three different pieces and shot out of the door to land with a crunch on the tiled floor.

His white-knuckled hands came out from behind Sean's back and he waved as if shooing away a flock of pigeons. Both glass doors swung silently open and he stepped aside as the children started slowly filing into the mall.

"Show-off," Alyosha whispered with a smile as he walked past.

The corner of Sean's mouth turned up in a grin as he fought to slow his breathing. The concentration and strength required to perform the trick were often greater than he let on – he knew it would take him just a few moments to recover, but at the moment it felt like he'd just sprinted a hundred yards.

"You'd didn't use the, the, uh, mind movement power – how do you call it? The telekinesis this time, did you? Some kind of audible force – a sound wave of some kind?" Viktor stammered in English as he walked with Sean through the open doors.

"Something I picked up from Svyeta – probably that first day we met," Sean replied in Russian, nodding to the girl walking a few paces ahead.

"But, I've never done that – if I'd tried I would have only shattered the glass," Svyeta responded.

"I, uh…" Sean searched quickly for the word in Russian, "improvised. I bet you could do the same thing – you just have to really concentrate on focusing the sound and then just let it slowly build."

Viktor nodded, his bushy brows knit in concentration. Svyeta smiled faintly then continued walking, pulling her sister Zhenya away from a store that used to sell bright-colored children's clothing.

Sean silently chided himself – he'd momentarily forgotten that his abilities occasionally made the other kids, especially Svyeta, nervous, even sometimes frightened. She rarely used her power – only when absolutely necessary. It was still something that she didn't understand and would have actually preferred not to have at all. The fact that Sean was already better at it than she was made her all the more uneasy. The other children were merely awed and somewhat fearful of the range and variety of Sean's powers. Some of the kids hadn't yet exhibited any sign of a newfound ability and those who did only had one such strange gift. As if his foreign nature hadn't been odd enough… now he had something else that kept him separate from the other kids.

"Have you been able to reproduce Kostya's little feat from last night?" Viktor asked as they walked into a shop filled with black, leather coats.

Sean thought back to the previous evening's incident. Kostya, a spirited four-year old who was usually assigned to water duty for the work crews, had somehow managed to ignite an entire tapestry in the hotel conference room where the children slept. Several of the others had witnessed the event, describing how the boy had become angry during a game of catch and waved his arms violently, causing a stream of flame to shoot from his hands at the tapestry. They'd managed to get the fire out, but it had scared Kostya and many of the other kids – including Pyotr and Ivan.

Sean shook his head. "Haven't had a chance yet, maybe later today when we're out on the street."

He glanced at Viktor out of the corner of his eye as they pulled leather jackets into large baskets that some of the girls had brought in with them. Sean thought it somewhat strange that they had become such close friends in so short of a time. But, this is a different kind of life, Sean thought. Nothing like being in school back in Pasadena. Still, he mused, we share something – more than anything we have in common with the others. We're both different: me because of being American and all of my powers and Viktor because he's handicapped and has a speech impediment. Neither of us fits in here.

Sean watched the boy limp around the store pulling down coats with his weak arms. Viktor had said that both his movement and speech impediment had been much worse before Ilya, or Jerry, landed and claimed that the meteorite's fall had somehow healed him. Sean tried to imagine his friend confined to a bed, not being able to get around very well by himself. And here he was now, able to work and converse fairly normally. If it was the meteorite that healed him, Sean thought, then I guess Jerry's arrival wasn't all bad for everyone.

"Have you felt anything from Ivan yet? Has the rushing feeling been there when you're around him?" Viktor asked as he dragged one of the full baskets out of the store.

"I don't know," Sean said as he waved at one of the other boys to take the basket up to the truck waiting on the street outside. "Maybe, but there are always so many other kids around it's difficult to tell for sure. I could have felt it at some point, but I haven't seen him do anything special."

Viktor paused to catch his breath and rested his hands on his hips.

"Remember Pyotr's ability to sense people's emotions or even my heightened ability to learn things quickly. You acquired both of those powers and were able to use them before you consciously knew what was happening, correct? It could be the same here. It's even possible that Ivan himself doesn't know what his power is, but he may already be using it and you may have already picked it up."

Sean nodded silently and watched his friend continue to think.

"It's important for us to know his ability now. What's your phrase? Sooner rather than later? I like that. Yes, we should find out what he can do so that we can use it to our advantage."

Joyful shouts echoed through the mall, coming from the direction of a central atrium where daylight poured in from above. One of the girls ran out of a store shrieking in excitement, a red bustier over her shirt and a long, blue-beaded necklace around her neck. One of the gang members chased her, laughing and squeezed her in a tight hug when he caught up. They both laughed hysterically, then staggered arm in arm to the next store. Laughter from younger children drifted up through the atrium from the floor below.

Sean picked up a plastic garbage sack and the two headed for a jewelry store where Svyeta and Zhenya were carefully unlocking one of the glass cases with a key they'd just found behind the register.

"Find any diamond-encrusted platinum lockets?" Sean asked as the boys walked into the store.

Svyeta glanced up, smiling. "If I do, I certainly won't turn it over to Pyotr. I bet the prize is an extra can of sardines for dinner. Not worth it."

"I hate sardines," said Zhenya, holding up a pudgy hand now adorned with three too-large gold rings.

As they were pulling out the most expensive looking pieces of jewelry, Alyosha sauntered into the store, a garbage sack in his hands.

"Hello, fellow looters. Any tasty trinkets?" he said loudly.

Svyeta smiled and added another necklace to the two already hanging from her neck.

"How's it going out there? Anyone getting any work done?"

"Not much. I saw Sergey and Nastya going back to one of the changing rooms and haven't seen them since. I get the feeling that the Black Scorpions themselves don't get much relaxation time either."

"Hopefully, today won't be too bad. I'm tired of the apartments – there's never much there anyway," Viktor mumbled quietly.

Alyosha glanced over his shoulder, then whispered, "Something's going on with Pyotr and Ivan. I heard him talking on his walkie-talkie and they were arguing about something. They kept talking about 'the Yozh.' You guys hear anything about that?"

Viktor turned to Sean. "It's the name of an animal – small, furry, has hair that sticks up in all directions."

"A porcupine or hedgehog?" Sean asked in English.

Viktor shrugged.

"Anyway," Alyosha continued, "I didn't tell you guys about this before – I haven't had the chance. About three days ago, I was with Volodya and Kostya waiting on the street for the truck to come back and pick up our stuff. After a while, we see these four boys who we've never seen before, pushing this big crate of food along. It was on a wheeled cart or something and they were just pushing it down the street. We talked to them for a second and they said they were taking it to the Yozh. He's some guy who has this big gang somewhere here in the center of the city and said that anyone who brings him a lot of food can join his gang. We asked them if they keep you prisoner and force you to work there and they said no, you're not a prisoner, but you do have to help out. But, it didn't sound like how the Black Scorpions do it."

He watched Sean, Viktor and Svyeta, then cast another glance over his shoulder and continued speaking in a hushed tone. "Maybe this Yozh guy is building some big gang and giving Pyotr and Ivan some trouble. If we could find him or contact him somehow, I bet he would help us. He probably wants to get Pyotr out of the way as much as we do. Then he could rule the center of the city and we wouldn't have to gather all this junk anymore. We've already picked up enough food – it's all this jewelry and nice clothing stuff that's wasting our time. It's like Pyotr will never have enough."

"How can we find the Yozh?" Sean asked. "We're constantly watched during the day and locked up at night. They'd chase us down if we ran away."

Alyosha nodded, then stepped out of the store and looked around briefly before coming back to stand next to the counter. "Watch this," he said.

The thin boy stood next to the display counter and held his hands above it. Closing his eyes tightly, he drew in a few deep breaths. Sean swayed slightly on his feet as the rushing sensation filled his mind and he had the feeling of a large, slow river pouring over the edge of a cliff. Alyosha took a step toward the counter, holding his body very still otherwise, then took another and another until he was about to bump into it – but, then he just kept walking and passed right through it like it wasn't there.

The boy continued walking, the counter passing through his midsection and legs until he came through on the other side of it and opened up his eyes, smiling. Sean, Viktor, Svyeta and Zhenya all stared at him in amazement.

"When did you learn to do that?" Svyeta asked, still staring at the boy.

"I was just taking a quick break after working a couple days ago and was leaning against the wall. I got really relaxed and just thought about lying back to just sit down for a minute. I took a few steps back and then realized that I'd walked right through a wall into the next apartment. I was lucky I didn't go through one of the outside walls or I would have fallen to the ground!"

They laughed gleefully and walked around the counter to pat Alyosha on the back and to see with their own eyes that it hadn't been some kind of trick.

"I can't take anyone else with me though. I kind of tried earlier with Kostya – I went through, but he just stayed on the same side of the wall, like normal. But, this way I can get out of the hotel during the night and find the Yozh. I can tell him where Pyotr and Ivan are holding everyone and he can come help us escape," Alyosha said excitedly.

"It would be better to have him and his gang come while we're out working. We'd have a better chance of getting away," Sean said. "I think I have an idea for how we can cause a distraction…"

Sean was cut off by the thundering sound of an engine roaring through the halls of the shopping plaza. At first darting out of the store to see where the sound was coming from, Sean and the other children immediately jumped back as a beat-up Soviet-era Lada sped by. The car screeched to a halt about thirty meters past them, leaving black tire marks on the white flooring. Pyotr, a fifteen-year old heavily made-up girl named Natasha and one of Pyotr's guards, a sixteen year-old named Kiril, stepped out of the car smiling.

"What are you doing with a car in here?" Svyeta shouted at the boys.

Pyotr walked up to the group that had just emerged from the jewelry store, Natasha on his arm as he flashed a malicious grin at all of them.

"Ivan told me you were having some trouble getting into a few of the stores. No disrespect to your unique abilities, my American friend," he said nodding toward Sean, "but, we thought it would be more fun to use a battering ram."

Ivan, walkie-talkie and machine-gun in hand, rounded a corner and stopped when he saw his leader. "Down this way – we've got a couple gates over a big jewelry shop and a make-up store."

"What do we want with make-up?" Sean asked as they began walking in the direction Ivan had indicated.

"My young friend – maybe when you're older you'll realize that ladies have... needs," he said nuzzling Natasha behind the ear. She let out a nervous giggle and they continued walking. Kiril got back into the car behind them, turned it around and followed.

Ivan pointed down at one of the stores at the end of a long, wide hallway. Some of the other children had taken a break from their work to come see what the commotion was. They stood back as Kiril revved the engine a few times. Finally, the old car lurched forward with a painful screech and sped down toward the make-up store at the end of the hallway.

As the vehicle gathered speed over the short distance, Sean and the others watched in a mesmerized state of excitement and fear. He's either not going to get through that metal gate or he's going to send himself through the windshield in the process, Sean thought to himself as he watched the car race along. Probably both.

When the car was about thirty feet away, speeding along at roughly fifty miles per hour, a restroom door right next to the make-up store opened up and Kostya, the four-year-old who had accidentally set the hotel tapestry on fire the previous night, emerged carrying a sack of loot. He began to cross in front of the make-up store, completely absorbed with the bag of treasure in his hands, until he heard the car's engine coming toward him.

The boy froze in place, his mouth hanging open as he stared incredulously at the vehicle driving very fast in a place where he knew cars weren't supposed to be. Kiril slammed on the brakes, not having any time to veer to the side for fear of rolling the car right into the store front. Sean and the others looked on in horror from the other end of the hall, unable to do anything.

Suddenly, Sean was vaguely aware of the rushing sensation gathering force in his mind. A brief thought flashed that it may be Viktor's or Pyotr's power that he was picking up, when suddenly they saw that one of the other boys had come running out of another store at that end of the long hallway. They hadn't noticed him at first because their attention was riveted on Kostya and the car speeding toward him.

The quickly approaching boy was a ten-year-old named Aleksandr who Ivan and his crew had picked up and brought to the hotel just a couple days ago. His feet raced along the floor as he moved toward Kostya, trying to beat the skidding car that was now coming for them both.

Kostya, still frozen in place with terror, finally managed to drop the bag of loot and get his hands up in a vain attempt to protect himself from the oncoming car. In his panic, jets of flame shot out of his fingertips at the vehicle, engulfing the hood and windshield in fire, but without enough force to even slow the out-of-control car.

A split second later, Aleksandr slammed into Kostya, throwing him several yards to the side. Although Aleksandr's momentum was enough to get Kostya out of the way, the sudden ball of flame surprised him and he stopped his forward motion as he flinched at the explosion of fire. The last thing he did before the car slammed into him was to throw up his own hands in defense.

Although they couldn't be exactly sure from their vantage point, Sean and the others thought they saw the front of the car stop and bend around Aleksandr's hands. As the front of the vehicle stopped, the back end kept going and the car flipped forward upside-down, up and over Aleksandr and the trunk slammed into the front of the make-up store behind him.

The children raced down to the end of the hallway. Aleksandr had collapsed on the floor and was shaking violently, his light brown hair quivering as he stared at the ceiling in shock. Svyeta and Sean quickly knelt by his side and examined him for injuries. But there were none – he was completely fine. Kostya was sitting on the floor several feet away crying, so Svyeta ran over to help him. He also was unscathed – just very frightened.

"Hey, hey you okay?" shouted Pyotr at Kiril who now hung upside down from his seatbelt in the car. The front half of the vehicle was bent in a u-shape almost all the way up to the dashboard.

"Yeah, yeah, I'm, I'm okay, I think," mumbled Kiril. "Hey, what – did I kill that kid?"

Pyotr looked over at Aleksandr who Sean had helped into a sitting position. The boy's eyes were wide in shock as he stared down at his own body which was still shaking.

"No, no," Pyotr said shaking his head in disbelief, "I think he's going to be okay."

Sean glanced up at Viktor who had made it down the hallway just a few seconds ago. The Russian boy had quickly been assessing the situation as he limped along. Now, he simply looked at Sean, a small grin beginning at the corner of his mouth, and nodded.

CHAPTER THIRTY-THREE

"It had to be either the ability to withstand physical injury or some kind of amazing strength power," Viktor said quickly as he eased himself down into the chair next to Sean's cot. "Or, possibly some kind of force field... perhaps one that only affects metal..."

"You're back to the force field idea?" Sean said, smiling as he pulled on his shoes. It was still early morning, the day after the trip to the shopping mall. After the initial shock, all three boys – Aleksandr, Kostya and Kiril – were fine. Pyotr and Ivan questioned Aleksandr at length, demanding to know what power he'd used, how strong it was and how often he could use it. But, the young boy had pleaded ignorance, insisting that he'd never been able to do anything like that before.

"Have you noticed anything? With yourself, I mean. Any new ability?" Viktor asked as he carefully scrutinized Sean's features.

"No, nothing yet."

"Are you any stronger? Have you tried to lift anything heavy?"

Sean walked behind Viktor's chair and grabbed the seat with the boy still in it. After heaving and straining for a moment, he gave up and flopped back down onto his cot. "Still weak," he said smiling. "Of course, you are really heavy – maybe my new power just isn't strong enough yet."

"Very funny," Viktor replied. "What about resistance to injury?"

"You want to drive a car into me to test it?" Sean asked with eyebrows raised. "Maybe a gunshot to my leg?"

"Good point. That one would be difficult to verify." Viktor

stared off into space, squinting in concentration.

The sound of keys turning in the lock quickly drew everyone's attention to the door. Most of the other kids were up by now. Svyeta finished pulling on her sister's shoes and sat beside her on the cot, staring at the floor.

Ivan stepped into the room as Sergey finished pulling the keys out of the lock. The white-haired, young teen glowered at the room of children staring back at him. He was dressed in his customary oversized, black wool sailor coat, similar to the one that Pyotr occasionally wore. The sleeves usually covered his hands and the bottom dragged on the floor, but he wore it everywhere he went. That and the sub-machine gun slung over his shoulder.

Ivan gestured for a couple of the boys to step out into the hall for the breakfast. As the hungry children gathered around the long dining table, they set down boxes of orange juice, dry cereal and a few hunks of cheese. Wide eyes stared at Ivan, as they stood waiting. With a casual wave of his hand, he bid the children to eat. They quickly descended on the food, almost shaking with anticipation as they passed boxes back to the younger kids.

"I want milk," Zhenya whined to her sister.

"It's all spoiled," Ivan replied.

Some of the kids sat at the table to eat, while others returned to their cots. Within a few minutes, they'd devoured everything and sat around listlessly, silently wishing for more.

Sean heard a playful shriek down the hall and looked toward the door as a seventeen year old girl with heavy make-up around her eyes backed into the room. She was staring in mock pain at Pyotr who was trailing behind her, holding her hands with a mischievous smile on his face. This was a different girl than the one who Pyotr had brought to the mall yesterday.

"You brute, not around the children," she whispered loudly and playfully slapped his hands.

The tall, dark-haired boy said nothing, but continued smiling as he quickly glanced around the room.

"Lieutenant Fyodorov," he said to Ivan, "have the workers been fed?"

"Yes sir."

Pyotr kissed the girl's hand and stepped forward.

"I trust you all slept well, we have a lot of work to do today." The smile was gone now.

"Viktor, how many kilos of food have we collected this week?"

"Three-hundred fifty – roughly." Viktor stood beside Sean at the edge of the table, leaning against its edge to ease the weight on his left leg.

"How long will that last us?" Pyotr replied, smiling at Ivan and the others.

"Well, assuming each of us consumes about two kilos a day, then only another week or so," Viktor stammered quickly, his eyes moving rapidly back and forth as he made the calculations.

"Hear that, kids? Not long at all! We'll have to pick up the pace if we want to keep eating. You want to keep eating, don't you?" Pyotr said as he jeered at the frightened group.

The children nodded mutely. Sean opened his mouth to give Pyotr a few suggestions on how to improve the food gathering process, but a sharp look from Svyeta silenced him. She's so afraid of him, Sean thought to himself. That's probably wise of her, but if we're always afraid of him and his gang then we'll never be able to break free. They'll control us and keep us here forever.

Sean stared at Pyotr and the other boys, their new clothing, recently scrubbed skin and mirthful faces. He wondered how this could all be so funny to them, how they could hold them all captive, forcing them to do all the hard work, while starving and scaring them into submission. Sean agreed that food had to be gathered and stored, but there was certainly a better way than using slave labor. He knew that there were still thousands of children out there, deftly evading the gang's reach as they made their own struggle for survival in the recently abandoned city. Maybe they didn't realize how cruel they were being, maybe none of them had little brothers or sisters before and didn't know about how kids suffered.

He began imagining who they all were before all the adults had died. Many of them, including Pyotr and Ivan, looked like they'd already been living on the street before Jerry fell. Their confidence and bravado had served them well before and were serving them well again. But, some of the others who were part of the gang didn't look like they quite belonged in such a group of bullies and miscreants. They were probably just normal high school kids before, playing sports and working at after-school jobs. Several times he'd detected some hint of shame from them when Pyotr or Ivan would scold or punish one of the younger children for being too slow or making a mistake. Sean couldn't pinpoint the color that he saw that indicated shame, but he knew exactly what it was the first time he'd sensed it. It was a mottled mass of other colors that looked like they were folding in upon themselves, swallowing up the center of the person. Despite this, none of them ever appeared to resist the gang's leaders, and even joined in on some of the beatings occasionally.

Sean watched Pyotr continue talking, but he was no longer listening to the words. He was wondering if he himself had changed in the past few weeks since his parents had died, since he'd been left alone in a foreign city with no one and no way back home. He knew that he wasn't as afraid anymore – living relatively on his own and developing his rapidly increasing number of abilities had given him a level of confidence that he knew would have been difficult to obtain otherwise at his age. But, even more than that, he felt that he was somehow different than the bright, unsuspecting boy that had flown halfway across the world, trailing the father he adored and looking forward to a grand new adventure. Now, he didn't look forward to any big adventures, to any new discoveries. All he looked forward to was the next time he could eat or sleep, when he could rest his mind from the thoughts that continually raced through it, plaguing all his waking hours with worry about getting punished or being trapped in the hotel for the rest of his life. He suddenly realized that he hadn't really thought of Elizabeth much for the past several days. Am I forgetting her already, he worried to himself. How long will it be before I can't even remember her face any more?

"Svyeta, make sure your little sister only brings back the containers that aren't open," Pyotr said as he stood lecturing the group of children. "Just the closed cans and bottles, okay, Zhenya?"

"And the rest of you – you have to check the tops of closets for jewelry or anything interesting. You've been leaving a lot of valuable stuff behind. Remember how it goes?"

The children began to chant slowly together, their voices gaining volume as they went. "Get the food, guns and jewelry in coats, purses, bags, closets, desks, drawers..."

"And what do you do if you find a safe that's locked or a desk that you can't open?"

"Find Ivan," they all shouted.

"That's right," Pyotr said, flashing a smile over at the teenage girl.

The children waited on their cots and around the dining table, staring dully at the older boys who were sharing conspiratorial glances.

Suddenly getting very serious, Pyotr stepped forward and looked carefully at the faces of the children closest to him. "And, does anyone remember what happens if someone doesn't come back at the end of the day?"

None of the children said a word. Little Kostya fidgeted and flashed his large blue eyes around at the others, wanting to give the answer, but not sure if he was allowed. Pyotr looked down at the boy and pointed to him.

"Kostya, what happens if someone doesn't come back to the hotel?"

The sandy-haired boy smiled broadly and waved his arms as he shouted, "Don't come back, get no food!"

Pyotr smiled grimly and nodded. "That's right. If even one of you decides to hide somewhere and doesn't come back, then the rest don't get to eat until that child returns. None of you wants little Zhenya to starve, do you?"

Everyone was silent. Pyotr stared carefully again at several of the children's faces individually, taking a couple of seconds to scrutinize each one. Sean knew that he was reading their emotions, trying to see if anyone was angry or feeling a little rebellious, searching for anything besides what he wanted them to feel – fear.

Satisfied, Pyotr stepped back and put his arm around the girl and said, "Now we had some fun at the mall yesterday, but today – it's back to the real work."

He gestured to Ivan. The latter stepped forward, his heavily pronounced jaw clenching as he addressed the group in rough, mock drill sergeant tones.

"Igor's group will continue on Tverskaya today, starting with building 149. You'll have the main truck, so pack it tight. Svyeta – you and the girls finish the top floors of 147 and then start on 149 after the boys have the doors open."

His voice cracked slightly on the last word, but no one made any sign that they'd noticed. A couple of days earlier one of the girls had giggled when Ivan's voice cracked while he was barking orders at one of the teams. His first blow had knocked her to the ground and he would have continued on had some of the other gang members not pulled him off her. From then on, everyone completely ignored his changing adolescent voice.

"Viktor – you and Sean are with me. Alyosha – you and your boys start at the top of 149 and let Igor work up from the bottom... hey – Alyosha!"

Ivan stepped into the middle of the room and turned around, pushing kids aside as he walked. "Where's Alyosha?"

"Bathroom!" yelled out Zhenya.

"Sergey – check it out," Ivan ordered as he continued to pace the room. Sergey disappeared into the hallway. Sean and Viktor stared forward, not blinking. Although they didn't chance a look toward Svyeta, they could see from the corners of their eyes that she was doing the same.

A few seconds later, Sergey returned. "Not there."

Pyotr looked up from nuzzling the girl's neck and said, "Was he at breakfast?"

The five armed gang members stared dumbly at each other, throwing questioning glances as Ivan continued to stalk around the room, pulling blankets and pillows off cots. Pyotr pushed himself away from the wall where he'd been leaning with his bubble-gum chewing girlfriend and walked over to Svyeta.

"Where's Alyosha?"

"I swear, I have no idea, I haven't seen him this morning at all..."

A frightened yelp jumped out of her mouth as Pyotr grabbed it and pulled her face close to his. "Are you lying?"

She shook her head as much as she could in his grip, trying to avoid looking into the dark eyes only inches from hers.

"Yes, you are – I can see it! Where is he?" Pyotr screamed.

Sean stepped forward quickly. "He said he was going back to his apartment. He wanted to bury his parents – they're still there. He said he'd be back in a few days."

"How'd he get out?" Ivan asked quietly.

Sean turned toward the smaller, white-haired boy who was regarding him with a cold stare. The American boy was suddenly aware that all attention was on him.

"Through the wall," Sean said, knowing that he couldn't throw out too many lies without Pyotr catching on. With the ability to sense emotions, neither of them could really tell whether someone was telling the truth, but they could sense if someone was nervous or concentrating hard on hiding something. Sean exhaled slowly, letting his chest grow smaller and smaller as he cleared his head of any other thoughts or intentions besides the true fact that he was now telling.

"He just walked through the wall – like it wasn't there," Sean finished.

Pyotr looked accusingly at Ivan. "Did you know he could do that?"

Ivan shook his head and stared back at the tall, fuming youth. "Did anyone know he could do that?" screamed Pyotr.

His voice echoed off the vaulted ceilings and intricate chandeliers, reverberating in the silence. Pyotr swallowed slowly to regain his composure and walked back to the middle of the group of children.

"Does anyone know where he used to live? Around here?"

The children remained silent. Suddenly, young Kostya blurted, "Maybe he went to see the Yozh!"

"There is no damn Yozh!" screamed Pyotr.

Pyotr stared at the group of frightened children surrounding him, appearing unsure as to what to do next. Sean sensed a trickle of panic beginning to rise in the leader's mind, as he saw the operation that he had so carefully constructed start to crack. The feeling of loss of control was plainly evident as the tall, dark-haired boy walked back over to the double doors.

"Okay, new rule: anyone else escapes, and we shoot someone else here. For this one, Alyosha's going to get shot – as soon as we find him."

No one in the room moved. All the children just stared at

the floor, waiting for the next command.

"Ivan, get them out of here," Pyotr grunted.

Ivan gestured at the other gang members who began directing the children out of the room with their weapons. Each of them filed slowly past Pyotr and Ivan, not daring to look them in the face.

As Sean made his way to the door, Pyotr stepped back into the middle of the room and gestured to the American boy. Sean glanced at Viktor, then turned to talk to Pyotr.

The tall, dark-haired boy drooped his hand over Sean's shoulder and leaned down to look him straight in the face. For five seconds, he didn't say anything, only continued staring at him with his round, dark eyes. Finally, he flashed a large, toothy grin.

"You're smart, American boy. You've done pretty well so far, especially with that fancy trick you do with the doors. Plus, the other kids seem to listen to you – they'll do what you say. So, I've got a proposition for you."

Pyotr glanced over Sean's shoulder to Ivan who was still watching the children leave the room, making sure they weren't carrying anything with them that they shouldn't be.

"I might have an opening soon for a new second in command. Ivan there's great and everything – gets the job done, but he doesn't exactly have leadership capabilities. Doesn't have any of the soft touch, you know? Same with the other guys – they pretty much just do what they're told. I want you to keep your ears and eyes open, okay? You can find things out for me – stuff like this Alyosha's disappearing power, so we're not surprised like that again. You'll know what to look for – and when you find it, just come and let me know. If you continue to impress me, there's a place for you in the Black Scorpions. And I take care of my own – you remember that."

Pyotr straightened up and pushed Sean toward the door.

"You keep an eye on that one, Ivan," he called after Sean jokingly. "He's one to watch."

CHAPTER THIRTY-FOUR

The smell of new tire rubber drifted into his nose as Sean knelt on the sidewalk beside the car. His hand rubbed some flakes of dark blue paint away from the sizable dent in the front right fender.

"Maybe he won't notice," he said over his shoulder to Ivan.

The pale-faced boy stood staring out at the street and nodded. "He'll notice. We'll have to find a new blue BMW on the way back to the hotel."

Sean stood up and dusted off his knee. Ivan, turning to Sean and Viktor, said slowly, "Not a word of this to anyone."

The telephone pole a few feet in front of the car had a new streak of dark blue paint carved into its base at about knee level. Ivan had swung a little wide when pulling up in front of the U.S. Embassy. Still, Sean gave him credit for the expert way in which he handled the car on the way over there, speeding through the streets and making fast, but well-timed turns through the wide boulevards.

Ivan motioned with his small machine gun tucked under his arm for the two of them to start walking toward the entrance. There was a great deal of debris scattered on the concrete steps that led up to where the front door used to be. Stepping over large chunks of splintered wood and plaster dust, they passed the guard room that stood right beyond the entrance. The bullet-proof glass window was riddled with cracks. Viktor looked questioningly over at Ivan and paused in front of the door, balancing deftly on his right leg as he gingerly applied pressure on his left for stability.

Ivan shook his head. "There won't be anything left in there now."

The three boys continued through the building of compact offices. Portions of the wall were black from a fire that had raged through the room until the automatic sprinklers had switched on. All of the stacks of manila file folders and other stray documents were now dry, but warped with water damage.

They eventually found the door that led to an internal compound road behind the main building. Sean immediately recognized the road from his visits before. The memory made him wince as he thought about his excitement in coming here last time with his father, trailing along dutifully as they went to meet with the senior NASA and Embassy officials to discuss Jerry's descent. This time, he felt no excitement – only a pervading sense of dread.

Rows of two-story, non-descript buildings stretched down the opposite side of the road. The meetings that his father had attended had taken place in a building just like these, although Sean couldn't recall exactly which one – they all looked the same.

"What are we looking for again?" Viktor said.

The thick-haired boy stood half a head taller than both Sean and Ivan. He was still dressed in his heavy, waist-length wool coat despite the cool, but pleasant spring air. A backpack hung from his shoulders, its bottom sagging from the weight of several books.

"Any type of powerful weapon – bigger rifles and machine-guns, explosives, rocket launchers if we can find them," Ivan replied as he surveyed the abandoned and silent Embassy compound.

"I thought you had taken all the weapons from Red Square and the Kremlin. There must have been hundreds there. What will you do with more?"

Ivan's small, cold eyes studied Viktor. "Just in case."

"Do you know where weapons were kept?" he said, turning to Sean.

"I told you, I was only here a couple times, just for some meetings. I didn't see any weapons."

"Okay, it's probably best if we split up, cover more area. Let's meet back here in an hour." The short-haired boy re-situated the shoulder strap of his weapon.

"Viktor – keep your eyes open for anything... advanced or

complicated looking. They might have some secret missile systems here."

Turning halfway toward the two smaller buildings directly in front of them, Ivan muttered quietly, "And I know I don't have to remind you two about being on time."

Without waiting for any response, he began walking slowly toward the interior of the compound. Viktor turned to the right and began limping down the street, while Sean set off to the left. A faint wind continued to blow, rustling the scant leaves that hung from the spindly tree branches overhead.

CHAPTER THIRTY-FIVE

The plain brownish Embassy buildings stretched out in front of Sean for quite some ways before finally ending in a tall concrete wall. He had a vague idea of the size of the compound from having arrived at another entrance on one of his trips. The large concrete wall probably surrounded the whole place, he thought to himself. Still, that's a lot of space for just an hour. He continued walking, hearing Viktor's shuffling footsteps fading away in the opposite direction.

Finally, he chose one of the buildings on his right and opened the closed double doors. Daylight poured into the long hallway stretching before him. Most of the dark wood of the wall paneling was lost in large shadows and the deep red carpet seemed to suck up any noise from the outside world.

Sean stood in the doorway, his hands still on the doors, staring into the dark interior. There were a few doors coming off the hallway which met another corridor toward the middle of the building. He could feel the sun's warmth on his back and, at the same time, smell the stale air wafting out from the dark interior.

The boy bid his body to move, but for some reason, his feet stayed rooted to the pavement in front of the door. The dark, empty hallway loomed before him, offering no clues or hints as to its destination – only silence. What are you afraid of, he asked himself, still staring into the darkness. You've entered dozens of empty apartments and buildings before. What's different about this time, about this place?

He quickly brushed the questions away and told himself to stop being silly. Still, his feet and hands didn't move. He stayed glued to his position on the building's threshold, confused and afraid.

The wind behind him picked up a little and he stepped onto the thick carpet and fumbled for a light switch on the wall to his right. The florescent panels in the ceiling flickered to life and a cold, greenish light splashed into the hallway. Very much relieved, Sean walked forward into the building.

Most of the doors along the corridor were locked. Sean didn't expect that they contained any sort of weapons anyway – most were probably very similar to the conference room where his father had met with all the Embassy officials.

He followed the hallway as it turned to the left then the right, running alongside the outside of the building. Paintings and photographs of uniformed men adorned the walls, with inscriptions carved on metal placards beneath them. The hallway turned again to the right into a lobby at what Sean assumed was the back of the building.

The lobby was empty except for a few cases displaying military uniforms and ceremonial swords. To his left, daylight streamed in through head-sized windows in the double doors at the back of the building. Opposite them, across the lobby, was another set of doors.

Sean stood, staring quietly at this second set of doors that led to ... what? He couldn't take his eyes from them, as if they were bidding him to look, to open, to discover. He felt his pulse quicken, then swallowed a couple of times to wet his dry mouth.

The building was completely silent, the only sound coming from his feet treading carefully on the thick carpet. Then, he could hear his own heartbeat pounding in his ears and the breath slowly blowing through his open mouth. He took a few steps toward the doors, feeling as though they were drawing him forward, then stopped.

What could be in there, he thought? Another conference room, maybe some offices – what am I afraid of? I'm alone, he thought. Usually I go into the apartments with the rest of the kids, but this time I'm alone. You've always been alone, a quiet voice whispered inside his head. Sean nodded silently. Ever since Dad died, he mused, I've been alone. Nothing to lose now. He completed the last few steps to the carved double doors and pulled them open.

Outside light from behind him shone on rows of seats

sloping downward into the room. Sean groped along the wall until he found a set of switches behind a curtain and flipped the first one. Light from some unseen source slowly brightened at the opposite end of the room and shone on the edge of a small stage.

The theater had only a little over a hundred seats, but was tiered and had a second level balcony above Sean's head. He stepped into the cavernous room and studied the shadows draped over the black curtain that hung at the sides of the stage. As his eyes adjusted to the dim light, he saw that there was furniture on the stage – it was set for some type of play. A few lamps stood on end tables. A couch and arm chairs were nestled silently beside a set of fake bookshelves. He couldn't make out what period the little living room was supposed to be in, so he flipped another light switch.

Subtle lamps set in the floor at the back of the stage slowly burned to life and lit a bright red backdrop. Fascinated, Sean stepped forward to the edge of the first step leading downward and stared at the idyllic, little nineteenth century home.

It looked so out of place, so quaint. It didn't belong in this city of drab gray at all. Fake plants sat beside some of the arm chairs, their long leaves draping luxuriously over a festive carpet. It made Sean wish he was there, in that world represented by the charming little living room – somewhere warm and happy where people sat chatting and drinking tea and eating cookies. Somewhere very far from here.

In the center of the stage, toward the back, there was a large, leather-looking armchair. Sean couldn't tell what color exactly, since the backlighting cast deep shadows on the seat and arms of the chair. It was turned almost completely toward the red backdrop, its tall back facing the silent seats. The warmth and homeliness of the small stage set drew him closer and he began descending the steps.

As he walked deeper into the theater, he kept his eyes focused on the stylish armchair, its graceful curves reminding him of a time and place long forgotten. Getting closer, he could see the faint outline of something resting on the arm of the chair.

Sean stopped. His eyes darted quickly to the corners of the room, to the barely visible side wings of the stage behind the curtains. The theater itself was empty – only a few additional pieces of furniture and gaily painted backdrops waited silently behind the partially drawn stage curtain.

He stepped quietly to his right into a row of seats about halfway down the sloping aisle. The overhead theater lights were casting deep shadows that covered much of the armchair. It didn't look right, sitting there toward the back of the set, facing away from the audience. It was out of place.

Sean squinted in the dim light, trying to make out the faint shape he saw on the arm of the chair, but couldn't. The distance to the edge of the stage was short, he could just run down for a quick look, he would still be able to get back up the aisle out of the theater, in case... in case what? What was he so afraid of? I'm just being silly, Sean thought. I've spooked myself, I should just leave and go on searching for secret missile systems or whatever.

But, he couldn't leave. He stayed rooted to his spot among the empty seats for several minutes, staring at the armchair and the rest of the quiet set, a red glow illuminating everything. Clenching his jaw, he made a quick decision and started walking before his mind could summon up another argument as to why he shouldn't have a closer look.

He felt his feet quickly running down the few remaining steps and then leaping up onto the stage, his heart pounding, almost two beats a second. Sean paused again, almost confused as to how he got onto the stage so quickly, looking around at the warmly decorated couch cushions and the leather-bound tomes sitting peacefully on the rich oak shelf.

The armchair sat directly in front of him, only seven or eight feet away. He could make out the edge of some type of dark blue cloth, lying on the armrest, but still wasn't close enough to hazard any guesses as to what else might be in the chair.

As he stepped to the right, his feet inched carefully forward, drawing him closer to the chair. He watched riveted as his view of the blue cloth expanded to reveal a sleeve, and then a jacket and pants of the same material.

Sean was just a couple of feet away from the chair when he saw the ashen hand sticking out of the navy-blue sleeve, clutching a square-shaped, dull black pistol. From his position, the upward sloping sides of the armchair blocked Sean's view of the face that he knew must be there.

His mouth had gone completely dry and his heart continued to march rapidly in his chest. The silence of the theater and the dank air seemed to envelop him, locking him away in a small, separate world where only he and the armchair's occupant existed. Despite the fear he could feel rising higher and higher in his throat, he couldn't manage to tear his eyes away or keep his body from moving forward to see more.

His fingers lightly touched the thick chair leather and he looked down to see the man's face. The skin was a deep purplish gray and sagged like old, wet paper. There was a hole in the right temple and crusted blood was stuck to the side of the head down to the jacket lapel.

Sean stared at the ghastly scene before him. All his earlier feelings of home and warmth were gone, replaced now by the desperation and horror of the man's last act. His heartbeat began to slow and his breathing became more natural as he studied the pitiful shell in front of him, soaking up an almost overwhelming feeling of utter loss and hopelessness. He wanted to leave, to run out of the theater and its mocking scene of deceptive peace, and try to purge the entire picture from his mind forever. But, he stood and stared down at the body, his legs locked in position.

Suddenly, the rushing sensation filled his mind: the sound of wind and water swirling around inside his head, overwhelming his senses. Sean's eyes widened in terror as he stared at the dead man sitting in the chair. The rushing sensation was unmistakable – he knew it meant that someone near him was using their special power. Only now he was alone – alone in a darkened theater with a dead man, a suicide. Someone nearby must be using their power, but there was no one else here, no one except... except the dead man. That's impossible, Sean thought. He couldn't use his power if he was dead... unless he wasn't dead. Or, unless he *was* dead and was suddenly coming back to life!

Suddenly, with that last thought, Sean's legs found the resolve they'd lacked only moments earlier and he whirled around and ran toward the front of the stage, launching himself into the air as his heart thudded loudly in his chest.

Taking two steps at a time, he reached the top quickly, ran through the open doors and sprinted across the lobby. He slammed into the doors leading outside, wrapping his sweating hands around the knobs and yanking furiously, trying to get them to open, to let him out. He heard his voice start to rise at the back of his throat, the beginnings of a deep scream welling up within him. He pounded his fists furiously on the door, still seeing the sightless stare of the dead man's cold, lifeless eyes.

Strong hands grabbed his shoulders, pulling him backward. Sean screamed in surprise and fear as panic washed over him in a powerful wave. The hands immediately let go and the person stepped away, letting Sean fall to the floor.

"Easy on the screaming, kid, what're you trying to wake the dead?"

Sean stared at the uniformed man standing above him, his hands clamped tightly over his ears. The man was wearing an olive green jumpsuit and large, black boots. His short-haired head was bare and he had a rifle slung over his shoulder. The man was thin and had a clean young face.

Sean sat up quickly, his fear fading slowly as he watched the man shaking his head from left to right, still massaging his ears. The boy stared for a few seconds, studying the stranger's soft features. It wasn't the dead man from the theater, Sean could tell that much. No, this guy was entirely new, yet he looked somehow familiar, like they'd met somewhere before...

"I know you!" Sean blurted.

"Quietly, okay, you gotta keep it quiet, my ears are a little sensitive now," said the young soldier in an easy southern drawl.

"You're from here – I saw you here at the Embassy before... the day after Jerry landed. You were in that meeting..."

"Hey – right! You're one of the NASA guys' kid, aren't you? What are you doing here now?"

Sean sat staring in disbelief at the smiling soldier. The man offered him his hand, "Private McCaney – Ryan." Sean took his hand and was pulled to his feet.

"Sean Prochazek," he said distractedly as he stood shaking Private McCaney's hand.

"Pleased to meet you, Sean. Boy, it's been quite a while since..."

"Why are you alive?"

Ryan smiled, the left corner of his mouth pulling more than

the right. "Why shouldn't I be?"

"Because... all the grown-ups everywhere are dead. We haven't found any alive – no adults survived," Sean stammered.

Ryan nodded gravely and looked down, then back at Sean. "No one?"

Sean shook his head. "How old are you?"

"I'll be nineteen in a few months. I went into the Marines the day after I finished high school. I wasn't quite eighteen yet, but the recruiter back in Greenville was so excited to be getting any volunteer, he didn't exactly do a lot of fact checking. Had my birthday in Basic Training."

Sean continued staring in disbelief at the young soldier. "We haven't found any kids' bodies, just grown-ups..." He stepped away, hands hanging limply at his sides, and exhaled slowly, looking around at the decorations in the lobby.

"I got these headaches real bad – for like the whole week after Jerry came down. They put me in the infirmary because I kept passing out. I think I was out for like three days the last time, they had me hooked up to all these tubes. When I finally woke up, though, I felt fine. But, no one else in the other beds woke up. They was all dead, every one of 'em."

Sean nodded and looked around, still recovering slightly from the adrenaline rush of a few moments before. He gradually became aware of a sharp, steady knocking sound, but couldn't tell where it was coming from. The more he concentrated on the noise, the louder it became until he turned around toward the outer doors, almost expecting to see someone outside knocking on the window.

"What is it?"

"Do you hear that? Where's it coming from?" Sean said as he began to circle around the room.

Ryan paused and closed his eyes. Suddenly he opened them and looked down at his arm. Raising his wrist to his ear, he said. "You mean this? You can hear that?"

Sean stared blankly at the wrist watch. Ryan moved closer to hold his watch up to Sean's ear. Even before he got close, Sean could hear the ticking as clearly as a snare drum beating right by his head. He quickly pulled away as the sound became almost deafening.

Ryan looked in confusion at Sean. "You can hear it too? It's loud, ain't it!"

"I don't know," Sean said as he took his hands away from his ears.

"You know, ever since I woke up – it was on a Sunday I think – I've had the most amazing things happening to me. I can hear everything around me, like totally clear, like it's right inside my head. The lights buzzing, birds' wings as they fly by. And you know what else? I can smell everything! Like I can smell your sweat from over here and something, I don't know, something like, I mean, no offense, but you really stink."

Sean stared back at him. He began to notice that he was able to make out individual pores in the young soldier's face with startling clarity, as long as he focused. The stubble around his mouth danced rhythmically as he spoke, waving back and forth like hills of grain in the wind.

"And, this is the coolest thing, I think – I can sit up on the top floor of the main building and see for miles all around the city. I can read signs that are blocks and blocks away, it's the craziest thing. Well, not read exactly, I don't speak the Russkiy," Ryan continued, smiling broadly in wonder.

Sean finally managed to tear his gaze away from the hypnotizing sight of Ryan's face as it moved. He nodded.

"Yeah, weird stuff has been happening to us all."

"Shhh!" Ryan said suddenly. He closed his eyes and turned his head up and to the right, holding his hand out in front of Sean.

"Footsteps – coming toward this building."

Sean also closed his eyes and listened intently. Gradually, the steady rhythm of feet on pavement reached his ears. The footsteps were separate and distinct, one after another.

"It's Ivan – he's one of the Black Scorpions gang. He's got a gun."

"I saw him come in with you, him and that other kid with the limp. Sorry I scared you – I didn't want to jump out around the kid with the weapon – Ivan. He looked like he might scare easily."

Sean stood frozen, listening as the footsteps drew closer. It sounded like he was right outside the doors. He began to back away.

"He's almost here!"

"No, he ain't, he's still a ways down the street, you're just not used to this. You want me to go out there and talk with him — is he harassing you guys at all?"

"Listen," Sean said as he grabbed Ryan's arm, "he and a bunch of other kids have been holding us prisoner for the past few weeks, making us gather food and jewelry for them."

"Well, I can get you out of here easy…"

"I can't leave. Viktor and I have to go back with him or they'll kill one of the little kids. Pyotr said he would this morning."

Ryan nodded grimly, then flashed Sean his lopsided smile, "Well, then. It sounds like you kids are in need of an old-fashioned rescue, aren't you?"

CHAPTER THIRTY-SIX

Sean sagged wearily against the wall as Aleksandr pushed the now unlocked door open and stepped inside. Viktor, a large trash sack clutched in hand, paused to whisper a word of encouragement to Sean before entering the apartment. He was immediately cut off by Ivan's bellow from the stairs behind them.

"Keep moving! You've got another building to get through before dinner!"

They'd already cleared four buildings that day with Sean opening each one of the apartment doors with his telekinetic power. Although he was definitely becoming more adept at it with all the practice, after an entire day of constant concentration and mental strain plus the added effort of hauling canned food from apartments, even he was exhausted. That and the fact that he hadn't eaten anything that day except for a meager slice of old bread for breakfast had him on the verge of collapse.

As Sean gathered his strength to enter the apartment, a loud crash of glass came from inside. Sean winced and instinctively threw his hands over his ears. Viktor, who stood in the hallway just ahead, turned around and looked at the boy in sympathy. "Aleksandr just broke some plates in the kitchen – that's all."

Sean had been practicing reducing his newfound sensitivity to light and sound, but he was still caught off guard sometimes. It seemed to function almost like a volume knob inside his head, although the effort to turn it was much greater than a simple flick of the wrist. He knew it would become easier with practice, but it still seemed very inconvenient right now.

It had been two days since Sean, Viktor and Ivan had searched the Embassy. As far as Ivan and Pyotr knew, their trip had been unsuccessful. Sean had told Viktor all about Private

McCaney back at the hotel that night, leaving nothing out, including his powerful new senses. Viktor was very excited at first with the idea of the young marine coming to rescue them. But, as they began to concoct escape plans late into the night, they kept reaching the same difficulty: escaping without getting most of the other kids killed in the process. If just the two of them slipped away, the others would be punished. But, any plan that included liberating the entire bunch of forty children was always too risky and implausible. Sean and Private McCaney hadn't had more than a few minutes to talk, before he'd had to go back and find Ivan and Viktor. McCaney had just told Sean to watch for his signal.

Svyeta, Zhenya and a couple of the other girls stepped out of the elevator and made their way past Sean into the apartment, quickly and expertly combing the place for valuables and any other useful items. Sean watched little Zhenya's shoulder-length brown hair sway back and forth as she shuffled around the apartment, trying to help while also staying out of the way of the older children who rapidly moved from room to room. Once again, he was reminded of his sister Elizabeth when she was younger, when they were both so happy and carefree. That time seemed so long ago...

Some days Elizabeth was more clearly in his thoughts than others. During those times, he could plainly see her face, hear her voice and sense her closeness. It was different than when he thought of his parents. Although it still almost brought tears to his eyes when he thought of his mother and father, the memory of them seemed so far away and somehow finalized. With Elizabeth, the memory was much more vibrant and fresh, like she was still very much a part of his life, but somehow removed. Maybe I'm just hoping, he thought to himself. Hoping that she's still alive. And if she was, he hoped that she wasn't going through anything like what he was experiencing.

"Hurry it up, ladies. It'll be dark soon," Ivan said as he walked into the apartment. "Aleksandr," he called loudly, "you, Sean and Viktor go on ahead to the next one and get the doors open."

A deep boom sounded in the distance. Svyeta stepped out from one of the bedrooms with a blank look on her face. She stood motionless, her eyes on the ceiling as everyone in the apartment quieted, waiting for a second sound.

It came five seconds later. The dirty window above the stairwell rattled softly with the explosive crack in the distance. Sean could distinguish the several pieces of the noise that was bouncing off the concrete buildings throughout the city. It was a distinctive explosion followed quickly by shattering rubble. He couldn't tell exactly what it was, but it sounded closer than the first explosion.

"It's nothing. Back to work," Ivan ordered. Aleksandr exited the kitchen and handed a heavy sack to Sean. The three boys made their way to the elevator.

A few minutes later, they dropped the sacks of canned food to the ground behind the large truck and leaned against the back step to catch their breaths. Another boom sounded, echoing through the almost empty city.

Sean looked around the deserted little courtyard that was nestled between several connecting apartment buildings. They had come from the tallest – the others were only a few stories high and much older. A plot of grass surrounded a feeble tree that was struggling to reach up to the sun in one corner. Several car-wide passages led off the courtyard. The truck stood opposite the building they'd just exited, pointing through an archway out onto a small street.

Kiril and one of the other captive boys about Sean's age jumped out of the truck's cab, slamming the heavy doors. They barely paused to look at the three exhausted boys, before emptying the sacks of the cans and tossing them one by one into the covered bed of the personnel transport vehicle.

Just as they were loading the last of the food, Svyeta entered the courtyard, her oversized boots slapping quickly on the cracked concrete. Her thin, pale face was pointed at the ground as she walked, her sharp shoulders moving gracefully under the light jacket she wore. The plastic bag in her hands held a few tin cans of food. The other two girls quickly carried their canned goods over to the truck. Zhenya trailed behind, clutching a large jar of peaches in her pudgy hands.

"One-seventy-nine's clear," Svyeta called out to no one in particular. She set the cans and Zhenya's peach jar in the back of the truck. More footsteps echoed through the small courtyard as three or four younger boys and girls walked in from the street. Each of them held canned foods or packages of dried fruit and crackers.

Another explosion burst in the afternoon air. This time, they all heard a faint whistle after the blast, which was closely followed by the sound of shattering glass and metal slamming against pavement.

The children jumped at the noise and Zhenya immediately burst into tears. Kiril tossed the rest of the food into the truck and jumped out to the ground.

"What was that?" one of the girls asked, staring in wide-eyed fear at the gray sky above the apartment buildings that surrounded them. The few scattered leaves on the tree waved fitfully in the wind.

"Sounds like cannons. Or a tank," Kiril said as he walked around the side of the truck toward the cab.

"Missile launcher?" asked the younger boy following behind him.

"We found one of those a few weeks ago – shot off a few missiles. Those explosions sound much louder than a missile launcher."

Sean, Viktor and Aleksandr stepped further into the middle of the courtyard, ears trained to the wind as they searched the sky above their heads for additional signs of explosions.

"Is Pyotr shooting off cannons?" asked one of the younger boys who had just entered the courtyard.

"Don't know," Kiril called back as he climbed up into the cab of the truck.

Viktor leaned over to Sean and said in English, "Can you tell which it is – cannons or tanks?"

Sean shook his head. "I can hear it pretty clearly – that last one was loud. I can make my ears more or less sensitive if I think about it, but I kind of have to know when the sound's coming. I don't know what a cannon or a tank going off sounds like, so I don't know which it is."

The thunder clap of another explosion rocked through the enclosed courtyard. This one was much closer, coming from the direction of the street where the truck was pointed. Sean held his hands tightly over his painfully ringing ears. He had been straining to hear any additional noises – feet marching, orders being shouted, gunfire. But, he'd over-amplified.

Zhenya had screamed again at the blast, along with several of the other girls. Svyeta stroked the girl's hand rhythmically as she looked around, listening to the echoes of the explosion carry through the deserted streets.

Ivan burst out of the stairwell several meters away, his hand clutching a walkie-talkie to his ear as he ran.

"I'm not shooting off anything! I thought it was you!" he yelled into the mouthpiece.

He sprinted to the back of the truck and crouched down next to the group of frightened children. His fingers released the talk button on the black instrument and loud static hissed from it. A couple seconds later, Pyotr's voice was faintly heard.

"We're not doing anything either – it sounds like a tank. Who else is there with you –damn!"

Heads turned toward the sound of distant and rapid popping coming through one of the archways on the other side of the courtyard. Sean could tell that the gunfire was far away – but still too close.

Viktor shifted nervously from his right foot to his left and back. He wasn't sure if he should watch the street behind them or the archway just thirty meters in front of them. Sean was crouched low on the ground beside him, his hands over his ears as he strained to decipher what was going on.

Svyeta turned to Ivan. "Who is it? Who's shooting?"

"It's the Yozh!" blurted Aleksandr.

Ivan's left hand shot out and wrapped around Aleksandr's throat. Although Ivan was a few years older, both boys were roughly the same size. But, the humorless look in Ivan's eyes and the determination with which he squeezed the windpipe made it clear who would win in a fight. With a look of pain and confusion on his face, Aleksandr pried the fingers away and backed up, rubbing his throat.

Ivan continued staring at him, almost daring him to attack or say something else. After a tense moment, he spat, "There is no Yozh!"

A loud boom rattled a few of the windows of the shorter

apartment buildings. It was instantly followed by a faint, short whistle, then a splitting crack as chunks of concrete and dust exploded into the courtyard. A meter-wide section of the concrete ceiling that hung above the tall archway leading to the street was gone. The truck's windshield was almost shattered by flying debris, while thick, gray dust swirled in a cloud around the rest of the vehicle and over the ground.

With a little yelp, Zhenya broke away from Svyeta's grip and began running frantically away from the exploding concrete. She was heading toward the smaller passage on the opposite side of the courtyard that led out to the street.

"Zhenya!" Svyeta screamed, panic rising in her voice.

"Stop!" yelled Ivan after her. He took a couple of steps forward as she continued to run away, her little legs pumping toward escape.

"Zhenya, stop!" Ivan yelled again, more forcefully. He deftly swung the sub-machinegun that was slung over his shoulder to point at the retreating girl. "I said stop!"

Just as Svyeta began to turn to him, a shriek starting to build in the back of her throat, the gun cracked, spitting out a burst of rounds. Sean saw the tiniest cloud of red mist burst from Zhenya's back and she immediately crumpled to the ground, face down.

The echoes of the gunshot quickly died away and the courtyard was left in silence, Svyeta's dangerous scream dying in her throat. Ivan stared ahead at the small body lying on the pavement, twenty meters in front of him, his hands still clutching the firearm, holding its muzzle level with the ground.

Sean was faintly aware of the sound of a metal track rolling slowly over street pavement, mashing the relatively soft asphalt. He, along with the rest of the children, stared in silence at the small form, lying still in the middle of the courtyard, brown hair scattered in disarray over the back of the head, her little patterned skirt blowing slightly in the wind. It danced over her purple leggings, licking the tops of her softly cushioned boots.

Sean's eyes blinked once slowly, as he stared ahead, his heartbeat thudding softly in his chest. Her hair was brown too, he thought to himself. The image of his sister Elizabeth came rushing into his mind – he could see her going down the yellow, plastic slide on the old play set in the backyard, her long brown hair trailing dutifully behind her. He imagined her tiptoeing carefully through the house, peeking her head around the corner each time she entered a different room, searching it to see if anyone was there, her eyes wide in wonder and sadness. In her hands, he could see that she was holding a small green lamp, one of the old-fashioned kind that held a candle in the center and reflected the light through the entire masterfully crafted piece of colored glass. Her head turned slowly, as she stood in the front hallway, toward the large, white front door. Before she could take two steps toward it, the door began to swing open. Her deep blue eyes widened, the black, inky pupils dilating quickly as her chest filled with a slow gulp of air. The green lamp skimmed the tips of her hair on its way toward the floor, where it shattered at her feet in hundreds of tiny pieces, sending mismatched shards in every direction.

The image quickly faded away in a wash of light and brightness. Sean closed his eyes and reopened them again slowly on the quiet courtyard in front of him. He stared at the inert form lying in the middle of the pavement, helpless and pitiful. Her face was hidden, turned away from him with only the back of her brown-haired head visible as the wind blew through her skirt. The absurdity of a perfectly normal person lying outside on the ground reminded him of a few of the bodies he'd seen at Red Square – their mouths opened in silent screams and eyes turned upwards toward heaven in mute supplication.

No one had answered the prayers that had died on their lips when the last breath of life leaked out of their broken bodies. No one had come to save them at the last moment, to protect them from the inevitable approaching death they knew awaited them in sleep. No angel had come down to save little Zhenya, to deflect the bullets before they pierced her small, defenseless body. No one had been there to comfort Elizabeth when she found herself alone that morning, crying on the edge of her mother's bed for her to wake up, to say something. And nothing but the dead body of his father had been there to comfort Sean as he cried himself to sleep repeatedly during the night, each time waking, hoping that it had all just been a dream, wanting his father and mother to still be alive.

Sean felt a hotness pulsating through his neck and coursing down his legs and arms, warming his toes and his flexing hands. His jaw began to clench tightly as he turned his head away from Zhenya's body to Ivan standing at his right. Sean could see tiny flecks of sweat that had formed on his pale, sunken cheeks, could smell the blood slowing in his veins and heard the faint wheeze of breath as it passed over his lips and down his throat. Right at that moment, Ivan's eyes turned toward Sean.

They were small and dark, seeming to blend in with the rest of his face, so lackluster was their appearance. Suddenly, Sean detected the faintest gleam, a spark in the depths of Ivan's eyes that was barely reflected in a twitch of his lips. Even without the color of emotion that his power allowed him to see – a deep, bubbling pink surrounding Ivan's being – Sean knew what the boy was feeling. He'd seen that same expression and gleam in the eyes before – in the faces of Kyle and Paul, in the bullies at the hotel: enjoyment.

Sean felt a slight sliding sensation in his mind, as if a precarious section of cliff behind his eyes had suddenly given way, falling unstoppably to the depths below. Rage began to well up inside him, a swelling sensation that filled his stomach and seemed to feed on itself. His fingers dug into the palms of his hands and his knees began to tremble.

Several seconds had passed since the last echo of the gunshot had died away, but somehow that abrupt sound still resounded in Sean's boiling mind. He glanced down at the machine-gun in Ivan's hands. The white-haired boy saw his glance and began to bring the gun around to point at Sean.

Sean waved his hand quickly to the side and the gun flew out of Ivan's grasp, landing with a clatter several yards away. A savage scream erupted from the pit of fire swirling in Sean's stomach and he launched himself forward, bringing his right hand back in a fist.

At the same moment, the rushing sensation filled his mind like a powerful river of sound and energy. It seemed to be flowing into him straight from Ivan who was quickly attempting to bring his hands up in defense.

As Sean brought his fist forward, he felt a surge of power course through his body like he'd just been struck with lightning.

Ivan wasn't able to back away or get his hands up in time to block Sean's punch. The blow caught him right below the left eye.

Sean felt his hand sink quickly into the boy's face like it was a lump of bread dough and he was faintly aware of the sound of bones snapping beneath his fist. Ivan's head snapped back sharply and he immediately collapsed onto the ground. Sean's momentum carried him forward and he landed on top of the Russian boy.

A mindless scream still tearing out of his throat, Sean grabbed Ivan by the collar and began shaking him harder and harder, as if shaking him hard enough would somehow undo Zhenya's murder. Tears poured from Sean's eyes and nose as his scream turned into a miserable wail, punctuated by the limp motion of Ivan's head as it flopped back and forth.

Sean released Ivan's collar, dropping the boy's head to the ground, and he began pounding on his chest with his fists, painful sobs wracking his body with each strike. He knew the boy was dead. He'd known it the second he'd felt his fist connect with Ivan's face, feeling his hand almost go all the way through. Now, his previous grief and rage were being compounded by what he had just done, by the finality and irreversibility of his act. Still, he beat the boy's body in anger. As he began to raise his hands for yet another strike, someone grabbed his wrists. Viktor locked his other hand onto Sean's shoulder and pulled the boy toward him, hugging him close from behind.

"Sean, Sean, Sean," Viktor repeated in a choked voice as his own tears soaked his cheeks. He held Sean, rocking the boy gently as the strength slowly drained from his muscles and his wail quieted to spasmodic sobs.

Kiril had jumped out of the cab and come around the back of the truck just in time to see Sean attack Ivan. He stood still, staring at the pair of boys clinging to each other on the ground, crying. Svyeta stood motionless nearby, her blank face fixated on Zhenya's still form. Suddenly, Kiril turned back toward the front of the vehicle at the sound of a metal track rolling over asphalt further down the street.

Running footsteps echoed from the archway on the opposite side of the courtyard. The group of boys and girls, still in stunned silence, turned to look at the figures sprinting in from the street.

Pyotr's long, black overcoat billowed out behind him as he ran into the courtyard, a pistol clutched in his right hand. Two of his guards were right behind him, assault rifles in hand. Pyotr slowed as his dark-haired head turned to stare first at Ivan lying on his back, then to Zhenya just a few meters from the archway, then back again at Sean and Viktor kneeling huddled on the pavement.

Sean inhaled slowly, the breath catching in his throat. He was shivering and he felt like he was going to throw up, his lips and face aching as his mouth began to open wide. His head rose toward Pyotr and he stared at the tall teenager who stood by Zhenya's body, an alarmed expression on his face.

Viktor slowly let go of Sean and leaned back to stare in fear at Pyotr. A faint smile spread across the young gang leader's face and he pulled back his shoulders as he looked at the frightened children in front of him. His gun hand slowly began to rise.

Suddenly, it jerked straight up and the cold barrel smacked into his forehead, the muzzle pointed toward the sky. Pyotr's face twisted in confusion and his eyes darted about as he struggled to pull the gun away from his forehead. His hand, still grasping the gun, darted to the right and back again, waving wildly around in the air. Sean stared in fixed concentration at the bewildered boy as he caused the infinite number of tiny particles in the weapon to be drawn to the walls, the ground, the tree – anything that would pull it out of Pyotr's grasp.

The two boys behind Pyotr stared at him for a moment in confusion as his gun hand waved wildly around, then they saw Sean kneeling on the ground and pointed their weapons at him.

At the same moment, Svyeta began to wail, as if finally coming to life. She hadn't moved at all in the last minute since her sister had been killed. Now, her grief began to rise in her throat, transforming quickly into a piercing scream that reverberated off the concrete walls of the courtyard.

The sound broke Sean's concentration and he released his hold on Pyotr's weapon. The tall, dark-haired leader, hearing Svyeta's dangerous scream, dropped to the ground and covered his head and ears. The two boys kept their weapons trained on Sean, staring in confusion at their cowering leader.

Sean quickly became aware of a swelling sensation within himself as Svyeta's scream grew louder. It felt as though something within him was amplifying her voice, lending strength to her already powerful scream as the sound waves beat against the two armed boys.

Suddenly, Svyeta opened her mouth wider and leaned forward, hurling out a shrieking force of energy that felt and sounded like a high-pitched artillery shell exploding. The boys on the other side of the courtyard were thrown backward several meters, landing solidly on their backs. After the explosive scream, Svyeta's voice died on her lips.

A painful screech of metal scraping across stone tore through the courtyard. Everyone turned toward the sound coming through the large archway leading to the street. Kiril, from his vantage point at the side of the truck, turned quickly and screamed one word: "Tank!"

Pyotr rose to a kneeling position and brought his pistol up again as he chanced a quick look at the tank slowly rumbling through the just wide enough archway on the opposite side of the courtyard. His grip tightened and his eyes narrowed as he aimed it directly at Sean and Viktor still kneeling on the ground beside Ivan's body.

Only Sean heard the shots over the thundering of the tank's engine as it echoed in the tunnel. Pyotr's head snapped to the side and the gun fell from his grasp as he toppled forward onto the ground. Sean turned toward an open doorway that led to the stairwell of one of the apartment buildings across the courtyard. Out from behind the rifle barrel poking from the shadows stepped Ryan McCaney. He held his weapon pointed toward Pyotr as he emerged from the darkened doorway and glanced nervously at Sean and the tank that was slowly rolling toward the front of the truck.

The large green armored vehicle stopped just short of the truck's grill and the large turret swiveled toward Private McCaney. Kiril and Aleksandr quickly ran from their positions beside the truck to stand in front of the tank, waving their arms and shouting.

For a split second no one moved. Svyeta's breath caught in her throat as she stared at the two boys frantically yelling at the tank to stop. McCaney stood frozen in position, staring at the enormous barrel pointing straight at him.

The hatch on top of the turret flipped open and a young boy in a tight, canvas military cap poked his head up to look out at the group of children. "Everything alright?"

Kiril and Aleksandr looked at each other in confusion. Beside the tank driver popped up another head. Sean immediately recognized him as the boy who'd spewed forth gallons of water when he'd originally been captured by Pyotr and Ivan. He pushed his way up on top of the tank and quickly scrambled down its side to the ground, his oversized military jacket hanging loosely on his shoulders.

He looked questioningly at both Kiril and Aleksandr who were staring at him and the tank, their mouths hanging open. "Is Pyotr here?"

Kiril gestured over toward the young leader's body which was lying face down across the courtyard. The boy quickly ran to the corpse, rolled him over, scrutinized his face, then called out, "This is him!"

The boy glanced at the two other Black Scorpion members who lay still on the ground nearby. Holding his hand out toward one of the boys, he paused for a second before a thin stream of water shot out of his index finger and hit the boy in the face. The gang member on the ground didn't move. The boy from the tank did the same to the other one, with the same result.

He turned back to his tank crew. "Dead."

Svyeta didn't seem to hear the news that she'd killed both boys. She was sitting on the ground, staring at Zhenya's body as tears poured down her cheeks.

No one else in the courtyard said a word, but just kept glancing from the boy in the oversized jacket to the tank and back again. The boy walked over to where Sean and Viktor were still crouched and looked down at Ivan's smashed face.

"Who are you?" asked Viktor.

The boy blinked a few times, appearing surprised at the question. "I'm the Yozh."

CHAPTER THIRTY-SEVEN

Viktor carefully eased his left foot off the curb into the gutter beside the large American SUV. The vehicle's storage area was loaded with sturdy plastic containers, long duffle bags and a large assortment of foodstuffs and bottled water. He pulled the door open and slipped his olive backpack off his shoulder onto one of the rear passenger seats. The frayed drawstring at the top was loose enough to reveal the worn cover of an American novel translated into Russian – *Earth Abides*. Viktor peered in at the book, shook the backpack to resettle the contents and pulled the draw string tight.

A squeal of terror drew Viktor's attention quickly back to the hotel from which he'd just exited. He watched as Kostya ran through the large double doors of the Hotel National, a wide smile of pure delight on his face. Running behind him were a couple of the other young boys, all about five or six years old. They all were screaming in glee as they ran from Alyosha. He growled menacingly and held up his thin, claw-like hands – one of which held a small red ball.

"Alyosha's coming!" screamed the last boy through the door as the others ran out into the street. As Alyosha shuffled through the door, affecting a slow, awkward gait, he growled again at the group of boys that was waiting in a semi-circle in the middle of the street, smiling. Suddenly, he darted into the middle of the group and threw the ball straight at Kostya's leg.

The boy attempted to dodge it, but was too late. He grabbed the ball as it bounced on the ground and carefully wound up his arm, aiming straight for Alyosha's chest. The older boy stopped in the street and slapped his thin, cadaver-like chest. "Come on!"

From three meters away, Kostya hurled the red ball with all

his force, nearly toppling over with the effort. Alyosha stood absolutely still as the ball sailed toward him, a faint smile on his lips. It reached the center of his chest – and flew straight through him, bouncing on the street.

Alyosha burst into laughter as a couple of the little boys' jaws dropped in amazement. But, Kostya, a petulant frown on his little features, cried, "Hey – not fair! Using powers is against the rules!"

Viktor smiled as he watched one of the other boys grab the ball and toss it to one of his friends. They were so much more animated now, more like he remembered the children who used to play out in front of his apartment building. He would sit on his bed during the afternoons, watching from his window as the boys chased each other around and the girls drew chalk figures on the sidewalk. When he'd been younger, he'd whined for hours to his mother, begging her to let him go out and play with them. And what'll you do out there, she'd ask. How are you going to play with those kids? He could never answer her and would just turn back toward the window to watch until it got dark. Viktor looked down at his backpack of books and let out a slow breath. Now I can, Mama, he thought to himself. I can finally play like the other kids.

The hotel's glass front doors opened again and Ryan McCaney strolled out, rifle strap slung over his shoulder and a cherry lollipop in his mouth.

"All loaded up?" he said, his soft voice amiable and pleasant, his southern drawl stringing the words lazily together.

Viktor liked this new American accent. "All ready."

A jeep turned onto the street in front of the hotel and pulled to a halt behind the SUV. The boy they called the Yozh and a couple older teens jumped out of the back, rifles strapped to their shoulders. Viktor studied the young boy in the over-sized military jacket. His face was calm, but his eyes darted about as he walked, as if he couldn't decide what to look at. Viktor had learned that his name was actually Yevgeny, but his friends had always called him Yozh, the hedgehog, because of a particularly short haircut he'd had a few years ago. Sean had told Viktor about the first time he saw the boy. He'd been captured on Red Square with Sean and had started spewing out water from every body orifice because he was so scared. Pyotr had eventually let the frightened boy go, apparently with instructions to carry an invitation to the other children of the city: Pyotr and his gang would give them food if they'd come work. Oddly enough, it was Pyotr's own messenger who had proved his undoing.

Viktor watched as the three boys walked into the hotel, their steps casual but determined. He wondered how they would be as leaders. He didn't believe that they would ever become like Pyotr and his bunch, but feared what they might do in the name of preserving order. The tank crew had spoken of rival gangs that they'd run across in the southern part of the city, describing crimes and atrocities far worse than anything Pyotr and Ivan had managed to commit. The Yozh said that his group controlled most of the area around Red Square now, but that they would have to vehemently defend their borders if they were to maintain the finite food supply. War has returned to Russia, thought Viktor. But then, had it ever really left?

Sean stepped out onto the sidewalk in front of the hotel, Svyeta behind him, a backpack hanging from one shoulder. Viktor's American friend had managed to wash most of yesterday's dirt and tear stains from his face, but a forlorn, haunted look in his eyes had replaced them.

He nodded at Private McCaney who leaned against the Ford Expedition beside Viktor. A squeal of laughter erupted from the group of boys still playing in the middle of the street. Each of them glanced over to see a small ball of flame rolling across the asphalt away from Kostya. The little boy stared at the ball that he'd accidentally set on fire, his fingers tugging at his lower lip in embarrassment. Alyosha was holding his sides, laughing the loudest.

"I'm ready," said Svyeta. "How will we get to... where in America is it?"

Sean pulled his gaze away from the group of boys to rest on the young girl standing in front of him. He looked at her round face, punctuated by sharp cheek bones that stuck out from beneath deep blue eyes. Sean couldn't remember how old she was at the moment, and wasn't able to tell just from looking at her. He thought he recalled that they were roughly the same age, but he almost didn't believe it looking at the young woman in

front of him now. Thirteen year-olds don't look this sad and
serious, he thought.

"Pasadena – it's in southern California," he replied.
"Hopefully, my sister Elizabeth hasn't gone far."

"But, how will we get there?" She turned to Private
McCaney and said in English, "Are you a pilot?"

McCaney shook his head. "No, miss."

"We'll drive to the eastern shores, to the Pacific Ocean. We
should be able to steer a boat across the Bering Strait, then drive
down through Alaska and Canada to California," Viktor said
matter-of-factly.

Svyeta nodded and looked down at her feet, her mind
drifting back to the brief graveside funeral this morning. It hadn't
taken long for Sean, McCaney and Alyosha to dig the little hole at
the cemetery where her grandparents had been buried a few years
ago. Svyeta had covered Zhenya's body in one of the beautiful
lace tablecloths from the hotel.

"Are you sure about this? This is where you grew up.
California's a long ways away – and people talk funny there."
Sean smiled.

"There's no one left for me here anymore. And," she
paused, looking down the broad street, "I'm afraid that staying
here would always remind me of them, of how they… went. I
want to remember them from when we were all together."

She placed a hand on her backpack. "I have pictures for
that."

Sean nodded, his weary eyes still staring into hers. The
colors of her many, mixed emotions swirled around her small
body – sadness, longing, some fear. And within all of it he saw a
shade that had already been growing quickly in all of them over
the past twenty-four hours since the Black Scorpions had fallen:
hope.

They hugged and said goodbye to Alyosha and the others,
then climbed into the SUV. As Ryan McCaney drove them down
the street, Sean, Svyeta and Viktor looked back at the hotel,
watching as the boys tried to dowse the still burning ball.

- -

The large, black sedan was right where he'd left it. Nothing had been touched – even all the food was still there. From their forced forages, Sean knew that there was still a great deal of food left in the city that hadn't spoiled and wouldn't for quite some time. But, it would be increasingly more difficult to find as the weeks and months wore on. Someday, it would all run out.

Sean unzipped his suitcase and stared at the contents packed neatly in front of him – his old clothes. It was all familiar to him, but still seemed a world away, like it was part of something that had existed long ago.

Viktor stood patiently a few feet away, staring across Red Square. He tried to remember the last time he'd been to Red Square, before this had all happened. He knew Aunt Lydia had brought him here a few years ago on a sunny Saturday afternoon, but he couldn't recall exactly how the square had looked then. All he could see when he tried to imagine how it would have looked on that day was the destruction. It lay untouched like a monument to the final moments of futility as most of the human race slowly died out. This is how he would probably picture it forever.

Sean suddenly realized that he'd been staring at his suitcase for a while – he wasn't sure how long. He quickly glanced over at Viktor, then to Private McCaney who was standing guard by the SUV, its motor running, with Svyeta in the backseat. Sean grabbed a few changes of clothing and stuffed them into a smaller bag. His Boy Scout knife also went into the bag along with his father's letter. He reached for the duffel bag in the front passenger seat and pulled out the video tape of the scientists at the Jerry site. His eyes scanned the rest of the car's contents – mostly dry food, a few weapons. McCaney had loaded down the SUV with all that it could carry of that stuff, along with quite a bit of camping and survival equipment. He slammed the door and walked back to the Expedition with Viktor.

"There's one last thing, before we leave the city," Sean said as they began to pull onto the bridge leading away from Red Square.

– –

The door swung open lightly on its silent hinges and Sean stared into the hotel room lit by the orange afternoon light streaming through the windows. Everything was exactly as he'd left it. He walked slowly to stand at the foot of the bed where his father's bundled form lay.

His father's arms lay straight at his sides, the blanket that Sean had wrapped him in tucked tightly so that nothing showed. He stood silently for a moment, staring at the mummified body as he quietly explored the few thoughts running through his head. The overwhelming sense of loss and abandonment that he had felt on that morning after his father had died was gone, replaced now only by a small and abiding sadness at the reality he'd have to live with forever. Looking at the inert form lying on the bed, Sean was completely unsure how to express what he was thinking and feeling. The only coherent words that his mind could assemble were "My father is not here – my father is gone."

They dragged an undamaged couch from the ransacked lobby across the street to the park in which stood the large metal statue of the Soviet workers. The perfectly sculpted man and woman, holding their hammer and sickle, stood stoically by as the three positioned the couch in the middle of the narrow expanse of grass, amongst the trees.

Sean set the can of gasoline on the grass beside the couch, then wiped his hands with a rag and stepped back a few feet to stand beside Viktor, Svyeta and Ryan, the soviet statue behind them. The sun was just reaching the horizon in the western sky, its straight orange rays causing the shiny metal surface of the statue to appear as if it were on fire.

Sean stared silently for a few moments at the body of his father, lying on the couch. Viktor shifted his weight carefully, avoiding putting too much pressure on his left leg. His dark brown eyes clouded in concentration as he imagined the bodies of his mother, grandmother, sister and Aunt Lydia lying in their beds at home. At least they'd had that comfort, he thought. They were able to fall asleep in their own beds, all the familiarities of their life close around them, one last time. And that's where they'll stay, Viktor thought – forever.

Ryan McCaney watched somberly, his cap in his hands behind him, his head slightly bowed. He still remembered the pressure on his arms as he'd laid Sean's father carefully on the couch. He wondered how it had been for his own mother at the end – she was old and frail already, had warned him that she may not be around by the time he returned from his foreign post. Just in case, they'd said their goodbyes before he'd left – as much as any mother and son could anyway.

Svyeta's mind turned quickly back to the image of her mother's body in the hospital room where they'd left her – the memory still felt so fresh like it had just happened. Only now, these many weeks later, it wasn't as overwhelming as it had been before. Mixed with it and the oppressive feelings it had first caused were the images of her father lying on the floor in their neighbors' apartment, Zhenya's tiny form being covered in dirt in the ground. Somehow these other images lessened the terrifying power of the first, as if knowing that her parents and sister were now together in death was easier. She was the last one of her family left, but she was good at managing on her own. And, now, with these others who would be like family, she had people she could take care of – and who could take care of her.

Sean extended his hand, fingers pointing toward the figure on the couch. He closed his eyes and concentrated, imagining the electrons in the air entering an increasing state of agitation, heating up as they bounced off each other in countless indeterminate patterns. He was aware of a slight sucking sensation in the air around him as oxygen collected. Suddenly, a thin jet of flame burst in the air a few inches from his fingers and shot in a stream toward his father's body. It was just enough to ignite the gasoline and the entire pyre was quickly ablaze.

The four stood silently still as the sun slid slowly below the horizon and the smoke drifted softly into the air.

CHAPTER THIRTY-EIGHT

Sean backed into the door slowly, pushing it open with his shoulder blades as he balanced the box of canned food and army-issue packets of macaroni and cheese with his duffel bag slung over his shoulder. As he stepped into the spacious living room and kicked the door shut behind him, he heard the banging of pots and pans from the kitchen to his right.

"Whoever these people were, they sure knew how to live it up," Ryan McCaney called from the kitchen. He stepped into the doorway that led into the living room, holding a large, Teflon-coated, steel pan about a foot-and-a-half in diameter. "Much better than that place in Kez last night."

"Crime pays," Viktor said from the leather couch in the living room. He was lying back against a couple of large, colorfully stitched Uzbeki cushions, a large atlas on his lap and a couple other folding maps spread out around him. Svyeta was curled up nearby, leafing through an old magazine.

Sean set the box of food down on a chair next to the door and carried his bag over to the couch, plopping down next to Viktor. Ryan ambled over to the cardboard box of food and pulled out a couple cans.

"Chili-mac okay with you guys?"

"You're killin' me, man," Viktor said, smiling as he perused one of the maps.

Ryan chuckled and walked back into the kitchen, swinging the large pan over his head.

Svyeta looked up, smiling at the unfamiliar words. Her English had been improving greatly over the past couple days, but at nowhere near the rate of Viktor's. And most of the American slang was still way beyond her ability.

Sean sat staring tiredly at the large television screen in front of him. This was the second dacha, or country house, that they'd stayed in. Once they'd left the Moscow metropolitan area, the small country towns had been easy to spot along the road. Some were larger than others, but all had been entirely deserted, as far as the three of them could tell. The first night they'd stopped, Private Ryan McCaney had been ready to pull in at the first shack off the freeway, but Viktor had urged him to drive through town first to take a look at their options. He'd explained that a majority of dachas were very primitive – just a limited cottage where work-weary city residents could spend the weekends soaking up sun or gardening. But, many of the communities had at least one or two very nice, brick homes that would be fully outfitted with all the latest amenities – usually owned by Mafia members. Although the water wasn't working, the large, fluffy beds had been exactly what they'd needed.

They had been driving for three days straight, traveling over a thousand miles, but still had about nine thousand more to go – another month of driving. Viktor was impressed with the progress they'd made so far, despite a couple detours around the major cities and some blocked roads. The Russian teen was guiding them along roughly the same route as the Trans-Siberian railroad, which would take them to the coast. From there they had a couple options. Hitching a ride on a plane out of Vladivostok was a longshot, but one that they wanted to investigate before beginning the longer and more difficult trek north to a smaller coastal city. Viktor insisted a boat trip across the Bering Strait to Alaska was possible, despite the fact that none of them had any experience with seafaring.

Thinking about the distance they still had to travel made Sean even more exhausted. He'd managed to grab a quick nap during the ride that afternoon, but he'd awoken from the same dream that he'd had the night before. It always began just as his normal forest dream that had repeatedly visited him over the past few weeks. He was hiking through a dense forest, toward some bright clearing in the distance, but this time, as he was clawing his way through the underbrush, he ran into a body slumped against the thick bushes. The face was broken and bloody almost beyond recognition, but he knew it was Ivan. As he was looking at the face, the dead boy let out a horrid scream and lunged toward him. Sean had awoken in a cold sweat both times, his heart racing, plagued by a single thought. It was the same thought that had been racing through his mind for the past few days: I am a murderer.

"It's you," Viktor said suddenly, staring at Sean from the other side of the couch.

Sean stared in surprise at his friend, suddenly terribly afraid that he was somehow able to read his thoughts.

"What?"

"I think it's you – you're causing it. You remember how I told you two days ago that I felt like I was getting smarter? Even smarter than before? The combinations, the equations that I was seeing – nothing that I'd even imagined up to that point. And now... everything is suddenly more clear just since you walked into the room... I think you're causing it – you're strengthening my intelligence power somehow."

"How? I'm not doing a thing," Sean replied.

"You may be using this new ability occasionally without even realizing it... through some type of unconscious activation – just as I suspect Ivan did..."

Sean thought back to that horrible moment a few days ago in the courtyard. Just as he was about to hit Ivan, he'd experienced the rushing sensation, meaning that someone nearby was using their special power. Then, right after that his fist had connected with the boy's face...

"Ivan," Sean said aloud. "I felt it right before I hit him. He could have been using it without even knowing. He was panicking – he was being attacked."

"Yes," said Viktor quietly, "he amplified the power being used around him, accidentally causing his own death."

Pulling himself out of the disturbing memory, Sean turned to Viktor. "What power? My telekinesis? But, I wasn't using that – I was just punching."

"But, punching with all your strength – including the additional strength you gained from Aleksandr. You couldn't have caused that much damage with your natural strength alone."

Sean nodded as it slowly became clear. "That day at the mall. The car was heading right for him, but he blocked it somehow at the last second. It wasn't a force field at all…"

"No, Aleksandr's ability, it seems, was extraordinary strength. That's the only explanation – you haven't seen any other kids exhibit any similar power right? Nothing that can explain what you were able to do to Ivan's face. So, you must have picked up this powerful strength from Aleksandr. He himself didn't even know about it up to that point. And since you weren't aware of the power that he'd had, you weren't able to use it consciously. Not until…"

"Not until I was angry enough. Angry enough to kill," Sean finished.

"It wasn't your fault. You didn't know you had that extraordinary strength and you didn't know that Ivan was able to amplify it even further. Besides, Sean," Viktor said as he leveled his gaze at the American boy, peering at him through his thick, dark eyebrows, "he killed Zhenya – murdered her. He might have murdered us too if you hadn't stopped him."

Svyeta had only understood bits and pieces of the conversation, but she looked directly at Viktor at the mention of her sister's name.

Sean slumped back into the couch cushion, reliving in his mind, once again, that terrible afternoon.

Viktor stood up and hobbled over to the black-finish cabinet underneath the wide-screen television. It was packed full of video cassettes and DVDs, mostly American movies dubbed in Russian. He flipped through the movies casually, looking for something interesting. He turned back to Sean and Svyeta, holding up a copy of *Terminator 3*. "You like Schwarzenegger?"

Sean shrugged, not opening his eyes, and let his head fall back onto the leather couch. Viktor began pushing buttons on the VCR and DVD player, trying to come up with the right combination to make the system work. After a couple of minutes, he turned back to Sean.

"How is this thing turned on?" When Sean didn't reply, Viktor turned to glance at his friend who was lying still. He looked over at Svyeta and she nodded, mouthing "asleep" silently.

Viktor rose from his knees and walked quietly over to remove Sean's duffel bag that was still lying open on his lap, some clothing and a couple books spilling out. Viktor looked down curiously, moved the bag to the other side of the couch, then pulled out a video cassette and turned it over in his hands a couple times. Glancing again at Sean, he moved back to his position in front of the television and began searching for the instruction manual.

By the time Ryan McCaney and Svyeta began dishing out food at the table, Viktor had the tape playing. He'd never heard an English-language news broadcast before and was fascinated at the way the reporters' words jumped up and down. The cadence was almost lyrical – so different from the way Sean and Ryan spoke. He watched as the home video-quality recording of the scientists standing next to the large meteorite played across the screen.

"Hey," said Ryan as he scooped a ladle full of chili into a bowl, "do we get the news here?"

"Videotape from before."

"Yeka... Yekaterin....Yekaterinburg," he finally managed in his easy Southern drawl. "Isn't that about where we are?"

Viktor nodded enthusiastically. "We're right outside of Revda, which is a suburb of Yekaterinburg. The newscaster said that Ilya, or Elijah, crashed just a few hundred miles north of the city."

Sean opened his eyes abruptly, realizing that he'd been dozing. He focused on the images on the television – the scientists in their white, protective suits, tramping around the foliage next to the enormous rock.

"Wasn't it supposed to explode or something when it landed?" asked Ryan.

"It was," Sean said quietly, "but it slowed down once it broke through the atmosphere. It should have exploded into a million pieces, but it just crashed and rolled a little."

The four of them watched in silence as the broadcast continued. Finally, the report cut off and the screen dissolved into static. They continued to stare for almost a minute, the image of the giant unearthly rock turning over and over in their minds.

"That's when it all started, didn't it? That week when Ilya came down," Svyeta said.

"It must be responsible," Viktor said quietly, his voice suddenly sounding very deep. He turned to Sean. "Elijah has to be the reason for all this."

Sean nodded and leaned forward, still staring intently at the blank screen. It was supposed to have been such a monumental event, even before all the people started dying. The fact that an asteroid of such size was actually going to collide with Earth was, up until that point, the news of the century. Probably the most significant thing since the Apollo moon landing. His father had been so excited about all the possibilities – even the meteorite's fragments would be extremely important. Everyone had been hoping that the pieces would yield up some secrets about the universe. Never before had anyone been able to study such a large asteroid up close or even been able to predict with such certainty when the thing would come down – it was a fresh sample, untainted by the years. Luckily it hadn't been too big – otherwise, the crash might have been much more devastating. But, much smaller and they would have never even seen it coming. Jerry/Elijah was just right.

Sean looked over at Viktor, into the boy's large, dark brown eyes. He was chewing on his lip nervously as his mind raced back and forth. Sean could feel the excitement coming off him, the possibility of discovery. Suddenly he glanced up at Sean, the question hanging in his eyes.

The American boy rocked back and forth gently, his elbows on his knees. "It might kill us. The same thing could happen to us that happened to everybody else."

Viktor nodded and looked down, his large hands fidgeting as he concentrated. "Maybe, maybe… but, I think it would have already if it was going to. Distance or – how do you say? Closeness or, or – proximity!" He pronounced the word slowly. "Proximity didn't really have any effect on the rest of the world. Adults in America died just the same as people in Russia, even though we were closer. I think we would be okay."

Ryan stood silently, listening to the two boys. He set the pan down on the table. "Could we actually get to it? Do you know where it is?"

"The news person on the tape gave the longitude and latitude. We could find it on a map," Viktor said excitedly.

"I've got a GPS device – if it still works. I'm not sure about the satellites and all that," Ryan added.

"What are you talking about?" Svyeta asked.

"We could go find Ilya – it's still out there somewhere," Viktor said.

He turned back to Sean. "Don't you want to know? At least see it? Maybe your tricky eyes could see something."

Sean nodded and stopped rocking. They were in the area, it was only a little out of their way. Were they in any hurry anyway? It had already been weeks since his mother had died. There was no telling where Elizabeth was or if she was even still alive. She might have been captured by some gang too, there was no way to know. It was still going to take them almost another couple of months to get to California anyway.

He suddenly wondered what his father would do. Would he continue on? Try to get to his family as quickly as possible? Or, would he allow the detour for the sake of discovery – for science? Sean doubted that they would be able to find out anything from the big chunk of rock. They weren't scientists, they didn't have any specialized instruments to measure radiation or density or anything like that. Still, they were there – so close. They had the opportunity right in front of them. It wouldn't ever come again.

Sean could almost hear the excitement in his father's voice the first time that he'd come home and told the family about Jerry, how they'd discovered the asteroid coming for the planet. His mother had been terrified at first, asking Kevin if they were in danger. He'd smiled and reassured them, launching into a lightning fast explanation of trajectory and the speed of Earth that none of them had understood at all. His eyes were glowing as he spoke faster and faster. Finally, here was something real that he and his NASA colleagues could study – something close to home, not on some dead planet millions of miles away. Here was the opportunity to look at some piece of the universe that was coming right to them, something that may give some insight into how everything began or where it was going. Something that would validate his father's work and show all the critics of NASA that they were wrong, that there actually was something to be learned out there.

Sean looked over at Viktor and smiled faintly. He could feel just a glimmer of something awaken within himself, a spark of hope for the future. And he thought, maybe my dad isn't completely gone. Maybe he left a little bit of his curiosity behind for me. He would do this, I know he would. He wouldn't be able to resist.

"Let's go find Elijah."

CHAPTER THIRTY-NINE

A cool wind swept up the slope, causing the tree branches to sway gently, just as Sean reached the crest. Svyeta reached the top a few seconds later, stopping beside him to catch her breath. The deer trail that they had been following meandered through the copse of trees at the top of the hill and continued down into an open meadow of high grass. The ground in the meadow would most likely be covered by a couple inches of cold water and would be crunchy in parts where the ice was still thawing. Patches of snow clung to the exposed root networks deeper in the forest where the sun couldn't penetrate. Gray clouds hung over the expansive and wild forests as far as the eye could see in every direction.

Ryan McCaney crouched on the trail, halfway down the slope. He held the GPS device in the air, rotating occasionally as he deciphered the digital numbers on the display. The thermometer read 48 degrees Fahrenheit – certainly not typical mid-May weather for either South Carolina or California. The previous night had been cold, despite the three-season Marmot bags they'd slept in. Luckily, there hadn't been any snow, just a few showers during the early morning and late afternoon. Ryan took in a lungful of chilled, forest-scented air. He could almost pick out the smells of the different types of trees dotting the landscape. His heightened olfactory senses had seemed to come alive once they'd started hiking the previous morning and had probably saved them more than once. Both he and Sean had picked up a strong animal scent a few miles back and had to skirt around the area to avoid whatever it was. It could have been a deer like the ones they'd spotted earlier, but they didn't want to take the chance. Viktor had warned against a strong likelihood of bears or wolves in the area.

The Russian boy was having the most trouble of the four with the trek. He came through the trees a few minutes after Sean and Svyeta, leaning heavily on a stout walking stick he'd found at the house they'd stayed at outside of Revda. Despite the boy's difficulty with the wilderness trek and clearly evident exhaustion, Viktor never offered a word of complaint, just a weak smile as he carefully maneuvered his withered left leg. Ryan figured they'd covered twenty miles in the last day and a half and the strain was beginning to tell on all three kids.

Sean stood behind Ryan, surveying the meadow and stretch of forest off to their right. This was entirely unlike any Boy Scout hike he had ever been on. Any of the areas where he'd camped in the San Gabriel Mountains of southern California were usually well trafficked by other outdoor enthusiasts. The constant warm weather also helped to make his experiences there rather tame and controlled. He always had the feeling that if ever he were to get lost or injured, an emergency helicopter was only a few minutes away. Here, the land had a savage and forlorn quality to it. Once they'd parked the SUV, after it had gone as far as the narrow dirt road allowed, they'd entered into another world, seemingly untouched by any humans. The group had been quickly immersed in a land of hills and trees with no buildings, signs, wires, telephone poles or overhead airplanes in sight. Sean felt as if they had dropped out of the sky onto another planet – one that was governed by altogether different rules.

He had been worried that, as they set off that morning after a welcome breakfast of instant oatmeal, they were going in the wrong direction or had missed the landing area entirely. But, a few hours before they stopped for lunch, Ryan had come across an immense gash in the earth. It was roughly a football field long and almost half as wide. An entire area of trees had been pulverized and mashed together, forming a depression in the ground over twenty feet deep. Some of the surrounding foliage looked as though it had been scorched by an intense heat. The scientists on the news report had said that Jerry/Elijah had bounced and rolled before finally coming to a halt. The hole in the ground told them that they were at least on the right track.

His walking stick thudded against the wet ground as Viktor

came to a halt right behind Sean and Svyeta. He let out a wearied breath and waited calmly while Sean and Ryan sniffed the air. At least, that's what he called it. The day before, he'd burst into laughter several times when they'd stopped, held their noses to the wind and occasionally turned in various directions, just like bloodhounds. He hadn't been laughing as much today because of the pain coursing through his body. His muscle tone and coordination had come quite a long way over the past several weeks, but he was still in no shape for a cross-country hike. Especially for one that was turning out to be much longer than they had originally planned.

"It should be another couple miles that way," Ryan gestured across the meadow, "to the northwest. We're almost there guys."

Sean looked in the direction he'd pointed, squinting in concentration. "There it is!" he shouted suddenly, pointing at the forest. "That's it!"

Ryan stood and looked in the direction he was pointing. "That could just be a group of trees."

"But, see how long it is? And the top is rounded – a group of trees wouldn't look like that at the top."

Ryan nodded. "Could be."

"And what does that look like, a couple inches to the right?" Sean pointed, but Viktor and Svyeta couldn't see a thing. It all looked like a sea of green trees.

"Is that... are those windows?"

"It looks like a truck or maybe a building or something. The team would have set up some portable structures, wouldn't they?" Sean asked.

"Guess we'll be finding out pretty soon."

- -

The meadow they'd crossed an hour ago had been covered in several inches of water, just as Sean had expected. Their boots were soaked now and the wind had picked up. Sean pulled the collar of his coat up higher as they crossed over some fallen logs into an area of dense, gray trees. Staring at the tall, somber pines as they barely swayed in the wind, he suddenly recalled an old Russian fairytale that Viktor had related during the drive a few days ago. It was about a group of travelers that had been enchanted by a *Rusalka*, a beguiling and dangerous fresh-water siren that was said to inhabit the lakes and rivers of the wild. The group had followed her voice for days, believing it to be a lost maiden in distress, until the *Rusalka* finally led them to their deaths. Viktor had said that Russian folklore was filled with such tales of forest spirits. In fact, some people still believed they existed and that they had only been pushed back into the wild by the spread of humanity.

Feeling the weight of the almost oppressive forest silence bearing down on him, Sean eyed the dark shadows between the trees suspiciously. His mind began to race with ideas of what could be lurking in those forest depths – wild animals tracking their progress, waiting for the perfect opportunity to pounce. Or, possibly, other people who had arrived at the crash site before them, anxious to protect their prize. The dankness of wet soil and rotting wood filled his nostrils, making him almost giddy with the desire to slowly sink down into the dark rich earth and sleep.

The trail they were following became gradually more and more obscured by hanging foliage and fallen trees. It split off into a couple of different directions, but both of these appeared to quickly terminate just a few meters into the undergrowth.

Ryan quickly consulted the GPS device, then began forcing his way through a thin wall of dead twigs and branches. The other three stepped carefully behind him, attempting to avoid getting scratched by the surrounding gnarled, claw-shaped limbs.

His hands held high in front of his face to block any branches that might swing back to slap him from Ryan's passage, Sean stepped over a thick, fallen tree. He could feel Viktor right at his back, could hear his labored breathing as he tried to balance in the crowded thicket while keeping up his forward pace. Svyeta was right behind Viktor, helping to push branches out of his way. For a second, Sean thought he could hear Viktor's heartbeat quickening, the soft thuds followed by an almost imperceptible sound of rushing liquid as the organ rhythmically pumped blood through his body. But, he then realized that it was his own heartbeat he heard, the pounding becoming louder and faster as he trudged forward, deeper into the forest.

Sean saw Ryan un-shoulder his rifle and hold it out in front of him to help push away some of the branches that clung to their clothing and backpacks. The boy glanced up to the top of the trees, trying to locate the sun. Even if it hadn't been covered by the sky of thick clouds, the source of warmth and light would have been difficult to find through the thick branches and blanket of pine needles.

The sharp stub of a broken branch poked Sean in the side as he passed, causing him to jump back and nearly knock Viktor over. The Russian boy's large, ungainly hands came up to steady Sean, helping him regain his balance. Despite the wet cold, he felt sweat trickle down his temple as he glanced back at Viktor, then put another foot forward to continue following McCaney, who was already several meters ahead. Fear of separation instantly flashed through Sean's mind and he surged forward, attempting to quickly close the distance to the Marine. Viktor and Svyeta followed almost as quickly, the same sense of dread of being lost in the tangled prison coursing through their already clenched stomachs.

Sean frantically pushed away clumps of pine needles that clung to the branches in front of his face. He inhaled deeply, feeling almost unable to pull in enough oxygen. The ominous trees surrounding them seemed to be suffocating him, their weight and smell weighing down each step as he struggled onward. He felt Viktor's hand reach out to touch his backpack as the boy attempted to steady himself and keep up.

Suddenly, Ryan disappeared from sight altogether, having just stepped behind a thick tree trunk a little further ahead. The word "No!" screamed through Sean's mind and he sprinted forward, ignoring the sharp branches that clawed at him as he passed. He heard Viktor grunt in pain behind him as he stumbled on a tree root. Sean turned to see the boy leaning against the base of a tree with Svyeta trying to get his arm over her shoulder. She glanced up at Sean, weariness etched into her features. Her eyes pleaded for him to stop, to make it all stop, but Sean couldn't. He had to keep going and find Ryan and get out of the dark, clinging forest. All of his senses were filled with its smell, its dank coldness. All he could see were dark green swaths of vegetation and endless grayish-brown branches all around him.

Beginning to panic, Sean sped up and swatted at the branches reaching out to him. He couldn't see Ryan anywhere and began leaping over fallen trees and elaborate, exposed root systems as he rushed to escape the forest. Ahead of him, he thought he could see a lightening between the trees, a diffused brightness that beckoned to him, promising release from the dank heaviness that was weighing him down. He focused on that growing light and pushed forward, faintly aware of Viktor and Svyeta struggling to keep up several yards behind him.

Just as he was about to give voice to the terror that was building inside him, the fear of losing Ryan entirely and being locked in the clinging forest forever, Sean burst out of the trees at the edge of a clearing. Cloud-diffused sunlight shone brightly into his face like someone had just turned on an overhead lamp. Once his eyes adjusted, he was able to see the short, tough grass that spread from under his feet. The clearing sloped downward and to the left. Sean glanced at Ryan who was standing a few feet away and staring. Sean slowly followed his gaze. Beginning just a dozen or so paces ahead, a thirty foot high rock cliff extended through the middle of the clearing.

CHAPTER FORTY

Suddenly, Sean realized his mistake. The huge rock stretching out in front of him was no cliff – it was Jerry/Elijah. The meteorite's surface was strangely blackened and porous like hardened lava, with intricate pockets and perforations dotting its entire expanse. It was potato-shaped – long, almost rectangular – and stretched roughly 450 feet across, thirty feet high, about fifty feet deep and sat atop a group of flattened trees. There was a wide, muddy gash in the earth right in front of it where it had skidded to a halt. A clearing had definitely existed here before the space rock had crashed, but it was even larger now, the trees on the right side having been severely cropped by the meteorite's passage.

Sean heard Viktor and Svyeta emerge from the forest behind him. He reached back toward them, unable to remove his eyes from the awesome sight stretching before him. Svyeta took his hand and squeezed. Viktor limped forward and gripped Sean's shoulder, leaning for support. The Russian boy had a long, red scratch down the side of his face and was breathing heavily, but seemed alright otherwise. He and Svyeta now stared, transfixed, at the immense meteorite sitting in front of them.

Two large, transport helicopters sat on the far right side of the grassy area. Their twin sets of rotor blades posed motionlessly over the short grass. Several metal storage containers were positioned between the helicopters with cargo nets and wires lying strewn about everywhere. A camp of temporary housing was set up opposite the meteorite on the right side of the little clearing. Various types of scientific equipment – computer monitors, scanning devices, radiation detectors – sat in the back of jeeps and on wheeled carts. Not a soul was in sight. A cool wind blew across the area and rustled the trees.

Without a word, the four began walking forward simultaneously, their eyes still fixed on the otherworldly chunk of rock looming before them. Sean could smell its charred surface and could see cavernous depressions in its face large enough to hide a fully grown person. Portions of it were smooth with veins of dark brown iron grazing the surface. But, its most impressive feature by far was its sheer size. Although it did resemble a small cliff face, the meteorite didn't extend into the ground, but rather sat on top of it – mashing trees and moist earth into a pulp beneath its immense weight.

They stopped in front of Jerry/Elijah, their feet touching the edge of the ravaged ground that had halted the meteorite. Staring up at the face of it, they could see that it rested just a few feet below the level of the rest of the clearing, having carved away the top soil as it slid. Sean remembered reading in his history class about how glaciers would scrape tons of dirt up as they expanded, slowly transporting nutrient-rich soil to other parts of a continent over millennia. He had been unable to imagine how something could really be so large as to move the top layer of dirt over several miles. Now, seeing the deep swath cut in the earth by the meteorite's passage and imagining the pile of soil and pulverized trees on the opposite side, he understood.

Sean looked over at Viktor, then back up at the monolithic meteorite. This is from outer space, he thought to himself – this rock is not from our planet. He stared in amazement at its immensity, the overwhelming reality of its presence, towering in front of him. Then, he found his feet acting almost of their own volition as they stepped into the loose earth that sloped down toward the base of the meteorite. He walked the few yards slowly as Viktor, Svyeta and Ryan remained behind, watching him.

His hand reached up and touched the rough, blackened rock. It felt just as he had expected: sharp and crusty in some parts and smoother in others from where the heat of the atmosphere had fused portions together. Sean took his hand away and stared at the dozens of tiny imprints of the meteorite's face in his skin and the few bits of loose crust that had stuck to his palm. "I've touched another world," he mumbled softly to himself.

A wave of dizziness passed over Sean and he quickly reached

up to steady himself, placing his hand again on the craggy, black surface of the meteorite. His eyes refused to focus, blurring his vision. He remained leaning against the rock, hanging his head down as he tried to regain his balance. Must be the hiking, he thought. Not enough water. Dad always told me that I never drink enough water.

Gradually, the sensation passed and Sean raised his head, pushing himself away from Jerry/Elijah. As he did so, he caught movement out of the corner of his eye to the right. Turning his head, he saw something coming out of the edge of the forest on the other side of the clearing.

In alarm, Sean turned to his friends behind him, to shout a warning. Just as the sound was about to leave his mouth, the words caught in his dry throat. The slope behind him was empty – Viktor, Svyeta and Ryan were gone. Sean's eyes darted in panic to the wall of trees through which they'd entered the clearing only minutes before, but there was no sign of them. Had they already run away, Sean thought, without a word? How could they have moved so fast?

His feet slipped in the soft, loose earth as he whirled around to face the approaching creature. It was a man, he could see that clearly now. Sean began to scramble back up the slope, his hands grasping at clods of dirt and tufts of grass as his eyes remained locked on the man moving steadily toward him.

The man was of medium height, with brown curly hair, and was wearing a light jacket and some rumpled-looking khakis. His hand reached up quickly to adjust the thin-rimmed glasses that sat perched on his nose. Immediately, Sean stopped crawling and stared in shock at the approaching man.

Impossible, Sean thought. It can't be, something's wrong, it can't be. He opened his mouth to yell, to scream, to say something, anything that would help him make sense of this. Instead, all that came out was a whimper as tears began to slowly flow from his eyes.

The man smiled and continued walking straight toward Sean as he sat frozen in the shadow of the huge meteorite. The small smile remained on his thin face as he stepped carefully over the torn chunks of dirt before stopping just a few feet from the boy. Through tears, Sean looked up at the man smiling down at him, extending his hand. An emotion-filled sob tore through his chest as he reached up eagerly to grasp the hand of his father.

CHAPTER FORTY-ONE

Sean was pulled up from his position on the ground into his father's welcoming arms. Burying his head in his father's chest, he let the sobbing come full force now, giving in completely to the pain, fear and confusion that was racing through his mind, pounding relentlessly on the inside of his skull. His hands reached up to squeeze his father's arms, holding him tight out of fear that at any moment he would disappear, leaving him all alone again.

His father continued to hold him close as his crying gradually ceased, the tears drying up. Kevin straightened up, his hands on his son's shoulders, and looked down into the boy's face. Sean stared with puffy eyes at his father, still gripping his arms tightly.

"Dad?" Sean asked in a weak voice.

"Yeah, son?" Kevin replied. His voice was exactly as Sean remembered, the same voice that he'd been hearing occasionally over the past few weeks – but then only in his imagination. It usually came as words of advice or in the form of a memory of some joke his father had told. But now, the sound was in his ears, not his mind. He could feel his father's voice and the vibrations of the sound in his chest as real as he'd ever felt anything before.

"Dad, you, you're supposed to…" Sean swallowed another wave of tears that was threatening to overtake him. "You died. We covered you up and… and… we cremated you, just like, just like you'd said…"

"Shh, shh, son." Kevin pulled Sean close, holding him as he cried again. Sean quickly tried to regain his composure, pushing himself away from his father's chest and wiping his eyes, but still holding onto his coat sleeve with one hand.

He looked up into his father's smiling face again. He hadn't changed at all! His father looked like it had been only yesterday when he'd last walked around the hotel room, had last joked about his courtship with Sean's mother, had last laughed. But, now, his eyes were different somehow. Sean looked closely as he and his father continued to stand in the clearing, holding on to each other. His eyes weren't sad anymore, Sean thought. The last day or so of his father's life had been one of such sadness and grief. They'd learned of his mother's death only the night before and felt the terror of Elizabeth being left on her own. Sean remembered his father's attempts to prepare him for the inevitable – on what had turned out to be the last day of his life. He remembered that his father had found some small degree of peace at the end, in the knowledge that, for him at least, it would soon be over. But, he also remembered the fear and sheer helplessness that his father had felt at not being able to secure the safety of his children before he left. Now, in these eyes, these new eyes that were so familiar, Sean didn't see any of that grief. All he saw was happiness and contentment. And peace.

How is this possible, Sean wondered. A strange mixture of fear and hope passed through him as his mind began to wander through the possibilities, carefully grasping at each potential theory as if it were a tenuous lifeline being dangled to him as he hung over the edge of a deep yawning precipice.

Sean hadn't looked at the body's face. He hadn't wanted to, not wanting to remember his father as a corpse, but rather as a living, breathing man. That was it, that had to be it, Sean thought. His father hadn't really been dead, he'd only been in some sort of coma and the body that they'd come back and cremated had been someone else's! Somehow, his father had woken up and left and had been able to follow them here! Or, it was possible that whatever had given all of them their newfound powers had revived his father, had brought him back to life somehow. And, if he was alive now, then it was possible that his mother was alive! Maybe, even now, she was with Elizabeth, trying to contact them...

Sean looked up at his father, who was still quietly watching him, a faint smile on his face. Kevin hadn't said anything more since quieting the boy a few moments earlier. He wasn't offering any explanations as to how he got here, how he was still alive. He was just standing there, his eyes full of love and understanding.

"You aren't real, are you?"

Kevin's soft smile didn't waver as he continued staring at his son, standing in the shadow of the monolithic rock. Sean saw a darkness, a twinge pass through his father's eyes. It was as if a painful memory had just flashed through his mind and he was busily trying to push it away, barring it from entering his consciousness again. But, all the previous emotions were still held in his eyes too – compassion, understanding. Sean remembered that this was the same look that his father had given him on their last day together as they walked on the street. He'd begged Sean with his eyes to understand that he was going to die and that he wouldn't be able to protect him any longer. And that this – his helplessness, the fact that he was going to leave his son and daughter all alone in the world —was, above all things, the greatest regret of his life. His greatest failure. He'd silently asked Sean to shoulder this grief, to survive and carry the memory of this pain because Kevin no longer could.

Reaching up to stroke Sean's hair softly, Kevin said, "Come on, we've got some work to do, okay?"

Not waiting for an answer, Kevin walked quickly over to the meteorite, pulling out a small black bag from his jacket pocket. Sean stood dumbly watching him, unable to focus on any one thought for more than a few seconds. Kevin retrieved a hammer and a clear plastic container, setting the latter in the soft dirt at his feet before starting to chip away at the craggy rock.

"Could you come here and hold the samples?" Kevin asked as he squinted through his thin, wire-frame glasses.

Sean obediently walked over to stand beside his father, staring dazedly at the area where the hammer struck rhythmically. "What are you doing?"

"We need to collect a few crust samples first. It'll give us a basic idea of Jerry's composition and of the heat that it underwent upon entering the atmosphere. We'll have to find a larger drill to obtain some samples closer to the core, but I think the lead crash site team left enough equipment to work with."

The young teenage boy looked over his shoulder again at the spot where Viktor, Svyeta and Ryan had been only a few minutes before. The entire clearing was deserted. The tents, storage containers and helicopters stood abandoned. All Sean could hear was the wind blowing softly through the surrounding forest and the soft strike of the hammer.

"What are we doing here?"

Kevin stopped chipping at the rock and dropped a few black chunks into the plastic container at his feet, then knelt down to face Sean.

"Son, where are we?" he said, staring intently into the boy's face.

Sean thought for a second before answering. "I think we're in Russia..."

"Russia, right. Where in Russia?"

"Central Russia. Near Yekaterinburg."

"Where near Yekaterinburg?

"About two-hundred miles north north-west of the city."

"Exactly. And what's here? What is right here?" continued his father, excitedly.

"It's the crash site. Where Jerry landed," Sean answered slowly.

"That's it, Sean, that's it," Kevin said taking hold of Sean's arms. "We're at the crash site of a huge meteorite that just dropped out of the sky and landed on our planet. And now, you and I have the chance to study it, to look at it like no one else has before. What could we learn?"

"Things about the universe, about our galaxy, the history of our solar system," Sean said, speaking more quickly now. The familiar words felt so right, like a comforting litany that had once, long ago, dispelled fear and doubt, leading him and his father onward. "It could help us find out about how the planets and stars were formed. And, maybe, about how we came to be here."

Kevin stood up and held out the hammer, his broad smile beaming down at Sean. "That's it, my boy. The sky's the limit with this one. Now, let's quit standing around and get to work."

Sean stared up at his father, vaguely aware of the soft earth beneath his feet and the cool wind blowing the clouds through the sky. This is my father, Sean thought, staring at the man in front of him. But, my father's dead. He glanced again around the silent clearing, noting the position of Jerry/Elijah in relation to the trees and the equipment brought here by the first team to the site. I'm thinking clearly, Sean thought. I'm not dreaming. I think that I'd like to move my head and it happens – I can do it. I think that I'd like to stand up and walk over there and I do it. I'm really here. And it seems like my father's here too. But, he can't be. He can't be, but here he is. Somehow, this is possible. Right now, we're here and this is possible. In this moment, this space, this can all be happening. In this moment, I'm here with my father and we're going to do what we both came here to do. We're going to study Jerry.

Sean reached up and took the hammer from his father's hand.

CHAPTER FORTY-TWO

Sean couldn't tell how long they'd been working. At first, it had started to seem like a long time. He expected that he would soon be getting tired or hungry, but just as soon as he'd thought this, his body was filled with renewed energy and he was able to plunge into the work again. Within a few minutes, he was almost laughing at himself for thinking that he was growing weary. A few times, Sean looked up at the sky, expecting that it would be getting dark any moment, but it never did. The cold, cloud-filled heavens never darkened, but only turned over and over as the wind softly blew.

They'd accomplished quite a bit in a seemingly short amount of time. Already, they'd been able to take a few deep, core samples with a diamond-tipped drill they found in one of the tents. The first team to the site had brought quite a bit of geological equipment, from picks and chisels to elaborate imaging systems complete with ground penetrating radar. Kevin showed Sean how to use it all. This was the first time that he'd been able to work so closely with his father on a project. Usually, Kevin had just given him a cursory overview of what he was spending his time on at work. But now, they were doing actual field research, collecting data and forming some basic hypotheses as to the origins of the enormous meteorite. Sean was impressed with his father's knowledge of and comfort with all the complex geological equipment. Not for the first time in his life, he wondered if there was anything that his father didn't know.

As they sat at a portable work station just outside one of the tents, Kevin pointed to a few lines of data on the screen. "See, these ones here – no matches. It definitely has all the characteristics of some type of ore, but nothing that we've found here on Earth."

Sean blinked. "What does that mean?"

Kevin chuckled as he continued to stare at the computer screen. "Well, it could mean quite a few things. First, that these elements are in fact located somewhere on Earth, but we just haven't discovered them yet. Or, they don't exist at all here, but do in some of the other planets and asteroids in our solar system. Third, there's the possibility that this meteorite arrived here from somewhere outside our solar system, where these elements do exist. Or, it could mean that we just don't have any idea what we're doing and I've made a mistake somewhere."

Sean looked over at his smiling father. He was just as he remembered him: curious, overwhelmingly intelligent, but, at the same time, humble and always willing to admit the limitations of knowledge – the consummate scientist.

Suddenly, Kevin's smile disappeared as he winced and pressed the palm of his hand against his temple. A faint moan escaped his lips as he bent over, holding his head.

"Dad, what's wrong?"

"My head... just a headache... been staring at the screen too long..."

Sean put his hand on his father's shoulder, feeling panic start to rise within himself.

Kevin sat up slowly, hands still pressed against his head. "Okay, okay, it's going away, it's a little better." He looked at his young son whose face was awash with concern. "That's quite a migraine, but it feels like it's subsiding. It just came all the sudden—"

Kevin gasped and slid out of his chair to the ground, his fingers white from squeezing his head. Sean gripped his father's jacket as he slid to the ground and rolled over onto his back. "It feels like my head's going to explode..." Kevin managed to say between clenched teeth.

"NO!" Sean screamed as he knelt helplessly beside his father. "You can't die again! You can't leave me again! You're going to be okay, Dad, it'll go away, just hang on a minute, the headaches will go away!"

Kevin stared up into his son's eyes as he fought against the pain. "What's going on, Sean? What's happening?"

Sean couldn't remember exactly when he'd started crying, but he now noticed that painful sobs were causing his body to tremble as they tore through his throat.

"Nothing, Dad," he managed to say, "You're going to be okay, you'll be okay."

Kevin gasped as a new spasm of pain coursed through his head. He opened his eyes slowly and looked intently into his son's face.

"What's happening, Sean? Do you know what's happening to me?"

Sean clung to his father, rocking slowly back and forth as he choked down tears, shaking his head.

Kevin spoke again, more insistently this time, "I need you to tell me what's going on. You know. What's going to happen, Sean?"

All the merriment of the past few hours had suddenly drained away. Everything had changed again, so quickly, in the last few moments, making it seem as though none of the experiences they'd shared that afternoon had actually happened. Suddenly, it seemed, they were back in the hotel room, his father lying on the bed, cold and motionless, with Sean staring at his body with no idea in the world as to what he was going to do or how he was going to live without his father, all alone in a foreign country. Why is this happening, Sean thought. Why has my father been brought back only to leave me again? Wasn't once enough? He'd seen so much death over the past few weeks, why did he have to see more?

"You're dying, Dad. You're going to die."

Kevin looked up at the sky above him and exhaled slowly. Then, turning back to Sean, he said, "That's right. I'm going to die. But why?"

Sean blinked at the tears in his eyes. "It's because of the headaches. You get the headaches, then you die."

"Yes, but why? What happened?"

Glancing around the clearing, Sean's eyes were once again drawn to the enormous monolithic rock sitting several dozen yards away. "It's Jerry or Elijah – Ilya… once it landed, everyone started getting headaches and dying."

Holding his head carefully, Kevin pulled himself up into a

sitting position with Sean's help. He took off his glasses and rubbed his eyes, breathing slowly as he tried to clear his aching head. "But, you didn't die. Why didn't you die, Sean?"

"I don't know. None of us know. We kids – we didn't die. Just the adults. Jerry killed all the adults."

"But, you had headaches too, didn't you?" Kevin asked.

"Yes, I think we all did. But, they didn't kill us kids. What's happening Dad?"

Kevin slowly pulled his hand away from his face, keeping his head very still to avoid jostling it and aggravating his headache. He started speaking haltingly, as if struggling to find the words, but as he continued, they came more quickly.

"My brain is... is expanding. It's changing – getting just a little bit larger and it's developing more folds and wrinkles, increasing its surface area. New pathways are literally being opened up. It's making me smarter – a lot smarter."

Suddenly, Sean could literally see exactly what his father was talking about. He wasn't sure whether the images actually appeared right in front of his eyes like a television screen or whether they were just in his mind, but he really saw what was happening: a detailed cross-section of the brain beginning to change, ever so slightly. Its already wrinkled surface almost visibly pulsated as it began growing larger, the tiny folds deepening.

"The entire brain gets just a little larger, just enough to unlock and increase its already powerful capacity. That's what happened to you – all of you children."

Sean nodded, still seeing the image clearly, watching the brain change slowly, new permutations gradually developing across its surface. "But, why didn't we die too?"

"Because you weren't adults yet. Technically, you're only an adult once your skull is fully developed. There are several bones that make up the skull, which are held together by soft sutures. These sutures are not fully fused when we're born so that the skull can be slightly malleable at birth, in order to fit through the birth canal. They become fully fused at adulthood, usually around eighteen to twenty years of age. Jerry affected us all in exactly the same way – expanding our brains. But, only the children, whose skulls still had a little room to move and grow, were able to survive this. Those of us adults whose skulls were solid weren't able to withstand the growth. Our brains pressed against the inside of our solid skulls, causing hemorrhaging and... death."

Sean watched as the brain continued to grow, pressing against the hard inner walls of the skull. As it did so, small areas of red began to pool and expand, until the brain stopped growing and was filled with dozens of clots. Then, the image disappeared.

Kevin sat peacefully on the grass as he watched his son's thoughts dance across his face.

"That's how you're all able to have these wonderful new abilities now. Your brains were transformed in such a way so that you can now understand more about the world around you – and control some of it. It's not magic – none of it's magic. It's all done through basic scientific principles, irrefutable laws of the universe, most of which we just didn't know or fully understand yet. You can move things by just thinking about them – how do you do it?"

Sean had barely moved a muscle since the image of the brain had first appeared. He was still kneeling, his hand on his father's shoulder, staring transfixed into his eyes as he listened. At Kevin's question, he seemed to come out of a daze and looked around again quickly, as if trying to remind himself where he was.

"I, I don't know. I just think about something moving and... and it does. But, it only works with smaller things, I can't move heavier stuff."

"Yes, but how does it happen? What do you think about, what do you sense is going on when something moves from one side of the room to the other without you touching it?"

Sean swallowed before continuing. "I feel, when I concentrate on a rock or a plate or something, I feel like there are all these tiny little pieces in it, all of them moving very fast. Then, I think about where I want the thing to go and I concentrate on all the tiny pieces in that spot on the floor or in my hand. Then... I don't know, it's like there's almost a button that I push in my mind, like I just turn something on in both the object and where I want it to be. I make all the little pieces attracted to each other somehow, like a magnet. But, I have to do it gradually, just a little at a time or they smack together too quickly. But, I don't know how I can feel all those little pieces – the molecules and atoms, I guess. And I don't know how I can press that button and make them pull toward each other."

Kevin nodded. "It's basic electromagnetism. You're using the electrons in the atoms to pull toward each other, making it seem like something's flying through the air, rather than what's really happening. It's just moving toward another magnetically polarized area in a very controlled way. See, these are basic laws, basic building blocks for the physical world around us. Now, you just have the ability to know some of them – and to control them."

Sean nodded as he tried to imagine all the swarming electrons in the objects around him, inside him. It was almost overwhelming at first, thinking of all the trillions of tiny pieces moving in completely erratic and unpredictable ways. But, as he continued to concentrate and began to relax somewhat, they all seemed to slow down a little, just enough for him to have a better sense of where they were. It was almost like a dance of living water, like little eddies in a river swirling around millions of unseen rocks.

"But, what about non-physical abilities like Viktor's? He just knows things – he can remember everything he reads or sees. He's like a computer."

Kevin smiled and nodded. The thought of how much the same his father was struck Sean – the way he smiled, the movement of his mouth when he spoke. He even taught Sean in the same way that he had when they were at home tinkering around in the garage or hiking in the mountains. He kept asking Sean questions to make him think, to solve the problems himself, each question guiding Sean closer and closer to the answer. But, this whole experience was different somehow. Right now it was different. While they'd been working on collecting and analyzing samples from the meteorite, Kevin had been excited, practically bouncing around with the joy of discovery – just like he always had when he was working or learning something new. But, now, he was just telling Sean how it all worked. He wasn't discovering it with him, but rather, explaining something that he himself already knew, that he seemed to have known and understood for a long time.

"To each person is given a certain talent. Just like with other talents that everyone has like intelligence or athletic ability, each person has a certain degree of knowledge of how to influence the world around them. Some have a great deal of natural talent, some less. But, just like the ability to run great distances, for example, you can increase your talent and ability with time and practice. You may start with the ability to do something very small, but over the course of your life, you can develop this talent so that you are able to do truly amazing things."

"It works the same with Viktor. His brain has been changed in such a way that he understands how to learn things better than most people. He acquires and processes information much more rapidly and efficiently which allows him to understand and remember many, many things. As he continues using this talent that he's been given, he will get even better at it. He might even reach the point someday when he knows and understands just about everything there is out there. As long as he has access to information, he'll be able to remember it – and understand it."

"His body works better now," said Sean excitedly. "He said that he used to barely be able to walk and couldn't control his arms and hands very well. But, he just has a limp now. He's not strong or fast or anything, but he's okay. Was he healed somehow?"

"The same power that changed Viktor's and everyone's brains repaired damage that had been done when he was a baby. He suffered from cerebral palsy. This brain damage had left Viktor's ability to think and reason intact, but had prevented his limbs from developing normally and from receiving the right impulses and instructions. Now, the parts of his brain that regulate movement and muscle control have been changed to that of any regular person, so he can begin to develop his strength and coordination as most of us have from birth."

Sean nodded again, still holding onto the fabric of his father's jacket. "And Jerry did all this? How? Is it some kind of radiation?"

Kevin turned and pointed toward the large, mountain-like meteorite. "Look over there."

At first, Sean didn't see anything. He wasn't exactly sure what he was supposed to be looking for. Then, suddenly, he noticed movement on the rock face of the meteorite about three

ANDREW GRIFFARD

feet from the ground. It looked like some large insect or bird was crawling out of the craggy surface. Kevin stood and pulled Sean up with him, leading him toward the meteorite.

As they walked closer, Sean saw that it wasn't a creature at all, but rather a white, crystal substance that was slowly oozing out of the meteorite at about knee level. It looked almost like half-melted snow that had been refrozen and was forming thousands of tiny ice crystals. It leaked onto the soft, wet dirt and began to pile up. As it began to form a small heap, it more closely resembled some kind of sharp-edged quartz or other type of milky white stone.

Suddenly, the now familiar rushing sensation filled Sean's ears and mind, more forcefully than ever before, so much that it was almost painful. Gradually, he became more used to it, the feeling of an immense, powerful river flowing through his head, delivering and taking away bits of memory and thought like ice floes in spring runoff. He stared transfixed at the substance as it continued to pour out of the rock.

Kevin knelt on one knee to look more closely at the substance as it collected on the soft ground. Sean stared intently, faintly aware of some kind of force he could feel emanating from the substance. He realized that he had an almost overwhelming desire to put some of the crystal snow in his mouth, just to taste it, despite the fact that he was sure its sharp, jagged edges would slice his tongue to pieces.

"What is this?" Sean asked, staring intently as the mound began to grow.

"It's the source of the headaches, the source of your new abilities, the reason that everything here has changed now. For that reason, it's called the Source. It's what Jerry was sent here to deliver."

CHAPTER FORTY-THREE

Sean knelt down in the soft earth, watching in fascination as the white, liquid crystal substance continued pouring from the meteorite. There was no smell to it and only a barely perceptible sound of friction as it continued piling up. A minute later, it stopped gushing from the meteorite, leaving a two-foot high pile that, rather than reflecting the diffused sunlight trying to poke through the clouds, seemed to glow from somewhere deep within.

The boy held his hands outstretched, almost basking in the warmth of the Source like a campfire. It wasn't emanating any heat that Sean could feel, but there was a definite energy pulsating from it. He could sense it like it was a wall, almost like a magnetic field of some sort or an increase in sound volume the closer he moved. As he watched, the pile looked like it was getting smaller, as if it were melting. At first, Sean thought it was his imagination, but within a few seconds, he could tell that the pile was definitely shrinking.

"What's happening? It's disappearing!"

"No," Kevin said as he too stared at the white, crystalline substance. "It's seeping into the ground. It'll travel to the center of the Earth and become part of the planet. That way, everyone around the world will be able to feel and benefit from its presence equally."

Sean nodded, but he didn't understand. Not about the Source, not how it had changed them all or why any of this was happening in the first place. He especially didn't understand how he was with his father now, talking to him, after having just cremated his body only a few days before. As the pile continued to shrink away, all the questions continued to swirl around in his mind, effectively paralyzing him and preventing him from doing anything except staring.

Finally, the last trace of it slipped away into the dark soft soil. Sean looked up and stared around dazedly as if just coming out of a dream. The rushing sensation was gone and all he could hear now were the faint breeze and rustle of the tree branches surrounding the clearing. Kevin, still staring intently at the spot where the white substance had been only moments before, leaned forward and sunk his right hand into the soft soil. When he pulled it back out, his hand was balled into a fist.

"This part is for you. I want you to keep it safe. Someone will be coming for it someday, but I want you to hold on to it until then."

Kevin opened his fist and dropped a palm-sized, smooth crystal into Sean's outstretched hand. It was hard, unlike the white substance had been, but not sharp at all. It was almost clear in some parts and a dense milky-white in others. It was shapeless – just a chunk of hard, white crystal.

Sean looked up into his father's eyes. He didn't know why, but he suddenly felt incredibly, almost overwhelmingly, sad. His father simply returned his gaze, his mouth held in his usual confident, but warm, half-smile. There were still millions of questions that Sean wanted to ask, but at this moment there was only one that he could concentrate on, one that stole away all his concentration and very breath. But, it was the one, most of all that he didn't want to ask, because he feared that he already knew the answer.

"You're going to – you're going to leave again, aren't you?"

Not on that day on the Moscow street, not even on that last night as Kevin had related to him all the most precious memories of his life had Sean seen his father cry. Nor did he now. But, Sean thought he saw his dad, for just a split second, almost blink away a tear as it threatened to fall from his eye. Sean wondered briefly what would happen were any tear to fall – would it change who his father was or who he had been? In those last few days Kevin had been able to accept his fate. Sean knew it was partly because he felt it was inevitable – an entirely foreign power that he was unable to stop. But, mostly, Sean knew that he had come to accept his own fate because of the death of his wife. His life had simply ceased to have meaning or value for him once she was gone. He had to trust that his children would be safe, that somehow they would be able to find each other in the new world that the meteorite had created. But Kevin was no longer a part of that world and had no place in it. And now, Sean saw that same familiar acceptance in his father's eye. This was something that was going to happen, something entirely beyond his power. But now, Sean hoped, at least his father would have some kind of understanding why this had all happened and that this understanding would help make the pain a little less.

Kevin pulled Sean close to him in a tight hug. The boy felt himself shaking with sobs as he cried tears for them both, for his mother, for Elizabeth, for all of them – all those who had died and especially for all those who had been left behind.

CHAPTER FORTY-FOUR

Sean was dreaming. At least, that's what he assumed was the reason for his inability to move as he stood several yards away from the large meteorite. He was staring at the body of his father lying still on the ground. Only moments before, Sean vaguely remembered, they'd been standing together, his father hugging him. But, this now definitely felt like a dream. His limbs were almost weightless and occasionally the world would spin around without him moving or doing anything at all. Suddenly, he saw his father move.

That's how it appeared at first, but when Sean looked closer he could see that his father hadn't moved at all. He looked dead. Exactly as he'd imagined him looking under the sheet that day when they'd taken him to the park across the street from the hotel and cremated him, just like he'd wanted – a Viking funeral. Slowly, his father started to sit up.

At the same time, he was still lying on the ground. There were two of him. Sean tried to blink, unsuccessfully, in his dream. The result was that he just closed his eyes for several seconds, preventing him from seeing anything. Once he finally got his eyes to open again, his father was standing up, rising out of his own body which still lay motionless on the ground.

Sean watched as his father turned away from the meteorite, seemingly oblivious to his son's presence, and took several steps to a pillar of gradually brightening light. The light increased in intensity until Sean almost had to shield his eyes. Suddenly a shadow crossed the light and it appeared as though a figure had stepped from the pillar and now stood directly in front of it, turned toward his father.

It was a woman, young with blonde hair, just a little taller than Sean. It was his mother. His father took the few remaining steps toward her and their hands clasped together before both turned to look at their son, who stood staring back with wonder. They smiled and Sean's vision began to blur, whether from the tears that he could feel coming from his eyes or the intense light, he didn't know. Gradually, the image of them faded completely and all Sean could see was darkness.

- -

Sean felt hands on his shoulders shaking him. He was on his back, lying on the cold ground. The sharp smell of the forest around him hit his nostrils almost as strong as smelling salts, forcing his eyes open. Viktor, Svyeta and Ryan were kneeling over him, staring with concern into his face.

"Are you okay?" Svyeta asked.

Sean struggled, with their help, to sit up. He was lying several yards away from the meteorite. His father and mother were gone. The four of them were alone in the clearing.

"What happened? How long have I been asleep?"

Ryan shrugged, sitting back on his heels. "Can't say for sure. We just woke up ourselves. I don't remember what time we got here, but maybe a couple of hours have passed. We just came over to you a few seconds ago. Did you, uh, did you have any dreams?"

Sean stared back at the young Marine, trying to comprehend what had happened, the memory of all that his father had told him and the image of his parents disappearing into the pillar of light coming back to him forcefully.

"My father was here. We were talking, we were working right over there on the meteorite —"

Sean gestured toward the meteorite, at the area where he and his father had cut samples only a short time before. He stared in confusion. None of the holes they'd made with the drill were there. He looked over for the portable work station that they'd pulled out from one of the equipment tents, but it wasn't there either.

"It wasn't a dream though. At least, not the first part... that couldn't have been a dream! It was too real – he was here, he was right here!"

Viktor nodded. "I saw my mother. We talked. I don't know for how long, several hours maybe. She was different though, almost like I remember her when I was very young child. Softer, happier. She said goodbye to me, told me that I needed to watch out for myself…"

After Viktor's voice had trailed off and it was apparent that he wasn't going to say anymore, Ryan spoke. "My mom was here, too. She was right here, we talked about everything. But, it was like she knew what had happened to her. It wasn't like remembering what it would've been like to go back and talk to her, it was like it was right now and she knew everything that had gone on."

Sean looked at Svyeta as she knelt on the ground right next to him. "Did you see anyone? From your family?"

She nodded. "Mama, Papa … and Zhenya. They were alive – so happy. But, they knew they had died and it was like they were okay with that. Like it was something terrible that had happened and was over now."

Sean nodded. "My dad, too. He knew that he had died, he told me all about our brains and our new abilities. He showed me…"

Suddenly, Sean scrambled to his feet and ran over to the patch of churned up soil right in front of the immense meteorite. Staring down at the ground intently, he began to pace back and forth, stepping carefully. The other three came over to see what he was doing, staying several paces behind him as he searched.

Sean walked over to the exact spot where he remembered seeing the Source pour out of the meteorite. He carefully ran his hand over the surface of the moist soil, scanning for any sign. There was nothing there.

Leaning back in frustration and disappointment, Sean stared up at the sheer rock face. Had it all been a dream, he thought? Had he not spoken with his father at all, but only imagined it? This seemed somehow even worse to him than having to witness his father dying again. The idea that his subconscious mind had dreamed up a simple little explanation for all that had happened seemed like a horrible mockery of the last moments he'd spent with his father – both several weeks ago and also several minutes ago.

Feeling the sorrow returning to his tired frame, Sean bowed his head, noting the sting of the salty tears in his eyes once again. Suddenly, the image of his father's hand plunging into the soft earth came to his mind. He opened his eyes and stared at the clear ground beneath his knees. Trying to remember the exact spot where his father had reached, Sean thrust his hand down deep into the soil.

His fingers wiggled deeper and deeper into the soft ground. Finally, once his arm was buried up almost to his elbow, Sean touched on something hard in the dirt and he grasped on to it, pulling his closed fist out of the earth. He slowly opened his hand to see the white crystal rock exactly as he'd remembered it.

CHAPTER FORTY-FIVE

Glowing cinders floated upward into the night sky above the campfire only to finally disappear, their tiny lights winking out in the starry blackness above. Sean stared at the sky, trying to remember the last time he'd seen so many stars. It must have been on the last camping trip with his family. They'd sat around a campfire, just like this one, while his father pointed out the various constellations, his mother adding the history and background of all the gods after which they were named. It was somehow comforting to Sean that Russia, a land that had for so long seemed so foreign and far away from his own, also had such beautiful, star-filled night skies.

"Did he tell you who sent Elijah? Or who would come for this stone?"

Viktor's face was glowing red and orange from the fire in front of him. He held a long stick in his left hand and absently jabbed it into the coals at his feet. He looked tired, Sean thought. Then again, he probably did too. It had been a long day – a long several weeks since the meteorite had landed. Practically a lifetime.

"No. I didn't ask him – I didn't have time." Sean stretched out his hand which held, and had been holding for the entire afternoon and evening, the smooth, white crystal that he believed to be a piece of the Source. He'd just finished telling Viktor, Svyeta and Ryan about his experience with his father, relaying everything that he'd said about their brains, their new talents and the Source. As with Viktor, a million questions still filled Sean's mind.

Occasionally, theories and ideas would attach themselves as possible solutions to some of these un-tethered questions, but he seriously wondered if he would ever find the real answers at all. Viktor, Svyeta and Ryan had seen visions of their families too, but they had not relayed any of the information that Sean's father had. Theirs had been discussions of shared memories and experiences, apologies and confessions of love previously left unsaid, with little talk of the future or explanations of the past.

Viktor leaned back into the portable canvas chair that they'd found in one of the tents. He stared into the flames, mulling over the events of the day, Sean's explanation of what had happened to them and his own conversation with his mother. It had been real, it had to be, he told himself. It wasn't a dream. He'd been entirely aware and in control of himself the entire time. Unlike other pleasant dreams that had always revealed themselves once he'd woken up, this experience still seemed just as real hours later. He'd sat in this very clearing, talking with her in a way that he never really had before. She'd apologized – which surprised him above all else – for the way she'd treated him, for not being a better mother. But, he'd never thought of her as a bad mother. That's just the way she was. He always assumed that it was because of the difficulty of her life that she was always so short with him. Having to take care of him, his sister and his grandmother after his father had left. Viktor had always imagined the anger she must have felt at having her only son be born a cripple, unable to help in the way that he should. The fact that she had always pushed him, always been so strict with him had always meant to Viktor that she really loved him and that she wasn't going to allow his disability to be an excuse for not using the one thing he had that did function properly – his mind. But, apologized she had. Viktor supposed that all mothers probably felt that way – that they hadn't done enough for their children, that they had never shown enough kindness.

A small pit of anger began to grow in his stomach as his mind again turned to the cold, immovable meteorite resting just across the clearing. It sat, heedless of the havoc and destruction it had caused, the pain that it had wrought in the lives of billions. Sean's experience, his finding the white stone, their abilities all proved that it wasn't just chance, some freak accident of nature. Someone had sent it here for some unknown purpose. Someone had deliberately killed his family and had changed his life forever.

And how have they changed my life, Viktor thought. He glanced down at his body – his two hands, the straight fingers and fully movable wrists, his arms and legs. I was a cripple – only half a person really, Viktor mumbled to himself. And now I'm whole. I'm free to live a life that I thought I would never have. Whatever, whoever did this to us – they changed us. But, they've also given us new life. I would never have traded my family for this new body, this new brain, Viktor told himself. I could never have done that. But, the choice wasn't given to us – it was made for us. And how can we know how many other children's lives have been changed for the better? How many others like me in the world can now move and walk – even possibly run one day? And once all this death and grief and pain are further away, once we've learned how to live in this new world with our newfound talents, how much good and happiness could come then? How can we now know what greater good could someday rise out of the ashes of our former world?

Ryan McCaney stood and stretched, reaching his hands out toward the stars. He stomped his feet on the ground, trying to get the blood flowing again.

"You guys get enough to eat?" he said as he picked up the plastic bowls that had held their dinner – canned soup again. The three nodded and Ryan walked over to a bag of trash hanging near the entrance to one of the tents. He paused momentarily to stare at the dancing flames of the fire. They were probably still thinking about the exact same thing, Ryan thought to himself – remembering their families and their experiences of the afternoon. It's probably better this way, he mused. This makes it all a little better, in a way, for all of us.

"I'm about ready for some sleep – you ready to turn in soon?

Viktor stood slowly, stretching his back, dropped his stick near the fire and wandered over to the tent where they had found a few cots. Sean and Svyeta remained sitting, staring at the night sky.

"I'll be there in a few minutes," Sean said.

Ryan nodded and turned to walk back to the tent.

"My mother said something that surprised me," Svyeta said, staring into the fire. Sean waited for her to go on – she'd been so quiet all afternoon after their dreams.

"She thanked me for keeping the family together before Elijah came and... said she was sorry that I'd had to for so long, but that it was what I was good at. She said that it was something I needed too – taking care of people. I hadn't thought of it like that before, but now I think she's right. It made me feel good when I thought they needed me and when I could help them – Zhenya with school, my mom with the house and my father... with his problems. I know we all feel lost without our families and I miss mine so much..."

Sean nodded. "We have a new family now – all of us. And you can take care of us, because you are good at it. We need that."

Svyeta smiled and nodded, pulling her jacket tighter around her neck.

"We should go to sleep – it's getting colder."

"I'll be there soon," Sean said.

She smiled again and walked over to the tent.

Sean pulled his gaze down from the twinkling stars in the blanket of night to the alien stone in his hand. It was somewhat flat and round, almost like a small disc that had been melted by an intense heat. There was some evidence of its once jagged edges that had become multiple, smooth, tiny facets of reflective stone that had been molded and changed, trapped just beneath the almost translucent surface. Other portions were entirely opaque – just a dense, swirled cloud of milky-white rock.

Has it all been worth it for this, he wondered. How could this little piece, and the rest that had sunk into the ground, be so important that the lives of so many could have been so easily traded for it? Is there something that we're supposed to learn from all this? Some greater message that we're missing? What greater good can be accomplished from so much death?

Suddenly, the image of little Zhenya's fluttering dress came to his mind. He could see her, once again as he had so many times in dreams and waking nightmares over the past few days, falling forward, her hair spilling around her head. As soon as she'd hit the ground, she'd stopped moving. Sean had thought that so odd at the time, how the life seemed to be immediately forced out of her body right when she hit the pavement, as if

only her body stopped, but her soul kept falling, deeper and
deeper into the ground.

The anger he'd felt when he saw her fall returned to him
again, not quite as forcefully, but lined now with a greater sadness
and weariness than before. I killed him, he thought. I killed him,
not just to protect the others, but because I was angry. I
murdered him – I am a murderer. What greater good or purpose
can ever make up for that?

CHAPTER FORTY-SIX

The next morning, as Ryan, Svyeta and Viktor were sorting through the equipment and supplies left behind by the research team, Sean found himself wandering along a path that led out of the clearing, through some white pines that seemed to be standing as silent sentries along the way. His hands ran softly over the tall, wild grass that grew in patches, catching seed kernels between his fingers.

He stopped at a break in the forest, a grove of trees that lay to the side of the deer trail he'd been following. The morning sun was breaking through the branches, lazily soaring insects caught in its warm rays. Sean looked around the clearing to make sure that he was alone, then carefully knelt down on the ground.

His sleep the night before had been fitful, plagued by dreams of his parents dying over and over again, of Svyeta and Zhenya and all the other children in Moscow alone and starving. And of Elizabeth, left alone and frightened in their large, lonely home back in Pasadena. Finally, just before dawn, he'd given up on sleep and gone out to restart the fire for breakfast.

Sean pulled out the handwritten letter that his father had given him on that last day. He didn't read it again – he'd already poured through the words dozens of times over the past few days – but just tugged at its corners, absently wondering how long the paper and ink would last, how long he would still be able to read it. He could still see his father's face as he handed him the letter, his awkwardness in trying to explain it.

His dream or vision or whatever it had been came back to him now – both his parents smiling, holding each other as they disappeared into the brilliant pillar of white light. Sean imagined both of them together again as they had always been – trading jokes and teasing as they stood in the kitchen washing dishes or painting old furniture in the garage. Where were they now, he wondered. Were they happy? Were they happy with him? How could they be, Sean thought.

Svyeta's face loomed in his mind wearing the look of terror she'd had when Zhenya broke away, running. Her scream echoed hollowly, then was quickly cut off by the thundering sound of the gun.

Sean squeezed his eyes shut, trying to block out Ivan's bloodied face that came back to him unbidden, for the hundredth time already that day. He saw his parents again, imagined them looking on as he punched Ivan in the face. In his mind, he saw them turn away, their faces white and grave. Tears came now, squeezing out of his tightly clenched lids, and he buried his head in his hands.

He felt pain course through his body, wracking his chest and throat with powerful sobs. Ivan's body was again lying on the pavement in front of him and his mind was reeling, trying to grasp what he'd just done. He remembered the feeling of panic that had gripped him, seeing Ivan just lying there. He'd wanted him to stand back up, to have his face be back the way it was supposed to be and for him to be up and walking around again. But, he'd just lain there, completely still.

Sean heard a sound struggle up from deep in his chest, a pitiful, whining moan that came out high and ragged between his tears. He squeezed his palms against his temples, trying to force out the image of Ivan's face, desperately searching for some other thought to fasten upon, anything that would take the place of the dead boy in his thoughts. But, all he could feel was the finality of his act, the utter despair that filled him and the fear that he would always feel the stain of Ivan's blood on his hands, no matter how hard he ever scrubbed them.

A wind blew through his hair, chilling his wet cheeks. He opened his swollen eyes, peering at the sea of grass, waving ferns and tall trees of the immense forest.

Sean lifted his head to look into the pale blue sky above him, feeling as small as a stray speck of dust blowing through the vast forest. He cleared his throat and wiped the tears from his eyes.

"Mom, Dad," he began, but his words were choked short by

his constricted throat. "Mom and Dad, I don't know if you can hear me or where you are, but ... I saw you yesterday, somehow, in my dream. You were together and you looked happy...."

Sean paused momentarily before continuing, trying to regain control of the fluttering feeling in his chest. "I've done something... something terrible. And I can't fix it – I can't take it back even though I want to. I just want, I need to know if... if you can still accept me as your son... after what I've done."

Sean's eyes searched the empty blueness above, heedless of the tears that poured softly down his cheeks. He felt the wind blow through his hair, bringing with it the scents of the living forest around him.

Gradually, as Sean knelt in the grove of trees, he began to feel a small warmth spreading through his chest, filling him until it stretched out to his fingertips and down into his legs. His tears stopped and he was acutely aware of everything around him, the smells, the warm dankness of the earth and vegetation, the moisture of the ground beneath his knees. These thoughts of the vitality of the world around him drove all his previous fears and imaginings away. The death, fear and pain receded until all he could concentrate on was the sheer physicality and majesty of the forest around him as his body seemed to be entirely suffused with some inner heat.

Suddenly, the image of the falling green lamp that he'd seen right after Zhenya died flashed through his mind again. It fell so slowly, finally shattering into hundreds of pieces on the hardwood floor. He felt more than saw rapid movement in the background, sensed the hurried patter of feet, running, trying to get away. And a soft, helpless cry of fear.

From somewhere deep within, Sean felt the words the moment before he said them aloud, as if they had somehow been planted there and were only now blooming like a softly unfolding rose into the full light of day. Immediately as he felt them, he felt their truth as well and the unyielding sense of urgency and responsibility that they carried.

Sean opened his mouth and the words came out. "Elizabeth is still alive."

EPILOGUE

The brisk morning air filled his lungs as Sean rose from his crouched position in the tall, yellow-colored grass. His hands quickly adjusted the shoulder straps on his backpack and he shifted his weight as he gazed out across the clearing. The expansive blue sky held a few stray clouds that danced their way lightly across the horizon. Sun beams had just crested the tops of the trees, spilling into the meadow with the hurried excitement of a new day.

Ryan McCaney stood by the fire pit, pouring a bucket of water into the chunks of ash. He kicked dirt into the grayish mud and stamped it down lightly with his boot. His young hands pulled the pack tighter up on his back and he looked over at Viktor who was watching him intently, his own largish hands fumbling with the walking stick by his side.

"It's important to always douse your fire pit before you leave, even if you think there can't possibly be any more embers burning. You never know when a wind could come by and make it flare up again. Can you remember that?"

Viktor smiled, long strands of dark brown hair swaying in front of his eyes. "I won't forget."

Svyeta was humming to herself as she stuffed a couple last food packets into her backpack. She stood, testing its weight then set it back down as she glanced around the camp area to see if they'd forgotten anything.

It was the next day – they'd spent two nights at the crash site. None of them had experienced any more waking visions, just the usual dreams while they slept stretched out on the cots left behind by the research team. Sean hadn't expected anything more to happen. He had a feeling that if his father had been able

265

to tell him any more, he would have. And Sean already knew what he had to do now. His experience in the grove of trees the day before had been as real as anything he'd ever known. Everything was suddenly very clear to him and he was anxious to resume their journey.

Viktor walked over to Sean, leaning heavily on his walking stick. He was already breathing heavily – the return hike wasn't going to be easy for him. The two boys stood silently as they looked at the large, immovable meteorite. Once again, they both thought – this thing has changed us. Changed our lives and our world forever – will we ever understand it?

Ryan turned away from the meteorite and started walking toward the trail that he'd picked out the day before. He was sure this one would lead them in a more direct route back to where they had left their vehicle.

Svyeta turned to follow him then called back to Sean and Viktor.

"Are you two coming or are you going to stand there staring at that rock all day?"

Viktor glanced at Sean, a smile on his face. "Time to hit the road?"

Sean turned away from the meteorite to smile back at his friend. "Yep. We're on the road again."

Viktor paused before forming the English words carefully. "We better ske... ske...˝

"Skedaddle," Ryan called from ahead.

Viktor smiled and nodded. "Skedaddle."

As they walked slowly through the calm trees and gently swaying wild grass, Sean's questions and fears slowly began to fade as his mind turned to the journey ahead and the thousands of seemingly insurmountable miles that lay between him and his sister. Imagining Elizabeth reminded him of his mother's face, its lines of care delicately etched into each feature. She was always so beautiful, he thought. His hand calmly gripped the white piece of crystal, and his father's calm, reassuring glance came to mind. The sun's warmth on his back drove away the chill of the clearing, sending a feeling of warmth and well-being throughout his body. Sean raised his head and drew in a deep breath of fresh morning air.

ACKNOWLEDGEMENTS

I owe thanks to so many without whom this book would never have come to be. Thank you all!

Bonnie Fulmer, Karen Parker, the Griffard clan, Pete Amador, Rob Lee, John Payne, Ken Wzorek, Chris Schoebinger, Golden Fillmore, Nephi Fillmore, Carol Thompson, James Egan, Katie Lynn Markham and all my Kickstarter supporters.

And to Kathy – thanks for joining me on the journey.

ABOUT THE AUTHOR

Andrew lives in Seattle and when not writing is busy doing online marketing, wrangling kids, hiking or making things out of leather. *Elijah's Chariot* is his first novel.

Made in the USA
Las Vegas, NV
14 December 2020